Ana Takes
Manhattan

Ana Takes Manhattan

LISSETTE DECOS

FOREVER

New York   Boston

Copyright © 2023 by Lissette Decos

Cover design and illustration by Holly Ovenden
Cover copyright © 2023 by Hachette Book Group, Inc.

Forever
Hachette Book Group
1290 Avenue of the Americas, New York, NY 10104
read-forever.com
twitter.com/readforeverpub

First edition: February 2023

Forever is an imprint of Grand Central Publishing. The Forever name and logo are trademarks of Hachette Book Group, Inc.

Library of Congress Cataloging-in-Publication Data

Names: Decos, Lissette, author.
Title: Ana takes Manhattan / Lissette Decos.
Description: First edition. | New York : Forever, 2023.
Identifiers: LCCN 2022042093 | ISBN 9781538706756 (trade paperback) | ISBN 9781538706763 (ebook)
Subjects: LCGFT: Romance fiction. | Novels.
Classification: LCC PS3604.E26 A85 2023 | DDC 813/.6—dc23
    /eng/20220902
LC record available at https://lccn.loc.gov/2022042093

ISBNs: 9781538706756 (trade paperback), 9781538706763 (ebook)

Printed in the United States of America

LSC-C

Printing 1, 2022

Para mi madre

CHAPTER 1

Now would be the perfect time to turn into someone else. Doesn't have to be someone completely different. Just a chilled-out, easier-going version of myself would be nice. Someone whose shoulders aren't way up by her ears. Or whose right eye doesn't feel like it's about to start twitching.

Why does it have to be *him* down on one knee? I can think of at least three other guys who could be doing this right now. And he's way closer than he needs to be. With little effort, I could run a hand through his thick brown hair with all those natural golden streaks.

"Marry me, Ana," he whispers calmly.

The words shouldn't surprise me, but they do. Especially the way he says my name. Like he's holding a small bird. I tuck a stray, frizzed-out curl behind my ear just as the cool mist from the fountain reaches my face.

Come on, Ana. Loosen up. This is the perfect day for a proposal. It's still early in the summer. Not too hot. Mostly clear blue sky. Central Park's Bethesda Fountain and the small lake nearby look both luxurious and welcoming.

"Thanks again for volunteering to do this..." I never even got his name after he delivered our generators this morning. Maybe it's Chad. Or Jack. He looks like a Jack. Jack from the Midwest. Corn-fed but also a little bit savage. Like one of those young Abercrombie & Fitch models who should be able to afford food but always looks famished.

"You're probably wondering why I do the rehearsal myself," I say to help ease the tension between us. *I hope I'm not the only one feeling tension.* "I just think it's not much of a camera run-through if the cameras don't get the chance to actually run through things exactly the way they're meant to go. When you're dealing with a surprise proposal, the rehearsal is really critical. And as the producer, I'm responsible for all the details—know what I mean?"

He licks his lips but doesn't respond. His scent is intoxicating. Like bubble gum and the sea.

I force my shoulders down and shake my head around like a boxer about to enter the ring. Problem is, the clock is ticking and my mind has gone completely blank. Mostly because his V-neck T-shirt is exposing a beautiful triangle of smooth, tan skin.

"So...what do ya think?" He sounds playful but also a bit worried.

There's an undeniable heat between us. It's like we're in a warm bubble and the world has stopped and nothing is happening. *Wait, why is nothing happening?*

I look around and realize he isn't the only one waiting

for my response. The entire production crew is waiting. My response is everyone's cue to begin this rehearsal.

I have no idea how long I've been out of it, but now I'm very much back in it—and no doubt visibly flushed.

It's fine. No biggie. But if I open my mouth right now, I'm pretty sure a high-pitched *YESSS* will come out. So I nod.

Finally, a smile spans his square cheeks just as a Spanish guitar glides into the silence. I look up at a dozen or so rowboats dotting the lake behind him. On the boat nearest us, a young man wearing a white tuxedo struggles to stand. He steadies himself, takes a deep breath, and begins belting out "O Sole Mio."

A wave of activity ripples across the other boats as men and women put down their oars and reveal hidden violins, clarinets, flutes, and a tambourine. Within seconds, the lake has turned into a concert hall.

"It's now or never..." A children's choir joins in with the English version of the song. Little girls wearing long pink tutus and boys in gray suits and bow ties walk toward us, each holding a glowing candle inside iridescent flower-shaped holders. They surround us, circling the fountain.

The performance comes to a sudden stop. The sound of wings flapping makes us all look up. Some of the children gasp as five snowy white swans swoop around us to land gracefully in the fountain. As soon as the last swan settles, the music picks back up where it left off.

Right on cue, *he* stands up and pulls me close. His fingertips slide up my forearm, and I'm completely undone. Losing my balance, I roll my ankle. *How does one roll their ankle when one is standing still?* Luckily, he catches me before I tip over.

"You okay?"

"It's fine. I'm fine."

Before I can say anything else, he tightens his grip around my waist and starts to spin me into a dance around the fountain.

I'm feeling everything at once. Excitement. Nerves. Joy. My senses are on hyperalert. When the sun tucks behind a cloud, I can even feel the slight change of temperature and notice the children's candles shine brighter.

A small crowd has gathered. Families, joggers, and even the soapy bubble street performer have all stopped to watch. I'm outside my body, watching us too.

I feel his strong hands on my back, guiding me. This can no longer be considered dancing. More like caressing on the move.

I'm not sure if the cameras are getting the right shots or if we're anywhere near the marked spots we're supposed to be landing on. Now we're back where we began, and I notice my hands have migrated from his shoulders to his waist.

The song ends just as he dips me over the fountain. He holds me there as if he doesn't want this moment to end. I wish I could think of the perfect thing to say right now. Something clever. Or cute. Something other than "What's your name again?"

"You could use a little kick." Chuck, our lighting director, has appeared and flicks his beloved electronic meter in my face. I imagine him out to dinner at a restaurant, shoving it into people's faces and arguing with the hostess about inaccurate exposures. The thing beeps loudly as it glides from my forehead to my mouth like it's mining for gold. I'm just glad it can't read my thoughts. *It would pick up things like: Did anyone else notice what happened a moment ago? Did he feel it too? Will he be handling all of our lighting and power needs from now on?*

"Those clouds should be gone in a few, and the sun will be just above the bridge." Chuck slaps me on the back. "Your timing is right on."

"Thanks," I croak.

Chuck walks away, and I'm left alone with *him*. "And thanks. That was perfect...you." Hopefully someone will mention his name today.

"Anytime," he says teasingly.

"Okay, well, see ya."

I leave him standing there and speed-walk toward the trees where we've set up our video village, an outdoor control room with nine monitors tucked behind an Astroturf wall. The moment I sit down, every muscle in my body softens. Even the little ones on my forehead loosen, relieved to be behind the scenes again.

I pick up my clipboard from a narrow table set up in front of the screens and check off "Proposal Run-through" on my list. Two sets of walkies are also on the table, one for the crew and one where I can hear the talent microphones. I nudge the crew walkie earpiece in my ear while simultaneously checking out the monitors.

"Ana for Jackie."

"Go for Jackie."

"Let's get the kids and swans back to starting positions."

"Copy that. On it."

On proposal days everyone switches from reality TV crew to undercover agents.

"Jackie for Ana."

"Go for Ana."

"The trainer wants us to start with the swans in the fountain."

"What? Why?"

"She says they're tired."

"That's not going to work." *Swans in the fountain preproposal? Puhlleeeze.* "Help her with the birds, Jackie."

"Copy that. On it."

My phone vibrates with the message I've been waiting for.

Jorge: Leaving the cafe now.

"Ana for Chuck."

"Go for Chuck."

"Maria and Jorge are on their way. Are we good to go?"

"Two minutes. Just adjusting the crane to get more of the fountain."

"Okay, well, hurry up," I say and quickly text back: Go to the spot where we rehearsed yesterday. And after you've danced around the fountain, dip her!

I hit send and then add: But only if it feels right.

This will be the perfect season premiere of *Marry Me, You Fool!* The rest of this season's episodes were all filmed, edited, and ready for air. So why have I waited until the last minute to cast the most important slot? And why does it *have* to be this couple?

Real love.

It's the one thing you can't fake on reality TV. No matter

how extravagant I make the surprise proposal, if the couple isn't deeply in love, the episode won't be special. It'll miss that secret *something* that makes you root for a couple and then cry in relief when it all ends happily.

As soon as I watched Jorge's casting video, I knew he and Maria had *it*.

It wasn't simply because Jorge had a great idea for their proposal. But you can tell a lot about a person by the way they're planning to propose. Most people go on and on about how much they love their partners and how I should pick them because their proposal idea is so big and original and whatnot. Most of the time they're way off the mark.

Marry Me, You Fool! automatically rejects the following:
1. Cooking the ring into a chocolate soufflé
2. Dropping the ring in a glass of champagne
   (The ring should not come into contact with *any* edible items.)
3. Creepy lipstick on the bathroom mirror proposal
4. All scavenger hunts and puffs of airplane exhaust
5. Placing the ring in a box within another box and then having the audacity to suggest *that box* be placed inside another box
6. Anything involving seashells

The truth is, Jorge's casting video stood out because it was . . . insulting.

"I'm going to be honest. I hate your show." Jorge started his casting video with a slightly bitter look in his eyes. "I think pretty much everything on TV exploits instead of educates the masses in a positive way..." At this point in the video, he peered over his shoulder to make sure he was still alone. "But my girlfriend loves your show."

Here, Jorge softened his gaze. "This is Maria." He held up a picture of a happy graduate in her cap and gown. "She watches every single episode of *Marry Me, You Fool!*, including the reruns. She's a neonatal nurse, and even after she's worked all night, she still watches an episode before coming to bed.

"I restore art and historic architecture. Sometimes I volunteer for low-income communities, and she's always so supportive. I think we could tell her that you're doing a before-and-after show about a project I'm working on in Central Park. Even though she's extremely shy, I know she'll do it for me." After a long pause, he continued. "If it were up to me, I'd propose in a more intimate way. But I want to do this for Maria because your show makes her happy. And all I want to do is make her happy."

From the moment I met Maria, I understood what he meant.

"Sorry about the mess." She greeted me nervously at the door of her apartment. Her hair was up in two braids that wrapped loosely around her head and met in the back.

As the crew set up the lighting for her interview in the living room, she showed me all the cards and photographs on her fridge. Dozens of adorable children she's cared for since she started nursing and still stays in touch with. That's when I had the idea to hire a professional children's choir for her surprise proposal.

Maria was fidgety when she sat down under the lights.

She kept checking her hair, worried the braids were coming undone.

"I was about to delete my online dating profile when I saw his. I was working nights at the time, so we messaged each other for weeks before we finally set a date to meet in person. We had been so uninhibited in our texts, I felt like I already knew him. We met at Riverside Park in the Bronx. He had a bottle of rosé champagne and miniature gourmet sandwiches set up on a rowboat for us. As I stepped onto the boat, he said, 'Is it too soon to ask you to marry me?'" She was more relaxed in front of the cameras, and her eyes started to water. "We both laughed, and I was so happy. It was such a relief to know we were feeling the same way."

That's why we're re-creating an enhanced version of their first date. Jorge told me he calls Maria his sunshine, so I hired the Harlem Symphony to perform "O Sole Mio." The swans were my idea—a completely unrelated, last-minute addition for a little *oomph*. Bringing them and their professional trainer in from Canada made us go *slightly* over budget. We had to house them in New Jersey for a month and pay hefty park fees to close off the area until the swans were trained to land in the fountain.

But everything will be worth it. Because after producing this show for eight seasons, I know how to make the predictable flow of each twenty-four-minute episode still feel shiny and new.

Minutes 1–3: Introduce a couple in love.
Minutes 4–6: Find out one of them is plotting a big surprise proposal.

Minutes 7–20: Drama ensues from all the hiding and secrets.

Minutes 21–24: Just when you think all is lost . . . surprise proposal!

I jam the talent earpiece in my other ear and quickly scan all the shots on the monitors. I see the swan trainer and Jackie shooing the last swan out of the fountain. On the crane's wide shot, I catch a glimpse of Generator Hottie running for the trees on the other side of the fountain. *Such a graceful runner. Like a gazelle.*

On the center monitor I spot Maria and Jorge walking hand in hand along the final stretch of Poets Alley that leads to the fountain.

I take a deep breath. *I love it when things come together exactly as I've planned.* I've learned to trust my gut when it comes to finding the perfect season premiere. And this is it.

CHAPTER 2

Jorge and Maria are about a hundred yards from the fountain. They stop to watch a Rollerblader expertly weave through a row of small orange cones. Out of nowhere, I get this terrible feeling that I've forgotten something. I scan the list. Cameras set. Swans and children fed. Full camera run-through done.

On the monitors, Jorge and Maria are now walking under the tunnel that leads out to the fountain. My eyes race down the list faster than I can read.

"Ana for Jackie. Ana for Jackie," I say, making an effort *not* to sound like I'm freaking out.

"Go for Jackie."

"Do you have a twenty on the park official?"

"He's right next to me." I see Jackie on one of the monitors, peering out from behind a bush.

"Great. Have him shut off the fountain and add the dye."

"Copy that!"

Seconds later, the fountain stops flowing, and I scratch the item off my list over and over until I break through the paper.

"...and we're still working out what tool would be best for cleaning this ceiling." Maria and Jorge are now within range of our audio engineer's soundboard, so I can pick up their microphones.

Maria believes the small camera crew following them is making a documentary about restoring the bridges in Central Park. I even made up a title to give it authenticity: "Fixing the Bridges: No Walk in the Park."

I click on my walkie. "Here they come."

The large crane kicks on and makes a sudden jolt, but thankfully Maria doesn't notice. "Too bad the water's turned off."

"Uh-huh, yeah, that is bad." Jorge sounds agitated.

Slowly, he gets down on one knee, right where he's supposed to. The park goes silent.

The cameramen step out of hiding for close-ups. On the monitors, I now have a two-shot of Jorge and Maria, singles of each, and a beautiful wide shot of the entire scene, including the fountain.

Jorge clears his throat again, and I really feel for him. The whole thing is riding solely on him now. The proposal is the *one* thing I can't control.

Whoever is holding the ring is usually so nervous at this point—only the most important moment of their lives thus far—that they can barely remember the things *they* mean to say, let alone anything I would write for them.

Sure, soon there will be singing and swans and rosé-colored

water flowing over the fountain. In the edit, we'll heighten the tension and extend the pause before she responds for dramatic effect. But for the proposal, I allow myself to be surprised by his words too.

Nothing brings it home like a man at his most vulnerable as he expresses his undying devotion to the woman he loves. So as hard as it is for me to *not* control what he says, I give in and let real love do its thing.

Somewhere behind the bushes a swan lets out a bellowing grunt.

"Jackie, calm the swans," I whisper into the walkie.

"Believe me, we're trying." She sounds out of breath, like she's been wrestling with the birds.

Maria's gaze is full of tenderness for Jorge. There's also a hint of fear in her eyes. She's clearly in shock. It's obvious she had no idea he was going to propose.

"Mari, Maria, mi amor." Jorge's words are slow and deliberate. "The day we met, I saw our future. I knew that all the broken promises and letdowns in my life had to happen because they led me to you."

After a few moments, it's all over. My skin is tingling. Jorge has nailed the proposal. Well, it will appear that way after my editor, Nina, takes out a dozen "ums" and when he called Maria "butterful."

The camera slowly zooms in on Maria as the hint of fear in her eyes intensifies to low-grade panic. The tenor stands and puffs up, waiting for his cue. The whole park is standing still, and a traffic jam of tourists on horse-drawn carriages have stopped to watch.

As Maria opens her mouth, I click on my walkie. "And in five, four, three..."

The crane begins to lower. "No, wait!" I say, causing the crane to stop and bounce in place.

Maria's lower lip is quivering now. She could start crying at any moment. *Yes, this is good!* I love it when little unexpected things like this happen. You can plan the entire moment to a T, but if you're lucky, they'll do something to make it more special. Nothing big—a tear, a yelp, a little hop. Any bit of unexpected reality makes it better.

I scan the monitors and let out a silent scream. Bright, gooey, pink liquid is starting to drip down the angel's face on the fountain. The whole idea is for the fountain to be glamorous and overflowing with what appears to be rosé champagne, but right now it looks like the angel is oozing blood out of a head wound.

"What is happening? Can we stop the fountain?" I scream out in a menacingly controlled walkie whisper.

Jackie has clearly heard me and told the park official because the pink goo stops flowing, but now it's threatening to drip off the angel's nose.

I watch Maria, hoping she hasn't noticed, but she's just standing there looking at Jorge, ignoring the giant crane approaching her from above as well as the half dozen crew and cameramen encroaching from all sides.

"Mari?" Jorge looks like he's about to cry too.

"I'm sorry," she says.

Huh? I raise the volume as high as it goes on my receiver.

Maria shakes her head, turns, and runs off.

What in the . . . ? I lean in closer to the monitor Maria was just in, dumbfounded. The camera spins around wildly, looking for another shot. It settles on Jorge. His face is still holding on to a feeble smile that makes him look a little creepy but also gut-wrenchingly sad.

He gets himself up, looks around, and takes in the production crew for the first time. After a moment, he bolts after her.

My earpiece is flooded with crew chaos all at once.

"What do we do?" yells one cameraman.

"Should I follow them?" asks another.

"She's coming right toward me. Do you want me to stop her?" Jackie cuts in all bodyguard-like. I picture her CrossFit-obsessed physique tackling sweet Maria to the ground.

Everyone is waiting for me to respond, but I don't know what to do. I yank out my earpiece and hold it tightly in my hand, but I can still hear all the yelling and confusion coming through.

What is happening? I'm holding the walkie so tightly, the palm of my hand hurts. Everything is spinning, and I've lost all communication with my gut.

The crew sounds get louder in the walkie, and I hear wailing coming from under the bridge, where the children's choir is standing by.

I realize I've been holding my breath. I try to exhale, but the air comes out in broken gasps. It feels like too much blood has rushed to my head at once.

How am I not prepared for this? I had thought everything through. That's what I do. It's my job to be prepared. Producers should actually be called pre-producers. We overplan. We play it all out in our minds beforehand and have a solution for every possible calamity.

That's the whole point behind "the show must go on." It takes so much effort, money, and time to get us all to a tape day, we can't let a little thing like a canoe sinking hijack our tight schedule. It's why we rented only brand-new canoes. It's why we have cough drops, hot tea, and a saline gargle station for the tenor.

In all my worst-case scenarios, Maria never bolted. I don't know why I didn't even consider it. The only thing I know for sure is that she's gone.

I bring the walkie up near my mouth. "Let them go."

Nothing happens. I can see on the monitors that the cameramen are still holding their positions around the fountain.

"Just wrap it up, guys," I say in a more convincing tone.

After a moment, the monitors begin to switch to black, until there's only one screen following the action of the cameraman continuing to aim his lens at Jorge chasing after Maria, the ring box still in his hand.

CHAPTER 3

I have no idea what Gia's talking about. She's been rattling on since we sat down at this new Dutch restaurant in SoHo she wanted to try, but my mind won't stop replaying the grim final moments of this afternoon. *Why did I have to get Canadian swans?*

Things I never should have approved:
1. Pure Eurasian mute swans
2. Underwater slow-motion cameras to capture said swans landing in the fountain
3. Waterproof microphones for all that exciting &@★#★★ swan splashing

I'm going to get fired. When is this martini going to kick in?

"I don't look as old as her, do I?" Gia points to a woman sitting at the very next table.

"No," I whisper and take a bite of sauerkraut-encrusted corn bread that I've slathered in butter. Everything is a competition to Gia. She's VP of a production company that specializes in competition reality TV shows, and I think it's made her lose some perspective. That's why we're here, about to try the herring sashimi.

Gia always has to be the first to discover a unique new restaurant, underground electro swing band, or teen prodigy designer selling garments out of a dirty taco truck.

She smiles seductively at the young waiter pouring her a glass of water.

Gia was born in Brazil, which I believe is what makes her a man magnet. Today she's wearing a slim tie and a man's button-down shirt, and she *still* manages to look sexy.

When we first met, Gia tried so hard to get me to connect with my inner sexy Latina. I tried to explain that I was second-generation Cuban American, and my Latin spice had been watered down, or possibly left on the island altogether.

"What about him?" she says, pointing to a bohemian-looking guy at the table across from us. "He's been checking you out since you arrived." Gia's other full-time job is finding me a mate.

"Uh, no thank you," I say after he looks away.

"Why not? What's wrong with him?"

"Didn't you see his sandals?" My eyes discreetly motion under the table to his Birkenstocks.

"So what? You should give a guy a chance to *actually* disappoint you before you turn him down. Going on a date would help. I'm sure he has other shoes." I ignore her and help myself to her untouched corn bread. "You know what your problem is?" she continues.

"I'm too picky?"

"You're too picky," she says at the same time. "Believe me, there can be no other reason why you're still single."

Gia may be loud and egocentric, but she's always been there for me. We've been inseparable since the first week of freshman year, when she introduced me to tweezers and I introduced her to mojitos. And in my darkest hours, when my mom passed away in the middle of our senior year, she never left my side.

"What's wrong with sandals anyway?"

"Men shouldn't wear sandals in this city. It's dirty. And who wants to be exposed to caveman toe hairs on the subway? Man sandals are way up on the list." I pull out a thick black spiral notebook from my bag and flash the first page in her face. "See? No open-toed sandals."

"Whatever. Your crazy list gets longer every day." Gia grabs her cell phone. The screen is full of messages and missed calls. "I don't even want to know what's on there now. I can't believe you still have that thing."

I shut the notebook overdramatically and put it away. *I mean, she isn't wrong.* The list is ever-growing. But I can't help that there's always something mortally wrong with the guys I attract. And I can't be blamed for the urge to write those things down.

<u>Top 10 things I don't want in a man:</u>

1. Lives outside Manhattan
2. Uses the word "ciao"
3. Prefers tea to coffee

4. Wears open-toed sandals
5. Vapes fruity flavors (can't trust a guy who puffs a mango)
6. Adds salt and/or pepper to a dish he hasn't tasted
7. Wears cargo shorts (with more than five pockets)
8. Rides a moped, skateboard, or electric unicycle
9. Has a bar code tattoo (appreciate the ironic anti-consumerism, but now there's a bar code on your body)
10. Wears jade rings, bracelets, or belt buckles

And sure, I keep other lists. What's wrong with that? I just like to keep things organized. *It's not like I'm weird or anything.*

Fears to conquer (heights, grasshoppers, making coq au vin...)
Dances to learn (tango, tap, Bollywood...)
Difficult rap songs to memorize for impressing coworkers at Christmas karaoke party ("Rapper's Delight," "Nuthin' But a 'G' Thang," the fast part of "Despacito")
Show ideas to pitch (short list)
Show ideas boss has rejected (long list)

There's no better feeling than crossing off an entire list. When I've checked off every single task, I feel like I'm in command of my own ship. A sense of calm washes over me, and it's as if I've stepped under a warm waterfall. The kind where the pressure of it gushing over my head is so hard that for a moment I can barely breathe. *Okay, so maybe I'm a little weird about lists.*

"Besides, what are *you* wearing?" Gia peeps down at my shoes. I proudly cross my legs for her to admire the tan heels I switched into during the cab ride here. "Hmmph," she mutters, unimpressed. Gia is always trying to save me from terrible shoe choices. My closet has two shelves. Sensible and G-approved.

"A lot of men are intimidated by a successful, single woman. If a guy has the balls to ask you out, you should at least give him a chance." Thankfully, our next round of drinks arrives, so I can zone out during her speech.

Gia refers to "successful, single women" as if having a decent job takes some of the bite out of being single. But I'm not just single. I'm malnourishedly single. I'm so single I'm afraid my heart will start to eat itself soon.

"You need to be open to the unexpected because..."

I know she means well, but Gia has no idea what it's like to be a nondescript-looking person. She has literally never *not* had a boyfriend. And there's always an understudy waiting in the wings. A few years ago, she was single for all of twelve minutes. We went to a coffee shop to plan out what we would do now that we were two single ladies in the city.

"This is *exactly* what I need. To be alone for a while," she had said just as her phone double pinged with texts. "Oh wow. He's so crazy," she said as she texted back a response. "It's Nadim. He just bought me a first-class ticket to visit him." And just like that, she was off to Dubai to hang out with a billionaire sheik she had met the night before as she crossed the street.

Pardon me, that was just the sound of my aorta chomping on itself.

"We need to go wedding-night lingerie shopping on Saturday," Gia says, recapturing my attention and not looking up from her phone.

"I can't." I always thought I'd be a great maid of honor. But the truth is, I'd rather go out with caveman toes over there than keep helping Gia with her wedding. It's less than three months away and, as the big day approaches, my free time has been consumed with endless tasks for her wedding. Last weekend we spent two hours picking out the perfect shade of burgundy for her thank-you cards.

"My stepsister's wedding is this weekend."

"Oh right, I forgot. Sorry," she says, feeling genuinely bad for me. "Well, family is more important than anything else."

I sigh as our salads arrive. "You know me. I love weddings." My heart flinches at the memory of Maria running away earlier. Away from her proposal and away from my premiere episode. *Stupid swans.* We let them out as we were wrapping up all the gear, and they looked so freaking majestic flying around the fountain in perfect unison as the sun set all orange and pink. The tourists applauded, clearly unaware that everything was awful and my life was over.

I remember the hottie who'd delivered our generators—whose name I still don't know—and how he made me feel. Like it wasn't a rehearsal, but I was in fact the subject of his love and devotion. Maybe he's one of those actors who takes production jobs instead of waiting tables? *Is that a thing?*

I eye Gia suspiciously as she ignores her food and pecks away into her phone. I can tell she's typing responses to multiple guys. Gia's a huge flirt—always has been. But I don't approve of her encouraging stragglers when she's about to marry someone great.

"What are you wearing to the Bach Bach tomorrow?" Gia and Matt have decided to combine their bachelor/bachelorette parties. But I don't have the heart to tell her that calling it a "Bach Bach" (pronounced *Batch Batch*) is the equivalent of fingernails scratching down a chalkboard for me.

"Well, I don't know if it's the perfect Bach Bach outfit," I say, trying not to wince. "But I was thinking of wearing my little black dress. The one with sleeves."

"Sleeves?" she asks as if it's the first time she's heard the word. "Send me a picture in it when you get home. The entire wedding party is going to be there, so I want to get some group shots."

The restaurant fades out of focus around me.

"The *entire* wedding party?" I say, trying to remain calm.

"Yes, everyone."

It's happening? It's happening. Tomorrow. I'm going to meet *him*.

Let me explain. You know when you see someone for the first time and feel a wave of energy pass through your entire body where you don't know if you want to laugh or cry? Well, that's how I felt when I first saw Landon, Matt's best friend.

Okay, so it was a photograph of Landon. But still.

Gia's fiancé had met Landon when he went to business school abroad in England. I saw Landon's picture in Matt's home office a year ago. Both men are wearing tuxedos and standing on a dock with a grand sailboat behind them. Matt is the more conventionally handsome of the two, but when I saw Landon, my heart hurt.

He looked like James Bond. Smooth. Unstirred. Not the Bond they call for hand-to-hand combat or to disarm a bomb. Landon's more like the secret agent who talks art history and tangos with the gorgeous jewel smuggler at a ball. He's Intellectual Soiree Bond.

I picked up the picture frame that day and felt like my arms were going to fall off my torso. It was love at first sight. *Fine, photographic sight, but whatever, it counts.* I can understand how this must sound, but I felt a profound connection with the man in that photograph.

Over the past year, my feelings for Landon have only grown. *As have my online stalking skills.* His name is Landon Wright. He's a British nautical architect who designs luxury sailboats for a living.

Everything about him is unearthly and divine. His chestnut-colored hair. His dark-green eyes. The way his ears connect to his head.

Bizarre nautical dreams I've had about Landon:

1. Landon and I step onto his sailboat, and inside, it's a replica of my tiny New York apartment, so I get stuck in the narrow galley.

2. Landon and I are sitting on the sand. He leans in to kiss me, but a giant octopus comes out of the sea and chases us down the beach.

3. Seagulls attack my nosy doorman for trying to stop Landon from coming up to my apartment.

I haven't told Gia about my Landon dreams because the first time I asked her about him, she shut the whole thing down.

"Trust me. He's not your type," she said, and that was that.

But since when is "wonderful" not my type? If I told Gia how I felt about him now, she'd say something like, "Don't be ridiculous."

So instead, I've kept my feelings about Landon a secret. But soon he and I will be walking down the aisle together because in the luckiest break of all time, Landon is Matt's best man.

"I could wear the leather pants and silk turtleneck you gave me."

"No, wear the dress. You should show off your legs more."

Thinking about finally meeting Landon has me forgetting about how I may get fired tomorrow for going over budget with no episode to show for it. Landon smiling in a tuxedo could heal the world.

———

"Early night? Nice dinner? Why are you barefoot?" My doorman fires questions at me as I power-walk across the lobby and I try to answer them all before the elevator doors shut.

"Yes, yes. Dutch. It was good. You know me and heels!"

Having a doorman in Manhattan was supposed to be a luxurious upgrade, but instead it's like having a gynecologist appointment a few times a day. Felipe sees *everything*. He knows *everything*. I'm sure his face expands or contracts because he's judging my shortage of suitors and surplus of takeout.

I moved in a few months ago, but he already knows

everything there is to know about me. If I have a rare day off, he'll say, "Taking the day off and going for a run?" If I have a later shoot and miss his shift, he'll ask, "You had to work late on Tuesday, huh?" And when he hands me my dinner, he'll feel the weight of it first and say, "Let me guess, dumplings? No, no, wait. Salmon teriyaki."

On the flip side, the only thing I know about him is that the sleeves of his uniform are too short for his arms.

I open the door to my apartment and catch myself just before falling over a giant cardboard box in the hallway. I sigh and push the heavy thing into my kitchen.

Inside this box is the single most expensive thing I've ever purchased. In an effort to make my one-room studio seem grander, I ordered a state-of-the-art chandelier from Sweden. It's big. It's beautiful. It's impossible to hang. And in the meantime, there's no place for the thing to be that *isn't* in the way.

I'd stuff it in the closet, but there's no room in there since Gia's wedding dress moved in. That thing is enormous. It's $11,000 stuffed inside a bright white marshmallow garment bag with the words "Carolina Herrera" written in gold cursive letters. I can't believe I agreed to keep it in my tiny apartment until the wedding so Matt wouldn't see it. It's like having a pompous new roommate that doesn't pay any rent.

I open the closet and find my black dress with the small, slightly puffy sleeves. By this time tomorrow night, I will have met *him*. Just the idea of seeing him and suddenly I have an urge to try again to hang the chandelier. Sure, I have to go to work tomorrow, where I may potentially be fired and therefore lose this apartment, but the only thing that can calm me down right now is checking off "hang chandelier" from my DIY list.

I drag a chair into the middle of the room and pull the chandelier out of the box, sending Styrofoam balls spilling across the room. I step up onto the chair with the chandelier in my left hand, my pink wireless drill in the other, and a screw between my teeth. The chandelier is heavy, but I totally got this.

I *live* for taking on DIY projects. I've hung up shelves, leveled picture frames, painted walls, and even replaced the old moldings in this apartment.

My cell phone buzzes on the couch. I can see it's Gia calling, probably demanding that photo of me in the dress. I almost lose my balance, causing the chandelier's hanging glass crystals to softly tap against one another.

I carefully tuck the drill into my pants and grab the cable at the end of the chandelier. The drill is part of an all-pink toolbox my father gave me when I went away to college and, I have to say, it's come in handy. The phone buzzes again, then stops.

While still holding the cable attached to the lamp, I use the same hand to grab the screw out of my mouth and the drill out of my pants. *I've so got this.*

It's late, but I figure that a single, precisely drilled screw into the ceiling won't bother my neighbors. From the very beginning, the trick with this chandelier has been that it's Swedish. And apparently in Sweden, they don't include the specific screw you will need to fit into the tiny cable thingy that attaches your new chandelier to the ceiling. But after trying every hardware store within a twenty-block radius, I think I finally found what I need.

I've got to hold the cable thingy just so and place the screw in just so, and then quickly drill the little sucker in. But I see now it's a three-arm job because as soon as I place the screw in and let go, it drops onto the floor, but not before I've started drilling into the ceiling. The drill connects with the other holes I've been making for the past couple of months, and it sinks in deep.

I yank it out and take a chunk of ceiling with me.

The chandelier is still dangling in my hands unhung, but somehow I feel better. Patching up holes in the ceiling is my specialty. *I'll just put that on the list.*

CHAPTER 4

Things I will miss about Manhattan when I get fired today and have to move back in with my dad and stepmom in New Jersey:

1. Homemade Pop-Tarts in Union Square
2. The truck in Bryant Park that sells truffle-flavored popcorn
3. Tap It Out! tap dance class on Thursdays at Lincoln Center
4. The Single Girls Can Hike Club every second Saturday
5. Parlez-You French Lessons on Sundays
6. Medieval Fight Club every other Wednesday at the Cloisters
7. Columbus Avenue
8. Park Avenue
9. Madison Avenue
10. The way the sun sometimes sets at the end of the block you're walking on, making you feel like the whole world is yours and anything is possible

Each season of *Marry Me, You Fool!* has eighteen episodes. After eight successful seasons on the air, we've had 144 happily accepted proposals. One time a girl fainted when her fiancé proposed, whacking her head on a baby grand piano. But even *she* said yes when she woke up in the ambulance with her adoring boyfriend by her side—along with two cameramen, a sound operator, and me. *Second-best-rated episode, thank you very much, fainting girl*.

But you're only as good as your last episode, and right now I don't have a last episode. And yet I managed to spend a lot of the company's money.

As I approach the conference room for our monthly pitch meeting and see most of the staff through the glass walls settling in, I consider fainting at *just* the right moment so my head will hit the copy machine.

Paper Cut Productions has multiple divisions spread over four floors in this building. Nuptials are on seven. We make shows about wedding cakes, celebrity weddings, big-budget weddings, and surprise proposals. I like to think of us as a love factory. Anything involving mud, trucks, and fried food is on floors eight and nine. Floor ten is our documentary division.

I sometimes feel like the folks on the tenth floor have a holier-than-thou attitude. I can feel it when we ride the elevator together. It's as if "telling the truth" gives them a license to be pompous.

But I think if there were a hierarchy, our shows would be on top. True love should be valued *way above* documentaries. Though last year, they made a film called *Life Is No Beach* about the tense relationship between pelicans and egrets that I did find compelling.

The only possible downside to working on our floor is it could skew your expectations just a tad. You know, make you feel deflated when wildly romantic things don't happen to you at the market.

Like in Episode #517, Dominic and Sarah. They were checking each other out while in line to check their luggage at JFK. He was hoping she would be on his flight but knew the odds were slim. She could've been going nearly anywhere in the world. He refused to let her get away. So he walked right up to her and handed her a note he'd written on the back of a baggage tag.

If you're not on my flight, will you still be in my life?

Four months later, he was proposing to her on our show.

"What happened? Why didn't that idiot say yes?" Bianca calls out as I walk in the door. Bianca was recently promoted to senior producer, though I've been here *way* longer than she has.

She always takes a seat right next to our boss, Edith, who's thankfully distracted at the moment with her cell phone. Sitting around the hip, metallic table are the junior producers, editors, and coordinators. Standing along the walls like vultures waiting for someone to die (or call in sick) so they can nab a seat, are the production assistants and interns. Thankfully, my lead editor Nina always has my back, so I take the seat she's been saving for me at the table.

Edith hadn't sounded too upset when I called her from the park yesterday, but then again, I was strategically standing near the swans being loaded onto a pickup truck. There was so much hissing and honking, it drowned out most of my explanation.

"I have no idea" spills out before I have a chance to think.

Bianca looks confused. "What do you mean? Didn't you ask her?"

Edith looks up from her phone.

"Why didn't you just get her to fake it for the cameras? That's what I would have done." Bianca's long red hair bounces in perfect waves as she speaks. "I would have lied to her and told her the contract she signed legally bound her to finish the taping. I would have forced her to just nod, put the ring on, and be done with it. Who cares if they don't get married in real life? Why didn't you just make her say yes for the show?"

I imagine Bianca dragging Maria back to the fountain and forcing her to say yes to Jorge against her will. Maria would have nodded and cried. Jorge would have cried too, and their emotions would have been real enough for the viewers at home. The orchestra would have played, the children would have sung, and the swans would have landed in the rosé-flowing fountain. And the season premiere episode would have been saved. *I'm pretty sure Bianca sold her soul for the shiny Emmy on her desk.*

I consider saying the truth. But then, "I let her run away because I felt bad and wanted to give them their privacy" sounds like the most non–reality show producer thing to say right now. *Maybe they give Emmys for Most Spineless Producer?*

"They won't return my calls," I say, sounding convincingly disappointed. Because I *am* disappointed. Through the years, there've been plenty of couples I thought should not be getting married, but Maria and Jorge were not one of them. And frankly, it's annoying Maria would dismiss Jorge like that. I use my frustration to convey an angry vibe. "And ugh." I slam my fist on the table. "I'm so upset about it."

"Ana, we should..." Edith takes extra-long pauses in the middle of her sentences, so you never know if she's going to say something good or bad until she's done, causing you to stress out either way. Right now I'm filling in her pause with "fire you and get a real producer."

"...find a way to use the material you shot."

"Top Ten Most Embarrassing Proposals," Bianca spits out coldly.

"Yes, perfect. Write up a pitch for that, Ana."

I nod at Edith.

"All right, people, pitch time. We still haven't heard if *Marry Me* [extra-long pause and critical look in my direction] will get another season. Who [mini pause] wants to go first?"

I'm ready to develop my own show. Something special like *Marry Me* but with more depth and meaning. Not that there's anything wrong with a show that culminates in a surprise marriage proposal. I just want to create something a little more life-altering. Some people would say marriage should fit that bill, but the couples on our show would eventually get engaged anyway. *Though, if you ask me, not all of them should.*

I want to make moments that help change the path of someone's life, not just throw a bunch of sopranos and swans at one that was going to happen with or without me.

I've been working on an idea I was planning to pitch today, but after Maria and Jorge's failed proposal, I'm not feeling my best. My freshly washed jeans are extra tight, and my hair is looking like one big flyaway. Overall confidence is about negative 6%.

"I've got two proposals." Bianca delivers pitches with gusto. Like she's doing us all a favor by telling us about them.

Marry me, You Fool! was Edith's creation, so for the past eight years I've worked on a hit show that wasn't my idea while Bianca has created two successful series since she started here. Nothing would be more rewarding than seeing my name at the end of a show with a created by credit.

"Mobster Brides. Imagine the potential scenes. Shopping for the gaudiest wedding dress, family feuds over seating arrangements, the bride's father is in prison so she has to walk down the aisle with her uncle, but wait, her uncle's gone missing on the wedding day, so we have an exciting crosstown manhunt trying to find him as the clock is ticking at the church."

"That is…"

…a ridiculously terrible idea.

"…fresh!"

Fresh? There is absolutely nothing fresh about mobsters or their wives. But I figure I should just keep that to myself right now because of my failed attempt to get two non-mobsters engaged.

"Great! My second idea is about women getting intensive plastic surgery before their wedding day. Nose, chin, boobs, complete makeovers to look the way they always wanted to look on their wedding day…like someone else! The goal is for the groom not to be able to recognize his bride as she walks down the aisle."

"Oooh, I'd watch that!" my editor Nina shouts out. I give her a look that says, *Et tu, Nina?* But she only shrugs.

Bianca looks so satisfied with herself.

"Love it. Get me budgets for both shows, ASAP. Anyone [medium-size pause] else?" Edith looks around the room.

I consider my options. I could take these color printouts back to my office and save my pitch for next month or...I could redeem myself. So I sit up a little taller and slowly scan the room.

"Um, I've got something," I say and begin to pass the documents around the room.

"Okay. So. This show would be called *What We Did with Our Wedding Budget* or maybe something...shorter. Um...the idea is that we take wealthy couples who are about to spend a lot of money on their wedding and put them in situations so they see what they could be doing with all that money instead. For example, bringing running water to an impoverished village in Ecuador or building a school for orphans in Myanmar."

The room is silent.

"It's like, um...a fish-out-of-water type show and they learn lessons and..." I can't remember how I wanted to finish that sentence. My jeans are squeezing my midsection, and I'm parched.

"So...once they've spent time in those places...with the orphans and locals, they have to decide whether they still want to go ahead and have the big, expensive wedding or donate the money to that community instead. Obviously, they'd always choose to do the right thing. And when they get home, they have a quick, albeit extremely meaningful wedding at City Hall."

I hear people shuffling around in their seats. I look up, and Bianca is admiring her nails.

"So let me get this straight." Edith holds up my printout like it's a dirty diaper. "This picture of a sweaty couple posing with shovels in what is clearly [long pause] the middle of nowhere, they're engaged?"

"Yes."

"And what are they doing?"

"Digging up toilets for a remote community in the Dominican Republic," I say, losing some steam.

"Toilets?"

"Yes. Well, I think it's actually more of an outhouse."

"So instead of planning a gorgeous wedding and exchanging their vows in front of their family and friends [unsettlingly long pause] in some divine and exotic location, viewers at home get to watch this couple dig [mini yet still extremely insulting pause] toilets?"

On the outside you can't tell, but emotionally, I sink deeper into my chair.

"Oh wait." Thankfully, I've remembered my favorite part about the idea. "The best part is that the couple will be even closer after what they've experienced together. The difficult circumstances will push them past their comfort zones, and they'll have to overcome any relationship issues they have with each other and—"

"They'll end up breaking up," Bianca cuts me off.

"Well, yes, I guess that's possible. But I mean, that would be a good thing, right? If they weren't meant to be together, that's a happy ending too. Isn't it?"

———

When the meeting is over I walk away quickly to avoid any further feedback on my show idea, but Edith calls out to me before I reach the door.

"Ana, since you no longer have a premiere episode [painfully long pause] to edit, Nina will be working with Bianca." *Oh crap.* Bianca pops up out of nowhere.

"Aaaand, Ana, it would be best if Nina just stayed with me for the next couple of months and helped me finish the new pilots."

"That's a great idea, Bianca [mini pause], whatever you need," Edith says, making Bianca smile.

I'm losing Nina? My favorite editor? We're the dream team. We have a system. We have our own language. And we're the perfect representation of our viewers because we're both single women in our thirties.

"Wait, who will I work with?"

"We'll sort it out. Once you [bitter, long pause] find a new premiere episode, we'll move people around."

I've lost the best editor in the world. I've lost the Maria and Jorge episode. And even *I* didn't like my pitch.

An uplifting, romantic song spills out of one of the edit rooms as I walk down the long hallway. If I were editing this moment, I would replace it with a more appropriately depressing tune. Maybe some jazz. Deep, dark horns. As I step inside my edit room, Nina's walking out.

"Can't work without my *Marry Me* mouse pad," she says, sadly waving it around.

"Yep."

"Lunch?"

"Sure."

I walk into the room and sit down. Everything we've shot so far for Maria and Jorge's episode has already been loaded onto the computer. I scan through and hit play on the day we shot Jorge picking up Maria's engagement ring.

Jorge looks so nervous as the guy behind the counter hands him a small box. He opens it and then walks right past the cameras over to where I am. The cameras follow him, so I see myself taking a bite out of a poppy seed bagel with cream cheese. I'm wearing my glasses and a big sweatshirt. I look right into the camera and push it away.

"What do you think? You've gotten to know Maria. Do you think she'll like it?" Our audio guy lowers the boom microphone down until it thumps me on the head, but I just brush it away like a mosquito. I can't look away from the ring Jorge has custom-designed for Maria.

My first thought was *There must be some mistake.* I've seen hundreds of engagement rings. Round diamonds, square diamonds, rectangular diamonds, pink and yellow diamonds, some with a diamond surrounded by rubies or other gemstones, but there's *always* a diamond. On Maria's ring, where the rock should have been, there was just a flat golden surface. At this point the camera zooms in on the ring, revealing three small circles etched onto it.

"It's the Mayan symbol for sun. That's why I call her Sunshine. She's my life source," Jorge says. The camera zooms back out and focuses on Jorge, who is now tearing up. I can see myself on the corner of the screen, tearing up too and nodding.

"It's perfect."

It really was perfect, and I knew Maria would love it.

Did she even see the ring?

"Perfect. Just like her." Jorge walks back to the counter to pay for the ring.

I'm always surrounded by future brides and grooms casually saying things like "I'm marrying my best friend" or "we balance each other out." A lot of times I feel like I have to work extra hard in the edit room to make sure what they're saying feels true. But when Jorge and Maria had said these things about each other, it had felt so real.

I pull out my phone to text Jorge and look up at my computer screen. It's frozen on an image of him walking out of the jewelry store looking so excited. Poor guy. I really don't know what to say. "I'm sorry it didn't work out" doesn't seem right. "What the $*@& happened?" isn't right either. Even "How are you?" feels pathetic, so I throw my phone back in the bag.

I stare at Nina's empty chair. She should be in here with me, working on Maria and Jorge's episode. Our small yet cozy edit room should be filled with tense music that builds up to rising cymbals, and up on the wall on the large TV monitors, Jorge should be kneeling in front of Maria. Nina would have swiveled around in her chair, high-fived me, and said, "Nice work!"

No problem. The show must go on. I switch on my desk lamp. I'll go through the rest of the casting videos selected for this season and find one worthy of being bumped up to the premiere slot.

"I can't wait to marry my best friend," says an attractive surfer-looking guy. *What could Maria have been thinking?* "When I'm with her, every moment is a dream," says a skinny guy in a suit and tie. *What's her problem anyway?* "Sometimes I watch her sleep at night and think about how lucky I am," says a guy whose muscles are bulging through his tight polo shirt. *I thought she loved Jorge.*

CHAPTER 5

I haven't worn red lipstick in so long. *Does lipstick expire?* I tap the red stain on my lips without fully committing to the richness of the color. Stepping back, I check myself out in the full-length mirror hanging from the bathroom door. *Tonight I'll forget all my work troubles.*

"What do you think?" I ask the large cardboard box crammed into the bathtub. I've decided it's the perfect spot for the Swedish nightmare that is my chandelier. *As long as I'm not in the shower.*

"I think so, too." The puffy sleeved black dress doesn't look half-bad. The built-in belt cinches at my waist, and the satiny fabric is playing nicely with my curves.

"Okay. Sensible or sexy?" I stand on one foot and then the other. On the left is what Gia describes as my "old lady pilgrim platforms," and on the other foot is a snakeskin, high-heeled, ankle-length bootie she forced me to buy last fall that I've yet to break in.

"It just doesn't *feel* like me," I tell the box. "Yeah, maybe that *is* a good thing." I sit on the edge of the tub and pull on the other boot. *What could possibly be wrong with letting Landon believe I wear sexy snakeskin booties all the time? Or that my hair is always professionally blown out?*

———

When I reach Gia and Matt's door, it occurs to me that Landon could already be inside. I quickly open the door in a move of wild bravery and walk inside.

Crap. Crap. Crap. Crap.

A sea of gorgeous women wearing obscenely small denim shorts and tiny cowboy vests fill the room. Six-foot-tall beauties. Their chests at eye level. I can't stop myself from staring at everything their tiny vests aren't covering. There's upper boob. Side boob. And even a little clavicle boob. *This is a nightmare.* My little black dress with sleeves suddenly feels Amish.

I had completely forgotten Gia hired the contestants from her fashion model competition show to be the servers at the party. Their outfits are the only hint in the room of the Western-themed wedding we're all here to celebrate.

A live ten-piece samba band of drummers and maraca shakers is jamming in the living room. They're not so much singing as they are screaming in Portuguese, and every once in a while someone in the band blows a loud whistle that makes me jump.

Gia and Matt's apartment has two levels and a large glass ceiling that stretches out above the dining room. Most of the minimalistic furniture is covered in plush sheepskin, as are certain parts of the floor. *Gia's big on sheepskin.*

Guests are dancing in the center of the living room, and the best dancer by far is Gia. She's wearing a short red slip and matching red heels with leather straps that wrap up and around her calves.

"Ana! Come, there's someone I want you to meet." Out of nowhere, Gia's fiancé, Matt, appears and tugs my arm, making one of my heels give way.

Wait. I just got here. I am not ready to meet Landon. *A lot could have happened to my hair in the cab. I had the window open. I need a mirror. I need a vodka.*

Matt weaves us quickly through the crowded apartment, and I think I'm going to be sick. I've been too nervous to eat much all day, so if I throw up on Landon it will be mostly coffee. Maybe that would make for a cute story to tell our grandkids? *No, probably not.*

We approach the couch and stop in front of an older gentleman wearing a sleek gray suit and purple bow tie. His face brightens as he stands up to greet me. My face brightens too. I have no idea who this is, but at least he isn't Landon.

"Ana. *This* is Philip." Matt emphasizes the word like I've been waiting for this introduction my whole life. "Philip, this is Ana."

I've never seen Matt so agitated and eager to please anyone.

"I was just telling Philip what a big fan of his you are."

I am?

"Yes, yes," I say, trying to play along.

"She's always talking about your work and how important it is. Aren't you, Ana?"

"Oh, yes. Very important. Critical, really." Maybe he works for a volunteer organization? "It's a pleasure to meet you, Philip."

"Please, call me Phil," he says, cracking a sweet smile, so I do too.

"Why don't you guys have a seat and I'll get us some drinks." Matt's trying so hard, I'm almost embarrassed for him.

"That would be great. I prefer to sit back and take it all in." Philip settles on the couch and crosses his legs. There's a sense of decorum about him, and he's completely unphased by the deafening live band performing just a few feet away from him.

"I totally agree, and so do my boots." I plop down next to him and scan the room. The fact that Landon could be here at any moment keeps me from fully exhaling.

"Helloooo!" Gia appears with a flourish and sits down on the other side of Philip. "Mr. Oberon, can I get you a drink?"

"Thank you, but your fiancé is already on the case."

"Hey! You look great!" I say to my friend.

"Are you excited about the exposition?" she says, ignoring me.

Exposition? Wait, what had she called him?

"Sure, sure." Philip sounds bored, and I've never seen *anyone* bored around Gia.

"With Matt's gallery opening, it would be such an honor to have you as our first artist. Won't that be amazing, Ana? He's practically said yes, haven't you, Philip?" *Oberon? THE Philip Oberon?*

I knew Matt was trying to get a painter with a recognizable name to show at his new gallery, but Philip Oberon is brilliant. His work is modern and captures important moments in history. One of my favorite paintings is called *Berlin Wall*, and though it's just a bunch of geometric symbols, the piece somehow screams "freedom."

"Are those snakeskin?" he asks, pointing to my shoes, shifting the subject.

"Yes. They're a little tight though. Feels like my feet have been *swallowed up* by a snake."

Philip flashes that smile again.

"Well, have fun, you two!" Gia says and heads back to the dance floor.

"Do you dance?" Philip asks.

"Not with my feet. No."

Philip laughs, revealing a dimple on his left cheek. "What part of you dances exactly?"

"Oh, you know, shoulders." I move one shoulder up, then the other. "Sometimes my chin." I jut out my chin and tilt my head up and down.

"Impressive," he says with a laugh. In every photo I've ever seen of Philip, he has a mustache and a goatee, but he's clean-shaven tonight, so I didn't recognize him. He was so handsome when he was younger. Now he looks like a mature Robert Redford. Like a really expensive, high-quality leather chair. Still classy but slightly worn in. A chair that, at the moment, won't stop staring at me.

"I was just at MoMA recently, and they have your *Self-Portrait* hanging just as you walk in. I love that piece. It feels light and funny for some reason. Actually, I've always felt there's a great sense of humor in your work..." I'm just babbling now, but I need to put an end to his awkward staring.

"Well, you should come by and see the studies for it sometime."

Before I can answer, Matt is back with two glasses of red wine. He hands us each our drink, along with a fancy linen cocktail napkin.

"What'd I miss?" he says eagerly.

"I'm anxiously awaiting the response to an invitation to visit my studio."

"That's a yes!" Matt practically shrieks. "The answer is yes!"

"As long as Ana comes along, I guess you can come too."

"Oh, right, of course." Matt laughs nervously.

I gulp down the wine. I should be mentally preparing myself to meet Landon, but I'm too busy getting hit on by *Philip freaking Oberon*.

"Do you have anything a little stronger?" Philip asks Matt.

"Yes, of course." Matt bolts toward the kitchen again.

"I haven't been to the MoMA in years."

"No?"

"I make it a point never to go below Fifty-Ninth Street."

I'm not sure if he's joking, but I can't help laughing. "They have a lot of your work right now."

"Oh yeah."

I look up and see Gia and some guy dancing directly in front of us, having a great time. He dips her over my lap.

"Hi!" she says to me, still on my lap.

"Hey!" As soon as I open my mouth, she rubs her tongue along her teeth to let me know I have something on mine. I panic. *Damn you, expired red lipstick.*

Santa Clara County Library District
1-800-286-1991
www.sccld.org

Terminal: CA-SELFCK5
Date: 07/20/2023 6:18:32 PM

Member: Y. Q***********
Membership Number: **********38

Current Fine: $0.00
On Loan:4 (0 Overdue)
On Hold:0 (0 Available to pickup)

Today's Borrowed Items: (4)

33305257173843
Mrs. Nash's ashes

Due Date: 08/10/2023

33305253707156
Colors of film : the story of cinema
Due Date: 08/10/2023

33305252302892
Know you by heart

Due Date: 08/10/2023

33305254603271
Ana takes Manhattan

Due Date: 08/10/2023

24/7 Telecirc: 1-800-471-0991
Thank you for visiting our library

"Pardon me," I say to Philip. "I need to go to the ladies' room."

When I shut the door and look in the mirror, I want to scream. There's practically more lipstick on my teeth than on my lips.

I scrub toilet paper over my teeth until I get it all off and take a moment before rejoining the party. There's been no sign of Landon yet, but that could change at any second. I check my teeth again. All good. I open the door and step out.

I can sense that something is different. The band plays more intensely. Everyone's chatting a little louder. It's like the room has received a boost of electricity.

And there he is.

By the front door. I catch glimpses of him through the people on the dance floor and tall models holding drink trays. I knew I would feel butterflies when I saw Landon in person, but what I'm feeling right now is more like a bunch of caterpillars gnawing their way out of my stomach.

Matt walks over to greet him, and the two hug. Landon is wearing a well-fitted dark-blue suit and a fresh buzz cut, which makes him look like he's preparing for another James Bond film. A more rugged 007, and he's pulling it off. He's just so *effortless*. He puts one arm on Matt's shoulder and says something that makes them both laugh. Landon has a big, open-mouthed laugh that is so inviting. I'm drawn to him. Literally. I've been walking toward the front door this entire time.

I'm inches away from them. Matt separates from him to greet a couple that walks in the door. This is my chance. If I give this any thought, I'll lock myself in the bathroom until tomorrow.

"Hi," I say, taking another step toward him. My heart is beating so loudly, I can't tell for sure if he's heard me.

"Hi." Our eyes lock. He definitely heard me.

"How are you?"

"Very well . . . thanks."

"How was your flight?"

His eyes shrink, studying me more closely. "It was fine . . . I'm sorry, have we met?"

"No, not officially. Or unofficially. Ha! I'm Anne. Ana. It's Ana." I put my hand out, but the space is so cramped between us, he doesn't see it.

"Nice to meet you," he says, meaning it.

"I'm the maid of honor. I'm Gia's best friend." *Please don't do that thing where you nervously spit out facts about yourself.* "Gia and I go way back, like waaay back. Since college. I live just across the park. I—"

I'm cut off by a towering blond cowgirl holding a tray of champagne. I'm so relieved because I've never needed a drink this badly. But when I try to pick up the glass, my hand shakes so wildly it spills all over the place, so I set it back down.

"And there's Gia now," I blurt, trying to divert his attention away from my shaky hands. "Doesn't she look amazing? She's basically wearing lingerie and calling it a dress, am I right?"

"Yes, she most certainly is. Gia, Gia!" he calls out. "Nice to meet you," he says again and walks away.

I live just across the park? What was that? Why not just ask if he believes in love at first photographic sight?

For the next two songs I stand against the wall and watch

him dancing with Gia. In her defense, she did try to get me
to dance with them, but:

1. I can't dance samba.
2. I can't dance salsa or merengue, either.
3. I'm missing the Cuban gene that allows hips and shoulders
   to move rapidly around in their sockets.
4. I can't even attempt to dance anything in these shoes.

Matt joins them, and Gia dances with both men. When Gia
dances samba, the Brazilian in her *really* comes out. She goes all
wild and primal, flailing her hair and arms around. Both Matt
and Landon are making every effort to keep up with her.

"Dance with me." I hear a familiar voice behind me.

"Fernando," I say and look over.

"Hey, beautiful." Gia's brother goes in for a hug. We do that
thing where I'm done with the hug *way* sooner than he is, so
then I go back to hugging him, but he's already pulling away.
The whole moment is awkward.

"It's been too long," he says sweetly. Fernando's shaggy hair
is still in need of a trim. He has Gia's genes, so he's not bad
to look at, but he's always squinting, which gives his brow an
intense frown. Like he's too sensitive to take in the harsh world
with eyes wide open. Last I heard, he'd just moved back from
California after getting a master's in Russian literature.

"It's good to see you. How do you like living in the city?"

"I could take the Harlem night and wrap it around you," he
says in his reciting-a-poem voice. "Take the neon lights and
make a crown." He looks at me, waiting for a response.

I shrug. "No idea."

"Langston Hughes. So, how are you? Still listening to the Grateful Dead?"

"Not at the moment, so you don't have to worry."

Since I've known Fernando, he's been a concert pianist, a yoga instructor, and a silkscreen T-shirt designer. I met Gia's brother our sophomore year in college, when she and I moved off campus. He came to visit her for a weekend and ended up staying on our couch for six months.

He'd be up all night reading Keats, Wordsworth, or Lord Byron and then would sleep all day with the books spread out on his chest like miniature blankets. Gia was so protective of him that I couldn't complain about the lack of access to our living room.

"He just graduated from high school and, you know, needs to find his way."

"Well, he sure found his way to Goodwill and bought a piano."

"I know. Isn't he talented?"

Fernando turned our apartment into an art house café with piano recitals, poetry readings, and spoken word slams. They almost always ended with him at the piano, so moved by the music he was unable to speak. While I considered him "excessively emotional," Gia called him "a free spirit."

I could tell he had a crush on me back then by the way he badmouthed my boyfriend, Sam, after we broke up. He and Gia would gang up on Sam if I so much as mentioned him or played one of his favorite Grateful Dead songs.

For a moment there, Gia was obsessed with me marrying

Fernando so she and I could be *real* sisters. I thought it was sweet in a weird kind of way, so I let him down easy with a list.

<u>Reasons I can't date you:</u>
1. My friendship with Gia is too important to risk.
2. We don't have enough in common.
3. No, a shared love of poetry is NOT enough to sustain a relationship.

A more honest and to-the-point list would have been:

1. After you go to the barber, your hair still looks uncut and it drives me crazy.
2. You have a perpetual frown, and you are not James Dean, so stop it.
3. I think you are an unstable, overly sensitive person.

"Let's dance," he says and inches a little closer to me.

"I can't, really," I say and point down. "You don't want to dance with me in these heels. Seriously. It's for your own good." He checks out my shoes and gives me a flirty grin.

We stand there and watch Gia for a moment as she shakes her shoulders and leans so far back it looks like she may snap in half.

"I still have that list, you know."

I turn toward him. "Really?" I try to sound surprised. *Only Fernando would keep a rejection list.* Behind him, I catch a glimpse of Landon heading toward the kitchen.

"If you look for perfection, you'll never be content." Fernando stares off into the distance. "Tolstoy."

"Ah...yes. So true. I'll be right back," I say before zig-zagging my way to the kitchen.

I find Landon talking to Matt, so I stop by the doorway. The band is so loud I can only hear bits and pieces of what he's saying.

"Not even buoyant...blissfully unaware...rev up some interest in..." Even his fragments sound brilliant.

"Ana!" Matt beckons to me again.

Is Landon smiling at me? As I get closer to him, I realize he's *definitely* smiling at me, and it makes me feel completely exposed. I want to spin on my booties and U-turn it back toward Fernando. Safe Fernando. Or safe Philip.

"Do me a favor," Matt says as I reach them.

"Sure," I try to say in a sultry voice, but it comes out "Churrraaa."

"Entertain Philip for me? You're the only person he seems to want to hang out with."

I look at Landon and then at Matt and then back to Landon. I'm secretly hoping he'll bust out, "Well, he's not the only one!" *Or something along those lines.*

"He hasn't shown new work in years." Matt sounds desperate. "Opening with Philip Oberon would start off the gallery on a whole other level. I tried to have one of the models chat him up, but he told me he prefers women who are more *subtle*. He was looking right at you when he said it."

"Ah, subtle." I repeat the word numbly. It sits in the air between Landon and me, and I wish it would just go away.

"Would you sit with him at dinner? I'd really appreciate it. Besides, you'd be surprised. I hear he still gets a lot of action," he says, impressed.

"Okay, yeah, no problem." I try to get out of the kitchen as elegantly as one possibly can when one has just been pimped out to a famous old painter in front of one's crush.

———

A long dinner table has been set up under the sunroof with white candles and tulips in porcelain vases. Fine white china place settings sit on a delicate cream-colored lace tablecloth.

I watch Landon sit next to Gia, while Matt sits on the other side of her. She's in the middle of a perfect man sandwich. I sit down next to Philip just as Fernando grabs the seat on my left.

"Thank you all for coming to our Bach Bach." Matt clinks a fork on his wineglass and stands up. "Three years ago, I found my best friend." He looks adoringly at Gia. "All my dreams came true that night." He leans down so he can kiss her on the lips and then pretends he's about to faint before getting back to his toast.

"So, we wanted to extend our luck to all of you tonight. We want your dreams to come true too. On top of your plates is a piece of paper. I bought these in Brazil a few weeks ago."

I pick up the small piece of paper. It's so thin I can almost see through it.

"This is magic, wish-fulfilling paper. Write down what you want more than anything in the world, fold it up, and hand it to the person sitting to your left. They'll hold it over a candle like this and..." As soon as the paper is on fire, Matt throws it up in the air and the whole thing disappears instantly.

Everyone applauds, and Matt beams with pride.

People get to work on their wishes. Next to me, Fernando is writing away. He's lost in thought, like he's composing a poem. Philip is done first. He puts his fancy pen back into his jacket and hands me his paper. It's not folded, so I can see what he's written on it.

Your number

I look at him and notice for the first time he's wearing a small diamond stud in his right ear. I make a mental note to add that to the list.

34. No diamond stud earrings

"So, what do you think? Is my wish going to come true?"

"Well, there's only one way to find out." I hold the paper over the candle nearest us, and as soon as the corner catches on fire, I throw it up in the air. It instantly evaporates. All around the table, everyone is doing the same, and the effect is pretty cool.

"Your turn," he says, pulling the pen back out of his pocket and handing it to me.

I look down at the thin piece of paper on my plate and look up at Landon, who has just handed his paper to Gia. He whispers something in her ear, and she laughs her flirty laugh. The one where she crinkles her nose like she's about to sneeze.

"Here." Fernando hands me his folded-up wish.

"You're supposed to go that way, to your left."

"It is not in the stars to hold our destiny but in ourselves," he says in one of his trances. "Shakespeare."

I watch Landon pour Gia another glass of champagne.

I don't want to feel sorry for myself. I really don't. *But I can't help it.*

Barely looking, I quickly light Fernando's wish and throw it up in the air with a thrust.

"Are you ready?" he says, looking at the piece of paper in my hands.

"Yep." I give the pen back to Philip and hand the paper to Fernando.

"You haven't written anything," he says, turning it over.

"Just burn it."

———

Although I hardly got to speak with Gia at the Bach Bach, as soon as I get in the cab, I'm bombarded with texts from her.

Helloooo

where did u go? u left w/o saying goodbye

omg philip oberon is in love with u!!

Ana Karina Oberon has a nice ring to it!

Please don't forget us on your fab yacht

where are uuuuu???

call me ASAP

CHAPTER 6

<u>Don't forget:</u>

1. Wedding gift
2. Film camera (*Loaded ahead of time.*)
3. Pajamas (*You never know—maybe I'll want to spend the night.*)
4. Toothbrush (*Who am I kidding? I don't even want to go to my stepsister's wedding*)
5. A positive attitude

I like to imagine that the island of Manhattan is an ancient castle surrounded by an unsurpassable moat and that we live in a time before bridges and tunnels.

"Round trip to River Edge, please," I say, leaning into the glass of the NJ Transit agent's window.

Unfortunately, going home is *way* too easy.

"Next one's in fifteen minutes." The attendant sounds irked.

"Thanks."

I've decided to ignore Gia's texts today, including the one she sent this morning:

Philip asked Matt for ur #!!

The train arrives right on time, and the doors shut as quickly as they open. I don't have a chance to hesitate. New Jersey Transit waits for no one, and if I don't attend my stepsister's wedding, my father will hear it from Jam-Hands.

Jam-Hands is what I call my stepmother, though her hands aren't particularly jammy. I guess I really needed to find something to *not* like about her, but when I met her, there wasn't anything to make fun of. So when she opened a jar of jelly that everyone else was struggling with, I kinda ran with Jam-Hands.

I find an empty row of seats on the train, and in just a few minutes, it's open sky, tall weeds, and telephone poles that sprout out of the earth.

I brace myself as the train approaches Secaucus. I remember how it felt when I came back home after college. How, at this stop, something clicked and it was all real. I was heading home, and my mom wasn't going to be there.

Now, as the train comes to a stop, I imagine what she would be doing to prepare for my visit. She'd force my dad to wash the windows and mow the lawn as if the queen of England were coming. I'd find her waiting for me outside on the hanging porch swing with her hair done. Making her happy was so easy. All I had to do was show up.

Twelve years later, I still brace myself for visiting the house without her. Maybe today everyone will be so focused on

Dana's wedding that I'll be left alone. There's even a chance I'll get through the day without someone asking if I'm dating anyone.

When I get to the house, the door opens and I'm greeted by my great-aunt Rosa.

"Ana Karina! You never come see me."

She loves to say my full name and complain about my lack of visits when she's in town.

"Roberto, Ana Karina is here. Ana Karina, have you met someone?"

I am technically standing outside the doorframe, and I've already been hit with the million-dollar question.

She doesn't even wait for a response. "I don't understand, Ana Karina. So many men in that city," she says as she leads me into the house. I know I should be immune by now, but somehow this line of questioning still agitates me.

"Well, you know the expression quality versus quanti—"

But she cuts me off. "And your *eggs*!" She refers to my ovarian eggs longingly. Like they're abandoned children and I am their neglectful mother. She's normally sitting quietly in a corner and observing the world, but complaining about something gives my great-aunt a burst of energy, and my lack of procreation really brings her to life.

"Ana Karina. You are running out of eggs."

"Tía, when are you going back to Tampa?"

She's been subtracting my eggs since I turned eighteen.

"Have you frozen them yet, Ana Karina?" she asks as she takes my arm to help her down the steps into the backyard.

"No."

"Why are you killing the babies, Ana Karina? Every month, you kill the baby." Her exasperated voice grows louder.

We are now within earshot of wedding guests—some of whom are turning their heads our way.

"I don't understand what you want me to do. Have a baby with the next man I meet?"

She considers this and then continues to walk down the steps. "Freeze the eggs, Ana Karina," she says sternly.

I can't bring myself to tell her that I actually *did* look into freezing my eggs last year, but it's extremely expensive, and at my age it would have slim chances of working. The brochure had a graph with the probability of success based on age, and after thirty, it dips down like an Olympic ski jump. Freezing is a young egg's game, and mine would rather spend their final years relaxing in a much warmer climate. My eggs are like Diane Keaton, sitting on the beach in white long-sleeved turtlenecks.

At the last step, my great-aunt walks away, leaving me alone to look around. The view still takes me by surprise. When my father got remarried to a former runner-up of the Miss Cuban American Beauty Pageant, two things happened: his Cuban accent became stronger, and his love of Jimmy Buffett went into overdrive. He converted our backyard into a cramped village of tiki huts that he christened "Roberto and Elena's Margaritaville Landing," but looked more like Havana on the Hudson. He hired artisan palm frond weavers to make the hut roofs as authentic as possible and had my uncle Caesar install sprinklers to bring them all up to code.

The smallest tiki hut houses a bar with a giant machine

that pumps out frozen margaritas. A medium-size hut has a double-decker grill, and his crown jewel is the largest hut with a hanging flat-screen TV, outdoor lounge furniture, and a domino table.

The ceremony is taking place in the center of the yard, and most of the guests are already seated on white rental chairs jammed up against one another in short rows. Every inch of the yard is being used up, so there's hardly any room to move around.

"Ana Karina!" my great-aunt calls out to me from the front row. Next to her is my uncle Caesar.

"Ana! Over here!" he yells.

I don't recognize anyone as I walk down the aisle. The guests all seem to be relatives and friends of Jam-Hands or the bride and groom. The men are wearing colorful Hawaiian shirts, and the women are in bright-colored dresses. The suggested attire on the invitation was "casual, happy colors," but I'm wearing a gray silk tank and a black skirt.

"Ana, check out the altar." My uncle points to the palm frond gazebo covered in fresh white orchids. "I helped your dad build it," he says proudly. My uncle is sporting a bright-green suit, which almost matches the margarita in his hand.

"It's great." I close my eyes and think back to birthdays and holidays celebrated near this spot. When it was just the three of us and we were a tight-knit, tiki-free unit. New Year's Eve was my mom's favorite. At midnight, Cubans act out a slew of rituals for good luck, and my mother had us perform each one with gusto and at a manic pace.

First we have to eat twelve grapes. This sounds easy enough, but when you've already had pork, beans, yuca, and plantains, twelve raisins would be a lot to ask. Next we throw a large bucket of water out the front door. This is supposed to help rid your home of any evil spirits it may have accumulated throughout the year.

And finally, to guarantee that you'll travel in the next twelve months, you have to run around the block with an empty suitcase. This would be fun if you didn't have to run by your American friends and their normal families innocently waving sparklers around on their front lawns.

I tried to boycott doing this one year when I was seven or eight. My dad, committed to the cause, scooped me and my suitcase up. He and my mom practically jogged along the sidewalk, denying the bitter cold while emitting pure joy and hope for a new year. I bounced around so much in his arms, all I could do was laugh and intermittently yell out, "Stop!"

Things are so different here now. Literally nothing feels the same.

A lone cellist starts to play, and I quickly realize it's "Cheeseburger in Paradise" and that any song can sound bridal if it's played by a classical instrument. The musician is seated near the altar wearing a hot-pink Hawaiian shirt.

Randy, the groom, makes his way down the aisle as he dances to the song. He's a big guy, so he doesn't have much room, but he's not letting that stop him. He waves his arms up above him until he reaches the altar. Then three bridesmaids walk down the aisle wearing bright-yellow dresses. They groove to the music, spin, and snap their fingers. Then Jam-Hands comes down the aisle while bobbing her head to the music.

"Now, *this* is what I call a wedding!" says my uncle and then sips his margarita.

I look around, and it hits me.

The Hawaiian shirts, the song, the margaritas, the giant parrot on Jam-Hands's dress. My stepsister, Dana, is having a Jimmy Buffett–themed wedding. *How did I not know this?* The invitation just had a cheesy sunset on it. *Jimmy Buffett is my dad's thing.* What if *I* wanted to have a Jimmy Buffett–themed wedding? *I mean, I don't. But I could.* Dana should have at least checked with me first.

I promised I'd take some backup pictures, which I could tell had gotten my dad some points with Jam-Hands.

I guess she heard some nightmare story about a wedding photographer whose digital camera went haywire and was only able to recover a dozen photographs of the bride's shoes by a window. So I begrudgingly pull the camera out of my purse, take the lens cap off, and tug the cord around my neck.

I'm scrolling impatiently, trying to find the manual feature, when I look up and see my father and Dana at the end of the aisle. He manages to look elegant in a linen guayabera shirt covered in black palm trees and beige linen pants. The cellist switches to "Come Monday."

When I heard that Dana had asked my father to walk her down the aisle, I hadn't really cared. Her dad hasn't been around for a while, and she's been living with my father since she was sixteen, so it only makes sense. But right now I feel a teensy bit jealous. *Okay, maybe a little more. What comes after teensy? I'm a wee bit jealous.*

Dana did ask me to be a bridesmaid, but I lied and said I

had to work, so I wouldn't be able to rehearse the down-the-aisle dance she had planned. Ever since she and Jam-Hands moved in with my father, I've used work as my excuse to avoid spending time with them. I've pretty much had to work every weekend for the past seven years.

As they make their way toward the altar, the bridesmaids start to sing, "Come Monday, it'll be all right..."

It's like I'm back in Central Park with all the little children singing for Maria, but this is real life and it's way sweeter and there's actually going to be a wedding this time.

Dana's wearing a short, tight white dress and carrying a bouquet of sunflowers that have been wrapped all along the stems with thick burlap rope. I snap some pictures of my dad and Dana and some of Randy watching her walk down the aisle. I also get some great pictures of my dad lifting the veil and kissing her gently on her forehead. My eyes water, so I look down and fidget with the camera. *Wee bit just kicked up to plain ol' jealous.*

"This is a big change in latitude, which I believe calls for a big change in *attitude*," says the minister, pausing for a moment to give people time to laugh, which they do.

———

After the ceremony, the photographer keeps the wedding party up by the altar for photographs. I make my way to the tiki bar for a margarita. I suck up the green slush so fast I get brain freeze. A line is forming behind me, so I ask for another one and step aside to admire the wedding cake set up on a table dangerously close to the barbecue hut. It's five layers tall with a pair of bright-yellow parrots carved out of sugar on top.

"Banana!" My dad appears and gives me a hug, but I just stand there, double-fisting margaritas.

"Hey!"

"There you go! That's my girl!" he says, nodding to my drinks.

"I think you've outdone yourself." I gesture toward the cake.

"Isn't she a beauty? Guava and cream cheese frosting."

"Que fancy!" We always say, "How fancy!" even when something isn't. If I put on strawberry ChapStick, my father would say, "Que fancy!"

Thank goodness I had a fast metabolism growing up because my afternoon snack consisted of leftover bowls of frosting and bread at my father's bakery. Now he's closed Mondays and Tuesdays and goes in for only a few hours on weekends to check on things.

"Hey! I'm so glad you were able to get out of work," Dana says sweetly.

"Of course! Congratulations!" *But about this Jimmy Buffett theme . . .*

"You look terrific." Jam-Hands gives me a kiss on the cheek.

The DJ kicks in a Buffett tune, and people start to groove on the makeshift dance floor they've laid out between the ceremony altar and the largest tiki hut.

"Come on, Dad, that's our song!" Dana grabs my father's arm. *Dad? Our song?*

My father tries to pull me toward the dance floor. "Come on, honey," his thick accent making it sound 'hoe—knee.'

"Oh, I'm going to sit this one out."

As the family joins hands and dances in a circle, I grab a seat right next to the frozen margarita machine.

By bouquet-tossing time, my lips are numb and green.

"Now all you single ladies! Come on out to the center of the dance floor!" Jam-Hands yells out into the yard.

Single girls are really afraid of only one thing in this world. And it isn't jogging in the park after dark. The absolute most terrifying moment in a single woman's life is when she's called out for being single and forced to compete for a floral arrangement.

"Ana Karina! Vamos!" My great-aunt can be heard across the yard.

"Go on, get out there!" says the bartender, who's been paid to watch me empty out the slushy machine for the past two hours.

I drag myself onto the dance floor and join two other ladies already standing in the circle of shame. One is our fourteen-year-old neighbor Tammy, who has a sprained ankle and is holding herself up with a pair of crutches, and the other is Jam-Hands's sister Dolores, who is *way* too old to be wearing braces.

Thankfully, Gia already told me she will not be doing a bouquet toss at her wedding. I can't imagine having to go through this humiliation in front of Landon.

Dana takes a good look at us and smiles. She turns around and tosses the burlap-wrapped sunflowers high up into the air.

Ever wish you could go back to a certain moment in time and do things differently?

Just as the bouquet is launched into the air, I feel all beady-eyed and defiant. Thanks, no doubt, to the margarita machine.

It's heading right toward me. To my right, Tammy drops one of her crutches and dives in the air. It hits Dolores, but she keeps her arms up in an effort to win this thing.

The bouquet is right above me. If I lift my arm, I can easily catch it. *But I don't want to.*

Guilt sets in at the last minute, so I shoot my arm up. Problem is, the bouquet is going way too fast. My interference only spikes the thing higher into the air.

Tammy slams hard on the ground and lets out a piercing scream. Her mom and dad jump in to help her, and a small crowd gathers, which is why it takes a moment for anyone to realize the bouquet has landed on the burger grill under the tiki hut, where it spontaneously combusts. *I think whoever used highly flammable burlap to wrap the stems is the real culprit.*

It's mayhem. Tammy tries to get up on her crutches, and my father kicks over chairs and pushes his way through the tight space. He finally gets to the barbecue hut and slams a large metal trash can lid on the blaze, but the dark smoke sets off the sprinklers.

The huts rain down on the guests, the food, and the wedding cake. The parrot cake toppers dissolve quickly, and in a matter of seconds they're just a couple of mustard-colored streaks.

———

After endless scrambling to shut off the sprinklers, my father brought out some tools and made the cake look less swampy. Everyone seems to have moved on.

Someone cracked a joke about rain being good luck, and no one has flat-out blamed me. *Then again, I really wouldn't know.* I quickly retreated toward the bar cart in the living room and ended up upstairs.

Jam-Hands has turned my old room into a fancy gift-wrapping station. Where my bed used to be, she's installed a great wall of paper roll dispensers, custom shelving for ribbons, fancy-colored tapes, and a clunky bow-making machine. She kept my old wooden desk to use as a workstation, so I sit down and look out the window.

I tune out the party music and focus on a patch of cloudy night sky glowing off in the distance. Below that glow is Manhattan. I used to sit here and look out on overcast nights. The bright lights from the city create a white haze on the clouds above. They say the phenomenon isn't good for birds as it's disorienting and makes them fly around in circles, but those glowing clouds meant everything to me. I believed that under them, anything could happen.

I lift the lid of the desk and feel relieved to find some of my things are still there. Novels, textbooks, old notebooks. I pick up a book of poems and see something peeking out. It's stuck, so I have to open the book and peel it gently off the page.

It's a paper napkin with my handwriting on it. *Of course. It's a list. Actually, it's The List.* I instantly remember where I was when I wrote it. The Denny's on the corner of our college campus. The whole thing was Gia's idea.

"You love lists. God, you have one for everything—why not *the most* important thing?" Gia was right. My list making was already in full effect back in college. Homework assignments, places I wanted to visit one day, favorite quotes, fraternity houses I had thrown up in...but *this* kind of list had never occurred to me.

"But why do we have to limit it to four things?"

"You gotta keep it simple," Gia said as she took a bite of a waffle dripping in syrup. I remember she was wearing a bikini underneath a white linen button-down shirt. Gia was always ready for the beach. And after a year of friendship, I already knew Gia was *always* right. She was right to be ready for the beach because we went to school on Long Island, and an impromptu beach rendezvous was very likely. And she was *always* right about guys.

"The key is to know what you want so you can go after it," she said with the assurance of a life coach. "Trust me, if you had this list, Sam never would have happened."

I still remember how much it hurt to hear his name referred to in the past tense. Sam wasn't just my first college boyfriend. He was my first boyfriend *ever*. He was super funny, a big flirt, and a total Deadhead, but I fell madly in love. After six months he dumped me for a Bosnian exchange student—just when I was starting to listen to the Grateful Dead and not hating it.

Gia was right about Sam. Even when we were dating, I knew he was unequivocally a total frog, but I just kept hoping he would turn into a prince or at the very least something not too slimy.

"How did I fall so hard for the wrong guy? And why is it taking me so long to get over him?"

"You were just unprepared. You need a road map. Something to guide you so you aren't blindsided again."

The thought of a magic list preventing me from the pain I was feeling was enough to get me to agree. Gia decided she was going to write her list too. *Not that she really needed one.*

I sat up straight and started to think of all the things I wanted in a man.

"It's not like he has to be perfect. I mean, it's not like I want Brad Pitt or anything," I said, taking the task more seriously than the essay on women poets I was supposed to be writing instead.

"Oh, but *I do!*" And so Gia began her list with "Brad Pitt."

I closed my eyes and imagined the perfect man. Fred Astaire appeared and began to spin me around a piazza in Rome. Wait. Is *that* what I want? A scene from a movie? Well, Gia said we could ask for *anything.* So I went back to Rome. With Fred Astaire spinning me and my big flowy skirt around the Fontana di Trevi.

I pictured us having espresso together as he read me poetry at a café. And when he wasn't kissing me, he was making me laugh. Yes, we laugh a lot! Like I did with Sam. But instead of being a lazy pothead, he was a passionate and creative genius who channeled his talents into works of art like van Gogh, but without the crazy cut-off-his-ear thing.

I also wanted to feel butterflies thinking of him, but not like I had felt with Sam. Truth was, I always thought Sam couldn't be trusted. He was too noncommittal. I always kept an eye on him at parties. My Fred Astaire wouldn't be like that. With him, I felt butterflies, but I also felt safe.

As I wrote it out, *The List* already felt sacred.

1. Makes me feel butterflies
2. Is a hopeless romantic (à la Fred Astaire twirling me around a piazza)
3. Is a talented artist
4. Makes me laugh

I looked up and admired Gia, sitting across from me in the booth, jotting away with careless abandon. I already felt stronger. We were two young women at the dawn of a new day. We were taking charge of our lives and declaring what we wanted.

"All right, let me see yours," she said, handing me her list, which was sticky with syrup.

1. Brad Pitt
2. ~~Rich!~~ VERY rich!!
3. 6'2"
4. Worships me

"Which one's Fred Astaire again? Whatever, here's to us and our men!" Gia said, cheering with her coffee mug.

Years later, Gia would meet a man that fit her list to a T. Matt checked off everything on that napkin. He wasn't Brad Pitt, but he looked a lot like Ryan Gosling—which, let's face it, is *today's* Brad Pitt. It was as if her list knew what was best for her and had updated itself. She now wanted Gosling, not Pitt.

Plus, Matt's a very wealthy entrepreneur with multiple businesses, including his own tequila brand, a protein-infused bottled water company, and an art gallery. He's about six two and, without a doubt, worships the ground Gia walks on.

I look at my list again, and my body stiffens. Images of Landon come to me in flashes. The photograph with Matt, his arrival at Gia's bachelorette party. *I mean, it really is uncanny . . .*

1. Makes me feel butterflies—*Only every time I think of him.*
2. Is a hopeless romantic (à la Fred Astaire twirling me around a piazza)—*He samba dances like a natural.*
3. Is a talented artist—*He's a nautical architect, for goodness' sake.*
4. Makes me laugh—*Ever heard of British wit?*

Landon completely embodies my list. A list I made almost fifteen years ago.

But he barely even looked at me the other night. There was only Gia. I can still see flashes of him dancing with her, making her laugh, keeping his eyes on her as his wish burned over the candle. Immediately, there's a dull pain in my chest. If the pain had a voice, it would be saying "never." As in, you will never have him.

The music outside has come to a stop. I look out the window and watch my father make a toast to the bride and groom. He's lifted his voice so everyone in the yard can hear, but I still can't make out what he's saying. A few feet away from him, the margarita machine attendant is still cleaning up the mess I made. There are large puddles on the cement floor under the tiki huts, and he's using a window squeegee to push the water onto the grass.

I redo the bouquet toss in my mind. This time I'm super cool and smooth and not bitter at all about being single. In this replay, I bring nothing but good cheer to the wedding, and when I catch the bouquet, I'm all lighthearted and chipper. Heck, I even do some good-hearted gloating. *In your face, Crutches!*

Off in the distance, the glowing patches above the city are gone. I squint but can't find them through the clouds that have rolled in. When I first moved to the city, I took some really big steps. Now it feels like I haven't gotten far at all.

My eyes burn, threatening tears. It feels like I've lost all momentum. Like I've been floundering for a while. I've been playing it safe at work and trying to find a guy that checks off this impossible list.

Outside, I watch Dana give my dad a tight hug. Whatever he said in his speech, it was good. The music starts back up again, and I hear the recognizable steel drums of "Margaritaville." Dana joins her groom for a slow dance. He's just the right height so that her head tucks underneath his chin. The song gets to the part about wasting away, and it feels like a personal snub.

I look down at the list and blame it entirely. The tears escape and slide down my face. It hurts to admit, but I *have* been waiting for someone that checks it off. *Like an idiot.* And where has it gotten me? Literally nowhere. In fact, trying to check this list off is not making me happy. It's made me a bitter tiki hut burner.

Grow up, Ana. Your dream life doesn't just come to you wrapped in a perfect bow.

Without looking at it, I ball up The List and toss it in my purse. Letting it go feels like surrendering a dream, but I also feel a sense of freedom. Like I've been under an oppressive weight I wasn't aware of until now.

I feel like I've been crying for hours. I'm exhausted but determined. From now on, I'm going to say yes to anyone who asks me out. Even if he doesn't check off a single thing on this list. Even if he ticks off a few from the other list instead. *Even if he's vaping while standing on a skateboard when he asks me. Or heaven forbid, wearing sandals.*

CHAPTER 7

It's been a week, and so far I've only said yes to a man who offered me his seat on the subway. As for romance, just after I got home from the wedding, I got a flirty text...from Fernando.

Favorite poem about summertime? Show me yours and I'll show you mine.

Obviously going out with my best friend's brother is not what I had in mind. Between that and this morning's missed call from Philip, I couldn't decide which one I was looking forward to returning the least. Philip checks off "talented artist" on my list, but when I wrote that back in college, I was thinking more along the lines of the lead singer of Pearl Jam. I wanted to be inspired by someone who lived and breathed his art. *I never imagined he would have been living and breathing it for this long.*

So I've focused on work instead. I even managed to keep it together each time I walked by Nina and Bianca's edit room and heard them in there getting along while I sat alone trying to find the new premiere episode. Thankfully, I've found it.

And it's going to be perfect. *Even if I can't stop wondering what went wrong with Maria and Jorge.*

Today is our first tape day with Elizabeth, the unsuspecting bride-to-be. She's a teacher at a junior high school for at-risk students in Queens, and the principal has allowed us to use an empty science lab for her interview.

"I'm so proud of him. Steven is the kindest person I've ever met." Elizabeth is crying, but she looks radiant.

The light is bouncing off the whiteboards beautifully. The room is filled with a soft glow, making her look gorgeous.

My production coordinator, Jackie, nudges me from behind with a box of tissues.

"Thank you." Elizabeth takes one and gently taps her eyes.

Everyone is waiting for me to ask another question, but I can't think straight. *Does Landon have feelings for Gia? I mean, it's possible. He's known her for a while, and I know they spent time together in London recently.*

I open my notebook and scan through the list of basic questions I haven't had to look at in years.

"What do you love most about Steven?"

"So many things. I love how supportive he is with my students and that he has such a good heart." Elizabeth looks more like a jet-setting princess of Monaco than a junior high school teacher. We've told her that we're covering a news story about professional athletes, and we're focusing on her boyfriend and his commitment to charity.

"He's my best friend." She's crying again. "He's everything I ever wanted...and more. He's just, he's...perfect. Did he tell you how we met?"

I lie and shake my head. Steven Davis, point guard for the New York Knicks, told me all about how they met.

"I was in the stands with my students, and he had heard we were there, so he came by during halftime to say hello. Can you imagine? The kids were so happy...and I was so happy for them."

"We were down by sixteen," Steven had said in his casting video. "And I could tell the crowd needed some rallying, just as much as my team did. So I ran up to the third row, where Coach said the special class was..."

Elizabeth continued. "And then he looked at me and said, 'How do you guys feel about me taking your teacher out on a date?'" She mimics her boyfriend in a deep, manly voice that is equal parts silly and sweet.

As she tells her version of the story, I have a thought. In the edit, we could cut back and forth between the two of them explaining how they met and fill in each other's blanks. Hearing both points of view will really help the viewers go back to that moment. Plus, Steven's already got the NBA's approval, so we'll have the actual footage to cut back to.

"I've taken over the halftime show. The cheerleaders are just standing there. It was unbelievable." In his casting tape, Steven gets more pumped as he tells the story. "I get this crazy idea, and I'm like 'Just run with it, Steven!'"

"It was as if no one else was there. Everyone just disappeared, and he was talking only to me." Elizabeth's face has a dreamy look on it.

"They were about to do the free-throw contest with a kid

from the audience, and I just took the ball from that guy and yelled out..."

"If I make this"—she's back to doing her adorable imitation of Steven's voice—"you have to go out with me, okay?"

"When she nodded, it was the most gorgeous smile I've ever seen. I just thought, 'That's her, Steven. That's the girl you're going to marry.'"

Elizabeth has to stop for a moment so she can cry again. That night, her students jumped up and down, and just as he was about to shoot, the entire stadium went quiet.

"I couldn't believe what was happening," she says through her tears. "I was so afraid he wasn't going to make it. I wanted to have a special telepathic power so I could somehow help make that ball go into the basket..."

"I mean, I can make that shot in my sleep, but I'm not going to lie; at that moment I said a quick prayer..."

At this point in the footage, Steven dribbles the ball and then closes his eyes. Clearly done praying, he opened them back up, dribbled again, bent his knees, and threw the ball with a flick of the wrist.

Is it a swoosh? Or a whoosh? What's the sound a ball makes when it slips right through the center of the net without any resistance?

The crowd goes wild, cheerleaders throw their pom-poms in the air, and the band starts to play, but you can't take your eyes off this handsome guy running back up the stands to this girl with her big bright smile walking down to meet him.

"It was like out of a movie," Elizabeth says, not bothering to wipe the tears racing down her cheeks.

When he reaches her, he lifts her into an elevated embrace that soon becomes a massive group hug when her students join them in one big celebration of spontaneous joy.

"I never believed in love at first sight." Steven is looking right at the camera in his casting tape, but right now it feels like they're talking to each other.

"It was the most romantic moment of my life."

"I couldn't believe I could feel so happy."

"...until that moment."

"...until then."

"Perfect. We're done!" I shut my notebook so hard I startle the emotional Elizabeth.

Jackie hands her a bottle of water, and the rest of the crew begins to break down the equipment. I turn my phone back on and see I have a text from Nina.

Bianca is the worst! She just watched my first cut and told me to "make it less shitty."

Nina would have done an amazing job with my idea of going back and forth between Elizabeth and Steven telling the story of how they met. Getting it right with a new editor will be so much more work.

Jackie walks over and whispers, "Is it one o'clock yet?"

I immediately understand our code and look over to see who is standing in that position. It's the world's hottest generator delivery guy. He looks directly at us, and I quickly thrust my neck all the way back to look up at the ceiling.

"Oh yes, yes. That *does* look like asbestos." I'm the last person anyone should ever tell "Don't look now, but..."

because I will look *exactly* where you just told me *not* to look and I'll also flail my arms around like I'm drowning.

"You are the queen of smooth," says Jackie. "But you know what? He doesn't seem to mind."

He's just standing there staring at me while he wraps a long power cord around and around his forearm. He's all angles. Chiseled jaw, sharp shoulders. I picture us dancing around the fountain.

"I think he just winked at you."

"What? No, he didn't. Nobody actually winks."

"Apparently they do in Minnesota. That's where he's from. He recently graduated from NYU. Film major. Did his senior internship at the rental house where we get our gear and now he works there part-time. He lives on the Lower East Side with three roommates. His name is TJ. I still don't know what that's short for, but I'm on it."

Oh good, hot generator guy has a name. Just wish he wasn't wearing a Mickey Mouse sweatshirt today.

"How could you *possibly* know that much about him already?"

"He's a vendor," she says, pretending to sound professional. "It's *my job* to welcome him and make him feel welcomed and welcome the spirit of teamwork." I roll my eyes, and Jackie's voice slips back to work mode. "So I have to talk to the principal about our next shoot. What time do you want to start? Hello? Earth to Ana?"

"Yes, sorry. I'm listening. Seven, seven a.m."

"Right. Enjoy the view, boss."

Jackie walks away, and I do a quick self-assessment.

This morning I threw on the first things I found, a loose-fitting white tank top and jeans. My hair was behaving for once, so I left it down. I realize now that the overall look might be . . . not bad. I lean against a desk and attempt to cross my legs seductively. I sense him coming my way and pretend to write notes about today's shoot.

"You never answered my question."

I look up, and he's standing next to me, holding a large light. My senses kick into overdrive. I'm pretty sure I can smell the tiny beads of sweat on his abs under that sweatshirt. So he recently graduated from college? That would make him twenty-one or twenty-two. *Here's hoping he was held back and he's twenty-three.*

"What?" is all I can come up with.

"I just want to know if we're engaged or not."

"Oh!" I say with a loud snort. *Real sexy, Ana.*

"I think we are."

"Ah . . . I never responded." I try to sound cool, but my voice just gets deeper.

"That's true."

"I mean, but we're also not *not* engaged." *That wasn't even in the neighborhood of sexy.*

"Hey, TJ, can you help me with this?" I'm saved by a crew member walking in holding a broken light stand.

TJ raises a finger, gesturing for me to "hold on a sec" as he turns and walks across the room. *Now, he can do sexy.*

I don't know whether to flee or wait to continue our conversation. My body is conflicted. My feet are frozen to the ground, but my hips are tugging toward the door. My head is turning away, but my eyes are stuck on TJ. I can't imagine what I must look like.

I stand there for a moment, contemplating words. Should I say anything? What does a goodbye nod look like?

I decide to make use of the distraction and focus on leaving the room without tripping over anything. Was I supposed to make a left? How do I get out of this school? I find an exit, and as soon as I step outside, my cell phone buzzes with a text from an unknown number.

Wanna kick it?

CHAPTER 8

I've hit snooze a lot because it's an hour later than it should be. I had too much to drink at my wine connoisseur class last night after work. You're supposed to sip and spit, but I focused more on savoring and swallowing.

Wanna kick it?

I checked online, and the text is from a Minnesota number. TJ must have found my number on our crew call sheet. What does he mean by "kick it"? Does he want to hang out? Or go out? Is this a new sexual reference?

I throw on the same jeans I had on yesterday, grab a gray T-shirt, and slip on the oversize blazer Gia gave me years ago. *Hmm, I like this outfit.*

Today's my first day with the new editor, so he'll just be sitting there wasting the company's money, waiting for me to arrive so I can get him started.

I walk into the room and find him sitting at the editor's station with his back to the door and cell phone pressed to his ear. The lights are dimmed, but I can still make out that he has light-brown hair and is wearing a scarf around his neck.

"... I'm supposed to have a say on the projects I work on." His voice is deep and slightly scratchy.

I haven't made a sound, so he hasn't noticed me. I feel a little guilty standing here eavesdropping.

"I get it, but I shouldn't be penalized because someone else makes a mistake."

Wait, is he talking about me?

"Listen, I'd love to help out, but I'm not sure I can do this."

I don't want to hear any more. I'll walk back out and pretend I just got here, but as I turn to leave, my bag catches on the doorknob and yanks me back in. When I look back up, he's looking right at me.

"Let me get back to you on that," he says and hangs up. "Hey, are you Ana?"

"Yep, and you must be Richard."

"Yeah," he says as he stands and shakes my hand, "that's me."

"Okay, this is great." *This is horrible.*

You see, I know this guy. And we have issues. Elevator issues.

It all started about a year ago, when we stepped onto the elevator at the same time. It was just the two of us, and I was closer to the buttons, so I intuitively pressed floor ten.

"Documentaries, right?" I said, looking over at him.

"Yes," he said hesitantly. "How'd you know that?"

How did I know? He was tall, tight-bodied, and had really great hair, but he also had this smug look on his face. Like he took himself way too seriously. Plus, he was carrying a satchel, was wearing a thin dark scarf, and a pale-blue sweater with leather elbow patches. Of course I could tell he worked on the documentary floor!

But his question had caught me off guard, so I blurted out, "It's the elbow patches."

He didn't react or move an inch.

"Sorry, it's just that—" I started to apologize, but he interrupted me.

"Are you going to ten?"

"No...oh." I had completely forgotten to press my own floor.

"Yeah, I didn't think so. Here, I got it." His arm stretched out in front of me and pressed seven. *With overdramatic flair, if you ask me.*

He was just in time, too. The elevator was approaching my floor, so it made a sudden stop.

"Reality shows, right?" He said, sounding obnoxiously cordial.

I felt insulted, but of course I couldn't show it. The doors opened, so I stepped off, turned around, and smiled politely like touché and all that.

But then, as the doors closed, he pointed at what I was wearing and said, "Yeah, it's obvious. Those shows are pretty forced. Just like that outfit."

My jaw dropped. I looked down at my I heart NY baby T-shirt, long prairie skirt, and clunky white sneakers. There was no other word to describe how I felt, other than aghast. *I was really, really aghast.*

A few days later, we ran into each other getting onto the elevator again.

"Please, allow me," he said curtly, pressing seven.

It was awkward.

That same night, I ended up working late. When I got into the elevator heading down, he was in it. Because of course he'd be in it.

"Let me guess. Lobby?" he said with a smirk.

After that we stopped pressing each other's buttons and rode the elevator in deafening silence.

"Sorry about that." He puts his phone away into his old-fashioned brown leather satchel. "I just found out yesterday about this"—he takes a breath—"arrangement. So you know..." He forces a smile.

I'm so used to avoiding eye contact with him in the elevator that it's hard to have to look right at him. His face is a little pale, half of it covered by an irritatingly perfect beard scruff.

"Look, I just never work on formatted shows like this. You know, with a formula down pat. I prefer more of a challenge."

His uppity attitude isn't surprising. He's just as pompous as I thought. Thankfully, he doesn't recognize me. Or if he does, he's pretending not to, which is a relief.

"I admit this show *appears* to be deceptively easy, but believe me, it's quite difficult for editors to get it at first."

"Just not what I signed up for." He turns around and starts to switch on all the monitors, computers, and editing equipment on his desk.

Does he also have to be so *honest? Him and his skinny jeans. And why does he always wear flimsy scarves? Indoors? What is he, a Rolling Stone?*

35. No skinny jeans

36. No indoor scarves

"So is this your thing? Wedding shows?" he asks, turning around.

My thing? Why would wedding shows be anybody's thing?

"This isn't a wedding show."

"I thought—"

I cut him off. "It's a proposal show."

"Right, but—"

"This isn't actually a show about weddings or even about marriage." I cut him off again and calmly recite my favorite lines from our official show description. "This is a show about a time-less moment filled with promise and possibilities. Things will inevitably get rocky, but in that moment everything is perfect."

"So how long have you worked on this 'promise and possibilities' show?" He tilts his head to the side, his eyes sizing me up.

I pause. "Eight years."

"Eight years?"

I sit up straight and try to look less exhausted. "Yep."

"Seriously? Eight years on the same show?" After a moment he adds, "Wow."

"What have you been working on?"

"I've just finished a doc project"—he leans forward as if genuinely happy to share—"and before that a couple of development pilots."

"Well, I develop shows too," I spit out and tap my fingers on the desk nervously.

"Oh yeah, anything I've heard of?"

"No . . . not yet. But I pitched one last week that got a lot of . . . interesting feedback."

"So, where should I start?"

"Well . . ." I open my notebook and turn the pages slowly until I find my list of scenes that need to be edited. "Here we go. You can start on a scene with the future groom, New York Knicks basketball player Steven Davis. Maybe you've heard of him? He volunteers with his girlfriend's at-risk students, so in this scene he's recruited a few of them to help him shop for a new outfit to wear for the proposal."

"You want me to edit a scene where a man goes shopping?"

"Yes," I deadpan.

"Are you going to want a montage where he comes out of the fitting room in a bunch of different outfits, all totally wrong for the occasion, until he finally comes out in the right one?"

What does he have against montages? So what if I *did* get shots of Steven trying out different outfits, and so what if we put the camera on a tripod so the shot looked *exactly* the same, and *so what* if I made him try on a bunch of bad outfits until he came out in the last one, which was perfect? *How else do people try on clothes on TV?*

"Have you ever watched this show?"

"No. I have not."

"Well, why don't we start there? I think it would be kind of a must since you'll need to make another one just like it."

I spin around in my chair and look at the oversize books lined up behind me on the shelf. I pull out the one that says

"Season 7" and plop it on my desk. I'm not looking at him, but I can tell he's watching my every move. I open the notebook and reveal four DVDs tucked inside sleeves on each page. Everything we've ever shot can be found online, but I'm kind of old-school and like to have everything backed up on DVD. It's nice having the shows in tactile form. Like a collection of great novels.

"Pick one," I say, like I've opened a delicious box of chocolates. "Each one's a winner."

He stares at me. This is going to be torture for him. He looks at the shiny DVDs and pulls one out carefully with his fingertips.

He's picked the finale, which is great because it kicks off with an impressive fast-paced and emotional montage of the season's best proposals: an exciting parachute-landing proposal on a *hopefully* dormant volcano, a dangerous shark–infested underwater scuba proposal on a shipwreck, and a touching last day of prison proposal. He slips the DVD in and starts watching the show on the large wall monitor with a pair of headphones.

I review the schedule for our next shoot, from time to time looking up to study the back of his head, but he barely moves.

The show is almost over, and I have no idea what he's thinking. *Not that I care what he's thinking.* But any reaction would be nice. He could be asleep for all I know.

On the screen, a slender guy atop a volcano looks up at the sky. A hawk lands on his arm, wearing a tiny scroll around his neck. *Okay, maybe this is a little over the top even for me.* Just as he's about to open the scroll to read his girlfriend's response, the door opens. The contrast between the bright hallway and the dark edit room blinds me for a moment.

"Hey!"

"TJ?"

Richard spins around in his chair, and now the three of us are waiting for one of us to speak.

"Richard," he says as he gets up to shake his hand.

"Oh. This is TJ. He works for one of our vendors. This is my new editor."

TJ is wearing another hooded sweatshirt, but this time he's also wearing a plaid shirt underneath.

"This is so cool." TJ sounds like a teen at his first Comic-Con. "It's way bigger than the ones at NYU."

He walks across the room and plops down on the couch but then gets right back up. He can't stop moving.

"So..." I say, trying to make conversation.

"So..." TJ mimics me.

Richard is just sitting there watching us.

"Can I help you with anything?" I ask after a pause.

"Jackie said you wanted to talk about the lighting equipment order."

I'm going to kill Jackie.

"Nope. Nothing. I...I took care of it. Just a few minutes ago."

"Oh, that's too bad," he says naughtily and leans on my desk. "Did you get my text?"

"Yes, yes, I did," I say in a proper businesslike manner. I take a sip of my coffee and try to think up ways to make this all sound like it's work-related. "And I texted you back." Another sip of coffee, hoping this looks totally natural.

"I didn't get it."

"Ah. Well. I said we will *not* be needing the extra light kit this weekend because...we will be just fine without it."

I hope I'm not being *too* cryptic. I still need TJ to get the point and leave.

"Are you sure?" TJ picks up my stapler and waves it around. "Because it would be really nice to have the extra lights this weekend. I think it will make a *big* difference, and you're gonna love how I...set them up."

He's not even trying *not* to sound sexy.

"Don't mind me. I'm just going to get back to work. See you around, man." Richard spins back around to watch the end of the episode. By this point my cheeks are flaming.

TJ sets the stapler back on my desk slowly and bites one side of his lower lip.

I know I made a pact. I'd say yes and stay open. Now I just need to follow through. *What's the worst that could happen?* Plus, I desperately need to get him out of here. "Fine! Yes, that does sound good. You sold me! What the heck, right?"

"Perfect."

When TJ finally shuts the door, I breathe a sigh of relief.

"That was definitely the right call." Richard swivels around in his chair, a subtle smirk on his lips. His tone is annoyingly professional and deliberate. "The proper lighting makes everything better. Don't you agree?"

My jaw is clenched, so I just say, "Mm-hm." I'm certain I detect a hint of sarcasm, but I'm not sure he's still talking about lighting. He could totally be dissing TJ or insulting my show. *Or both.* We do a bit of a weird stare off before he turns back around and gets to work.

"At the same time"—he's turned his head back slightly—"all the bells and whistles in the world can't save you if the content isn't any good."

CHAPTER 9

I ring Gia's doorbell with my elbow because I'm carrying an extra-large wedding planning notebook and a stack of new bridal magazines I've already looked through and marked up with ideas for everything from table settings to parking lot configurations. I want to forget about the fact I said yes to a date with someone *so much* younger and focus on checking off my list of things to do for Gia's wedding.

<u>Wedding Chores:</u>
1. Create schedules for rehearsal and wedding day.
2. Complete DJ playlist.
3. Follow up with pending RSVPs.
4. Update wedding website.

Gia opens the door wearing a floor-length silk kimono and high heels. "Welcome to my dungeon!" she says. Her hair must have extensions in it because it's a foot longer *and a foot wider* than it was last week.

"Uh, hi." I follow her as she leads me to the bedroom. "I brought the music list I started last night, but I think we should video conference with your cousins about the wedding-day schedule first. That still needs a lot of..." I come to a complete halt. It looks like my production crew is taping in her bedroom.

There are large lights set up all around the bed, which is covered in black silk sheets with matching red and black striped silk pillows.

"What's going on? I thought we were calling the twins to work on the wedding?"

"We are, but first I'm having boudoir photos taken as a wedding present for Matt." Gia slips off her kimono, revealing a red lace teddy with built-in garter attachments. "And look!" She grabs a leather riding whip and slaps the bed with it.

"You said you wanted us to work on his gift, but I thought you meant we'd look for something online *while* we worked on the wedding," I say, trying not to sound stressed out.

Gia has tasked her twin cousins, Emilia and Esther, with the wedding planning. The problem is neither of them has ever planned a wedding. Together they manage their parents' small chain of supermarkets. Plus, they live in Sao Paolo, and our video conference calls are not even remotely productive.

Gia only translates about half of what they say, so the producer in me is flipping out because I have no idea what's really getting done. When I told her that she should drop the twins and get a professional, she said, "No way. They really want to do it, and family is more important than anything else."

The biggest challenge with this wedding is that Matt and

Gia are getting married in Aura, a quaint little town two and a half hours north of the city. Just far away enough that people will need to spend the night and too far away for us to use any New York City vendors.

In Aura there's absolutely nothing in the realm of florists, photographers, DJs, or pretty much anything you could possibly need to put a wedding together. It's all apple orchards, horse farms, a decent diner, and one sushi restaurant. In other words, it's a production nightmare.

Gia decided to get married there because she was producing a new show about farm-to-table cookoffs. Which didn't make any sense to me because I thought the whole farm-to-table thing was about slowing down and taking your time to prepare a meal for optimum taste and nutrients. *Not about having chefs yank turnips out of the ground just to throw them into a food processor.*

As Gia was driving past an orchard after filming the show, she saw a lone black horse run up a hill and stop just as the sun was setting behind him, creating a dreamy silhouette. She decided that was *exactly* what she wanted for her wedding.

The problem is her "vision" really isn't much to go on. A horse. A hill. A sunset. That's more like a John Wayne movie. Or *Black Beauty*. Or *Seabiscuit*.

Now she's expecting the twins to create her wedding from scratch. In the middle of nowhere New York when they're all the way in Brazil. So far all they've done is rent out an empty barn they found online.

"I love it. All we need is a couple of chandeliers," Gia said when we were scouting the place a few months ago. Talk about oversimplifying. Does she have any idea how difficult it is to hang a chandelier?

A stocky guy in an oversize beanie walks out of Gia's bathroom.

"What do you think!?" Gia asks him as she kneels on the bed and cracks the braided leather strands of the bullwhip in the air.

"Perfect!"

"Enrique, this is Ana, my best friend and maid of honor."

Enrique is not excited to see me.

"Enrique won Race for the Raciest Bedroom Photo Season One. He's a boudoir master."

"No kidding. So, what time is Matt getting home?" I'm hoping this will all have to wrap up soon.

"He's out of town till tomorrow."

"We have a lot to do," I say, trying to remain calm.

"I know. We'll get to it."

Gia whips the bed, and Enrique gets to work. She lies back on the bed and opens her legs in the air just as the doorbell rings.

"That should be the sushi. Will you get it?"

I sign for the food, set it all up on a tray, and pour myself a tall glass of red wine. I take a deep breath and drink half of it before heading back into the room.

"An article in one of these recommends creating a schedule even before you have all the details down pat," I say as I flip through the magazines.

"I want one like this." Gia squeezes her boobs together until they practically pop out and takes a sexy selfie with her cell phone. Enrique snaps pictures of her taking pictures of herself.

"How about we start with the rehearsal day? Eight o'clock? Nine? Let's say eight for the wedding run-through." I can tell Gia's not listening. Instead, I watch as she carefully adds filters to one of the pictures she's just taken and sends it to someone.

"You're not sending those to Matt, are you?"

"No, of course not."

"We could have the catered brunch at ten a.m. I think that gives us plenty of time to actually practice with the horse."

Her phone chimes with a text back that causes her to laugh. "You have to see this guy's tilted penis." She turns her cell phone toward me, and I'm too late averting my eyes.

"Could you stop flirting with other men so we can plan your wedding?"

"I'm not flirting. I'm getting feedback."

I get that friendships shouldn't feel like a race, but I've always felt miles behind Gia. Now she's getting married, is ready to start a family, and has received so many penis pics she could make her own coffee table book. While I've yet to receive a single one. *Tilted or otherwise.*

Gia stands up on the bed, and Enrique turns on a large fan I hadn't even noticed was there, which makes her hair fly around. If we're not going to get any planning done, maybe I can bring up Landon. I may be open to dating someone who isn't perfect, but that doesn't mean I have to give up on the real deal. I'm just not waiting around for him.

In the meantime, I should be able to tell my best friend how I feel about a guy. Well, maybe not *exactly* how I feel. *No need to mention the playlist I created a while back for when I stalk his social media. Of mostly Gaelic tunes.*

"So, Matt's friend Landon was really nice. Did he have a good time?"

"Yeah, he's okay."

"Why just okay?"

"Matt said the dumbest thing," she says, avoiding my question. "He thought you might have a crush on him."

"I mean, I do think he's—"

"He's not your guy. Trust me." She wraps the whip around her neck.

"Yes!" Enrique snaps away.

"Why would you say that?"

"Trust me," she says in a way that makes me feel suspicious. What is she holding back? I hate when Gia acts like she knows everything and I just have to take her word for things.

"Maybe you're right. It did kinda seem like he was flirting with *you*."

"With me?"

"Oh, Gia, Gia!" I mimic.

"Please, he does that because he knows how much I hate it." The fact that she's now on her back and pretending she's a cat clawing at some make-believe yarn makes her lack some validity. I may be paranoid, but something about the way she's acting makes me feel like Landon could be one of the men she's sexting with right now.

"Yes! Bad kitty!" Enrique's loving life.

Gia's phone chimes, and the text makes her laugh again and go back to taking sexy selfies.

"You just need to trust me." Gia sounds a little stern suddenly. "Remember I was right about Sam I Scam."

I hate when she brings up my ex from college to win an argument. Five nanoseconds after meeting Sam, she decided he was "a bad idea." Sometimes I think she brings up Sam to convince me I can't trust my own feelings and only *she* knows what's best for me. It's infuriating. It's also upsetting that the nickname she gave Sam still has a fresh sting to it.

"Love me," Gia demands childishly and swats the whip toward me. She knows when I'm wounded. "With fondue," she adds, and I can't help smiling. She also knows how to butter me up.

"Some hot cheese on your head would be perfect right about now," I say, and she gives me a sore look.

Our friendship has gone through many catchphrases, but "with fondue" has stood the test of time. We came up with it back in college. I miss how it felt to be that version of us.

We had a news reporting assignment due for our TV production class. We could choose any subject to report on, and somehow we landed on smog. We had to do all the work ourselves. Research, write, operate the camera and audio equipment, and take turns being the on-camera reporters. It was so hot and sticky the day we were recording our assignment. We had decided to film our report from our school's observatory so we could have the sun rising behind us in the shot. But that meant we had to lug all the heavy equipment up seven flights.

"You know what would make this worse?" I said as we stopped to rest the cases for a moment. "If we had to wear high heels."

"Or snow boots."

"Ooh, that would be worse."

"What if we absolutely had to wear feather boas?"

"Ah! That's awful. It would stick to our sweat."

We slowly inched our way up the flights, making ourselves laugh to ease the pain.

"And with hot cheese fondue pouring down on our heads," I said, convinced my arm would be too sore to lift the microphone when we got to the top.

"Fondue? Who would be doing that to us?"

"The heavens. Because we've clearly upset them."

We were so exhausted, we were giddy. We fell to the ground, laughing hysterically. We practically missed the sunrise. *And unfortunately, it was a clear, smogless morning.*

Over the years, the notion of hot cheese on our heads has become a positive thing, and "with fondue" is now our equivalent of "with a cherry on top."

"And don't get mad." Gia is now sitting on the edge of the bed and putting on long black leather gloves. "But I'm the one who told Matt to give Philip your number."

"Whach?" I've just stuffed a large piece of sushi in my mouth.

"Give him a chance. I saw the way you two were getting along at the party. You never know. Crazier things have happened."

"I think those garters are cutting off the circulation to your brain. He invited me to his studio, and of course I want to go, but that's it." But she's right. It was so easy talking to Philip. While everyone else was working so hard to impress him, I felt so relaxed and at ease.

"Yes, that's perfect! You have to go!"

"You want a sexy photo for Philip?" Enrique whispers to me, motioning to the bed.

"No, that's not going to happen," I snap. "Besides, I may have actually met someone."

"Really?" Gia eyes me suspiciously. "Who? Where?"

"No one you would know. At work."

Gia squints her eyes like she's reading my mind. *Which is a power I do think she possesses.* "Well, just give Philip a chance."

CHAPTER 10

It doesn't seem real to me." Richard sounds exhausted.

But I'm the tired one. Editing a show with Nina was so much simpler, so idyllic. If I said, "Add more cymbals," she'd do it. If I said, "Longer drum roll," she'd say, "You're a genius." But Richard fights me on every little thing. He says he prefers to keep things feeling "less produced," and seeing as I'm the producer, I feel like what he's really saying is "less Ana."

"It's just an *overall* note," he adds, and I'm starting to think he's making fun of my outfit because I'm wearing denim overalls today, and it's the third time he's found a way to use the word in a sentence.

"My overall opinion is that more cymbals would be idiotic."

"Overall, I don't think we should have any more montages."

But overalls are *totally* back in style. I'm seeing them everywhere, so I pulled out my old ones from college and tied up my hair in a high ponytail.

As I walked out of my apartment, I felt so hip and bouncy,

which is *exactly* how I want to feel today. This afternoon we're taping a new scene for Steven and Elizabeth's episode indoors, which means we'll need lots of lighting equipment.

"They're just having dinner. What's so unreal about that?" I say, trying not to sound upset. Richard swivels around in his chair to face me.

"He's rented out the roof of the Empire State Building, which is in and of itself a completely unrealistic thing for someone to do, and he's gone through all this trouble with the wine and the fancy stuffed mushrooms, so she's *clearly* expecting it, and then he *doesn't* do it! Why would he set up such an extravagant dinner and then *not* propose?"

"That is *exactly* the point! He thinks that will make the *real* thing an even *bigger* surprise." I hope he doesn't ask me whose idea the Empire State Building rooftop was. Steven is a nice guy, but he doesn't have any great ideas for the show. Thankfully, he goes along with whatever I suggest.

"Sounds like he's torturing her."

"Stuffed mushrooms *aren't* all that fancy. I have them all the time. Besides, it's about setting things up. Proposing at that dinner is *exactly* what Elizabeth would expect. It's all part of their story. Steven feels like she sees him as this famous athlete who lives a lavish celebrity lifestyle, so he wants to show her he's more than that. That he can be sweet, too. He can be everything for her."

Take that, Mr. Documentary! How's that for deep and meaningful material? Sure, I had to make the whole thing up because Steven and Elizabeth's relationship is about as deep as a stuffed mushroom, but Richard doesn't seem moved.

"Don't roll your eyes at me, Brooklyn."

"Brooklyn? How do you know I live in Brooklyn?"

"Wild guess."

"What's wrong with Brooklyn?"

What *do* I have against Brooklyn? I've only been there twice, once to a work party at a loud, dirty bar in Williamsburg and once when I walked across the Brooklyn Bridge. I guess I just feel that if you could be in shiny Manhattan, why go anywhere else?

"We have too much to do right now to get into that. Back to this dinner...The whole point is that it's going to be an even bigger surprise when he shows up at her school and proposes in a sweet, low-key way."

"Well, I can't wait to see what you consider low-key, Manhattan."

"I take that as a compliment."

"Look, I just think we'd actually root for the guy if he weren't so obnoxious."

"But he's perfect. He's a gorgeous athlete with a multi-million-dollar contract who also happens to be smart and down-to-earth."

"What makes you think he's smart?"

"He wrote a book," I say quietly.

"Really? What book?"

"A children's book...about cyberbullying. Don't roll your eyes..."

Richard's cell phone rings. "Hey, Maxi," he says, sounding irritated. He stands up to take the call out in the hallway and shuts the door behind him. Maxi is Richard's poor, neglected girlfriend. I have deduced this by the way he always takes her calls and sounds even more annoyed with her than he does with me. *I miss Nina.* She never took her personal calls outside. We never kept anything from each other.

The producer/editor relationship is supposed to be sacred. Like the one with your hairstylist. You spend hours together in a small, dark room, so it's impossible *not* to bond. You create your own language and read each other's thoughts. You get into a smooth rhythm, and it's like you become one person, like an octopus with many hands working together to sculpt a piece of art.

But working with Richard is the complete *opposite*. It feels claustrophobic in here. There's no shared language. The whole day is filled with stops and starts. He thinks he knows everything, and I spend the entire day explaining why he's wrong.

He walks back in, and I notice his scarf is even thinner than the one he had on yesterday and that today's jeans are made of corduroy. Where does he even find such perfectly fitting corduroys? He must have them custom-fitted to his body.

37. Tight-fitting corduroys

Thankfully, I'll be leaving soon. He can just sit here and argue with his girlfriend all he wants because I have better things to do.

"Hello! How's it going in here?" Bianca lets herself in.

Richard and I respond at the same time.

"Terrific," I say excitedly.

"Fine," he says in a monotone droll.

"I'm Bianca, by the way. Senior producer. So nice to finally meet you." Bianca walks up to Richard's desk and rests her butt close to his console. "I've heard great things about you. So sorry your first project down here wasn't your first choice."

"Oh, it's okay, I was just a little disappointed at first—"

"Oh, me too, believe me. It's just that when Ana lost her premiere, I had to snag up her editor, who had *nothing* to do." Bianca is completely ignoring that I'm in the room. "Well, hopefully we'll get a chance to work together soon."

"Yeah, sure."

Bianca turns to me. "Don't work him too hard. Now that we've got the best editor in the building on our floor, we don't want to lose him. Well, gotta cruise!"

"Ciao," Richard says offhandedly.

Bianca shuts the door behind her, and he swivels his chair around. "So how does one lose a premiere exactly?"

"I didn't lose it..." I start out defensively, but thinking about Maria and Jorge has a sad, calming effect on me. "The bride walked out on her proposal."

"That sounds like a much better show."

"Not really," I say quietly.

"Listen, I can be romantic. I just don't think any of this stuff is romantic. Do you honestly think so?" I notice for the first time that Richard's scruffy beard has reddish streaks in it.

"I think it *could* be, if you would agree to adding more cymbals when the stuffed mushrooms arrive." He almost breaks into a smile, and I feel triumphant.

GERERRRRR.

The moment of victory is completely canceled out by the unmistakable sound of my stomach growling. And it's a deep, lengthy, boorish growl. Even Richard looks surprised.

It's especially embarrassing because the timing couldn't have been worse. It's as though my stomach overheard our conversation and got all excited: "Stuffed mushrooms? Did somebody say stuffed mushrooms?!"

"Someone's hungry."

"Oh no, that's just..."

GWRRRWW.

The second one is more horrifying than the first. And so robust. Like our sound guy has placed a microphone on my belly button.

Nothing I can say would help this moment feel any less awkward, but I'm racking my brain for ideas anyway. I could explain that while it's only 11:00 a.m. and I had a hearty breakfast, my body is ravenous again. And how my gut typically demands a second breakfast or an early lunch. Or, in a perfect world, a weekday brunch. *But I don't need to explain my corporeal quirks to Richard. Why do I care what he thinks?*

Richard is smiling now, which isn't helpful. "You okay?" His tone is unusually sweet.

I squirm around to try to prevent it from happening again. *Please don't happen again. Not here. Not in front of this guy, who should be mocking me but instead is making me feel like he thinks it's the cutest thing in the world that my stomach grunts like a wild hog.*

BZZZZRR.

My phone vibrates, and I almost drop it trying to answer it so quickly.

"Oh good, you're not dead," says my dad on the line. I've taken the call without noticing who it is.

"Hi." I purposely hold back on saying "Dad." *No point in letting Richard know my business if he doesn't share his. Plus, if he thinks it's a guy calling, that could be growl-redeeming.*

"What are you doing tonight?"

"Tonight? I don't have plans." I'm thrilled, and not only because the slight raise in his brow reveals Richard is definitely intrigued. I'm also thrilled because this could mean some one-on-one time with my dad.

"Great! We're going to the city to see a show. You can join us for dinner." *Us?*

"Oh . . . great. See you later." *A show?* My father's never seen a Broadway show in his life.

"Are you all right?" Richard asks.

"I'm fine."

"Are you sure? Because your *overall* countenance changed after that call."

————

The first time we taped an episode of *Marry Me* at Tiffany's, I was awestruck. It was a magical day. Everything was coming together. My career was as sparkly as all the rings under the glass because I finally felt like a part of New York's history.

But eight years later, it's feeling like an endless pale-blue fun house with way too many mirrors, and the equipment keeps reflecting off the glass display cases, making it impossible to shoot. Chuck can't stop waving his light meter around desperately in search of a good reading. Maybe this is a sign I'm ready to work on something else. On my own show.

The worst part is the place is swarming with tourists walking through the aisles. Have any of you heard of the Met? Or the Guggenheim? Get outside, people! Explore the city! I know you're looking for a bit of *Breakfast at Tiffany's* nostalgia, but I'm trying to work here!

Or more accurately, I'm standing behind a tall ceramic vase watching TJ through the windows as he unloads equipment from the van.

"Give me the word and I'll work my magic." Jackie appears from behind, startling me. I bump into the vase so it teeters back and forth until I wrap my arms around it.

"Huh?"

"Just give me the go-ahead and I'll let him know you're interested."

"Why would I do that?"

"News flash, he's never going to approach you first. He's going to need some reassurance," she says, looking at him from behind the vase. We watch TJ as he jumps out of the van and bends over to pick up a stack of light reflectors.

"I have no idea what you are talking about. I mean, besides, it's called *company policy*." I haven't told Jackie that I've already agreed to a date this weekend.

"First of all, life's too short to follow every single rule. Second, he's over twenty-one, so he's fair game, and third, you're not technically his boss. He works for a vendor."

"You think he's only twenty-one? Does NYU have a three-year program?"

Jackie looks up quickly. "No, that's not where we want the catering," she says to a delivery guy about to set two over-loaded plastic bags on a jewelry case. I'm left alone with the thought I have agreed to "kick it" with someone more than a decade younger than me.

Then again...there's *something* about TJ. He walks in and smiles right at me.

My phone buzzes, and I see I have a missed call from a number I don't recognize, but they've left a message, so I listen as I watch TJ's beautiful backside as he heads out to the van again. Immediately, I recognize the deep, raspy voice.

"Ana, hello. Phil Oberon here again. Hope this message finds you well. I would like to formally extend the invitation for a tour of my studio at your earliest convenience..." TJ walks back in and puts down a large case just a few feet in front of me. "Let me know if Tuesday works for you. You can reach me at this number anytime."

I fumble, trying to put my phone away, and drop it on the floor. TJ pulls out his phone. As I pick up my cell, it buzzes with a text.

ps1 saturday jam hot wanna?

I have no idea what it means, but TJ is watching me and waiting for a response. The text needs to be deciphered, but I'm still excited to receive it.

Jackie's right. Life is short, and I should live a little. Although I have no idea what TJ wants to do on Saturday, I text back: Sounds perfect!

CHAPTER 11

A warm breeze sweeps through the buildings as I step out of the store. It's only about fifteen blocks from Tiffany's to Times Square, and some fresh air will be good for me. I'm headed to a pre-theater dinner with my father and stepmother, yet I've got an extra bounce in my step.

I've made plans with TJ, and I may even see Philip, too. *Why not?* I have nothing to lose. I actually feel inspired. Like I've opened a bunch of doors, each filled with unlimited potential. They may not be perfect, but it feels like I'm sending the right message. Look at me, universe: I'm open for business! *In a nontransactional kinda way.*

"How About You" blasts in my headphones as I speed-walk through the packed sidewalks. Here's a fun fact: when you listen to that song in New York and it happens to be June, you feel like it was made just for you. *Who doesn't like a Gershwin tune? I mean, really?*

The song ends as I cross Forty-Seventh Street. Now all I

hear are taxis honking. This is why visitors find New York intimidating. They go to Times Square and don't realize this isn't New York at all.

Times Square is New York pretending to be something it isn't for tourists who want to eat at themed restaurants, be slapped by 360 degrees of computerized advertising, and see a musical that was once a decent movie. I forgive the city for giving in to others' expectations and walk against the foot traffic in as Zen a state as I can.

The Chinese restaurant I picked for us is packed with theatergoers waiting to be seated.

"Ana! There she is!" My stepmother's voice cuts through the crowd.

I turn around and see them walking in the door. My father always sticks out in New York. He's wearing a nice jacket and tie, but he doesn't look comfortable.

"I'm really glad you could make it," he says, rolling the *R* as though he were speaking Spanish, and gives me a bear hug that smells like Old Spice.

He's made big changes over the years, but at least he still uses the same aftershave.

They sit across from me at the table, and I notice the gentle ways my father treats his wife. Even the littlest things stand out to me, like the way he hands her a menu before taking one for himself or how he pulls her chair a little closer to his.

"Dana says they're having the best honeymoon. Randy booked a private sailboat. Can you imagine? They have their own captain and skipper, their own chef and housekeeper. Can you imagine how romantic it must be to be waited on hand and foot while sailing around the Caribbean? Dana says there are black sand beaches. Can you imagine?" My step-mother shakes her head like no one in the world can imagine anything.

"We have an announcement to make. Do you want to tell her, Robert?" Elena prods my father, but he looks stiff and hesitant.

"We sold the bakery," he says finally with a forced smile.

"Why?" I spit out the word without really thinking.

"Well..." He seems surprised and responds in the same tone as when I was a little girl and he carefully laid out all the reasons why I couldn't go to sleepaway camp.

"I was spending less and less time there, and we got a really great offer."

This sudden disappointment sits heavy in my chest. It's not like he shouldn't be allowed to do what he wants with his life. It just seems like he wants to strip off anything left of his old self. Especially the bits of him connected to my mom. What was wrong with the old him?

"Sounds great, Dad," I say, trying to sound genuinely happy for this person sitting in front of me. Whoever he is.

"Thanks, Banana."

"You know, there's something *different* about you, Ana," says Elena, narrowing her eyes and snapping her head to the side.

"Yeah. You know, I was just thinking the same thing," says my dad.

And then Elena yells out, "There's a man in your life, Ana!" Two elderly couples at the table next to ours are now waiting to hear if I'm finally dating someone too.

I tense up as if I've been caught doing something I shouldn't. The fact is she's right. *Sort of.*

The look on my father's face makes me even more anxious. He looks... *ecstatic.* Before I know it, I find myself nodding.

"I knew it! That's wonderful. I knew something was different about you!" Elena screeches and puts her arm around my father. "Well, what's he like? Tell us all about him!"

"I like him already," says my dad with a sweet, dumbstruck look on his face. "It's great to see you smiling."

What's he talking about? I smile. I smile all the time. Maybe not so much when I visit them, but that's their fault, not mine. I smile tons in the city. *Tons!* Well, maybe not at work lately, but that's because of Bianca mostly.

My father reaches across the table and grabs my hand gently.

I mean, maybe he's right. I don't smile enough. Maybe I *could* be happier. But I'm working on it. I definitely don't want him to worry about me. But I don't think he wants to hear about how I've quit waiting for my dream guy and started saying yes to anyone with a pulse.

"He's great, actually."

My father and Elena are hanging on every word.

"He's extremely talented, funny, and romantic."

"And what does he look like, dear?" she asks.

I imagine TJ's strong forearms as he lifts heavy production equipment.

"Gorgeous." I sound so convincing.

"He sounds perfect!" She claps her hands. My father looks like I've won the Nobel Peace Prize. Better, in fact. He looks *relieved.*

"Yep. Yes. He does...he is." The look of joy on my father's face makes me feel pathetic. *So this is what I've become. A grown woman who lies to her father about having a boyfriend.* I feel my eyes watering up.

"Oh look, Robert. She *is* in love."

Thankfully, love can look a lot like misery. And now they're both convinced I've met the man of my dreams.

"Oh, Anita. We're so happy for you!" Elena reaches across the table and takes my other hand.

This is awful. My father and Elena are holding my hands and think we're finally bonding and having this family moment, and I want to scream. I can feel my face twisting in a contortion of frustration and pretend smiling.

"Bring him around. We'll have him over for BBQ Sunday. Get a look at him." My dad says this so naturally and Elena nods so sweetly that for a moment I allow myself to believe this guy actually exists.

CHAPTER 12

I feel a lot better after the emotional moment with the parents. I must have been feeling stressed, between the situation at work and trying to make sure my best friend's wedding isn't a huge unplanned disaster. It makes me sad to think Dad has been worrying, though. There's nothing to worry about. I'm fine! Especially now that I'm ready for the weekend.

I was up early to prepare for whatever it is TJ has planned for us and came up with a list.

Main differences between college girls and women my age:
1. Body fat
2. Number of eyelashes

As we age, our lashes become thinner and thinner until they all fall off and never grow back. I think it's nature's way of saying the older the eyeball, the less it deserves protecting.

So that's why I find myself in the part of Chinatown

where they specialize in women's cosmetic insecurities. I pass the "No Happy Endings" sign on the door and hope it isn't foreshadowing.

"Cash only, one hundred dollars," says a beautiful young Chinese woman behind the counter. I comply, and another woman appears and leads me down a dark hallway. She opens a creaky door and...

It's like something out of *A Clockwork Orange*. The room is filled with as many narrow beds as they could cram inside, and on each one is a woman with her eyelids forced wide open with pieces of white tape. It's terrifying. What's wrong with these women? What's wrong with me? Where are my priorities? Why would I pay for someone (who is not a doctor) to stretch my eyelids up to my forehead and come dangerously close to one of the most important organs of my body with a faux lash dripping in glue?

An hour later, I barely recognize myself. I have so many long and thick lashes, they're almost in the way! Each time I blink, they bump into my eyebrows. These longer lashes are making me feel younger. *Hopefully no one will notice my lashes have sprouted like beanstalks overnight.*

When I finally get back to my apartment, I can't stop overthinking "kick it." Is this a date? Kick it could mean "let's hang out as friends." Why didn't I consult a young person? It's too late now.

I try on almost everything I own before I settle on an outfit. Weekend daytime events like this throw me off in the city. I have to dress for 3:00 p.m., but what I'm wearing also needs to be appropriate at 10:00 p.m. because I may not head home in between things. This outfit must transition seamlessly from day to night.

I'm not sure I've made the right choice. I'm wearing a short, white cotton minidress with an open back that makes me look like I'm headed to a tennis match.

———

TJ texted that we should meet by the bar, but right now I'm standing in the middle of a rave in broad daylight, and there is no bar in sight.

The garden of the PS1 Museum of Art in Queens has been converted into a summer beach house, with a DJ up on a platform spinning deafening techno music and hundreds of people crammed around a long two-foot-deep pool. Some ravers planned ahead and are wearing flip-flops and bathing suits and are dancing *inside* the pool.

I check out my expensive platform sandals. There will be no pool for us.

It took forever to decide what shoes to wear. If I went with flats, I wouldn't feel dressed up enough, while heels would make me feel old. So I went with a designer pair of beige platforms with soles made out of ropes. I bought them three summers ago for $420 (under Gia's influence, of course), and this is the first time I've ever worn them.

Tall towers of metal fans all around the garden are helping everyone stay cool as they bounce in unison under the sweltering summer sun.

I spot TJ walking toward me, parting a sea of regular-looking people. He's wearing a white T-shirt and cargo pants and carrying red plastic cups spilling over with beer.

"What a fox!" he says, handing me one of the red cups.

"Thanks!" The music is so loud, for all I know, he may have just said, "You look like a tennis trot." So I add, "For bringing me here!"

We both sip our beer, and the song shifts from one hypnotic drone to another slightly different hypnotic drone that makes TJ really excited. He slams back the rest of his beer, throws the cup on the ground, and grabs my arm.

"Come on," he says in a sexy take-charge kinda voice, leading me deeper into the crowd *and closer to the pool*. It feels nice to be led by him. To be here with him. For people to think a hot guy leading me to the dance floor is a regular occurrence.

But I'm tense and stiff, and no one said anything about dancing in broad daylight. I chug the rest of the beer and place it gently on the floor by the pool because *placing* is not the same as *littering*.

A couple of guys jump in, splashing me and my outfit, so I "dance" around TJ and position him between me and the water.

I think I've got a handle on the dancing. I'm pulling off a nice and easy side-to-side movement that goes with the slow drone beat.

"So you're from Minnesota?"

"What?" He leans in so close that I can feel his soft skin on my cheek. It's as soft as a baby's bottom. *And what is that smell? Vanilla? The sea? Do oceans smell different than seas?*

I'm forced to get closer to his bright, perfectly sculpted face and yell, "Where are you from?"

"Minnesota. Yes."

"Which city?"

"Minneapolis," he yells back. "Home of the Vikings."

"Oh, nice!"

TJ smiles and puts his hands around my waist.

"You know, the Vikings discovered America." *I'm kickin' it, all right. Kickin' it right into nervous-talking mode.* "Christopher Columbus gets the credit, but it wasn't him at all."

His hands are all over my white tennis dress. He's so close, my legs can feel his strong quadriceps.

"But it was actually discovered hundreds of years before that, by a Viking named Leif Erikson!" I scream the last two words as his hands discover my butt.

The dance floor is packed tight. It's the kind of crowd that makes you feel like you're invisible. Which is a relief because TJ leans in and kisses my ear. His lips feel so soft. And warm.

"But you know what?" The words are still spewing out of me nervously. "Who really knows for sure? *I* wasn't there. *You* weren't there. That's the thing about history. Who's to say what really happened and who touched what first? It's silly when you think about it. The land was already there; no one *discovered* it. You know what I mean? What about Indigenous peoples? What about the Incas?"

The song ends and TJ steps away from me, releasing his arms from my waist. The next song kicks in, and everyone in the crowd, including TJ, starts to jump up and down. I don't get it. As far as I'm concerned, this is the same song we just heard, only louder and quicker. The beat speeds up until there's a crescendo, and then a hurricane arrives in Queens.

It's now raining down on all of us. But the water isn't just coming from above, it's coming from all sides and it's coming in fast. The towers of fans all around us are spraying water so intensely they're quickly soaking the crowd. And everyone is loving it.

Every part of me is under attack by the fans. They're everywhere. And they're clearly programmed to go with the music because as the song speeds up, they spray us even more.

People are jumping in the pool and throwing their beers in the air, so every once in a while I feel a cold spray on my open back or splashing up from below. My ropy platform shoes are decomposing, and my white tennis dress is stuck to my skin and completely see-through. My new eyelashes are like upside-down umbrellas, collecting the rain and dragging my eyelids down.

I stop moving. My body is frozen stiff. I cannot even pretend to know how to kick it looking like this.

But then TJ locks eyes with me and takes his wet T-shirt off and tucks it on the side of his pants. His bare chest is quickly drenched uncharted territory, and it's beckoning me. He's not dancing anymore. Wet TJ is just a few inches away from my face. Shirtless, beautiful TJ is too much to take in all at once. It's like looking directly at the sun. He leans in.

"So, can I have your number?"

"My number?"

"Yeah."

"You already have my number."

"I know, but I want you to give it to me."

"What? Why?" I say, laughing.

"I don't want to have your number because I took it from the call sheet. I want to have it because you want me to have it. I want to do this right," he says, looking serious for a moment. *Do what right? What's he talking about?*

I feel like a completely different person standing here soaking wet in the sun. I lean in and whisper my number in his ear like it's a sexy secret. He already has it, so he doesn't have to write it down. He just listens as I say each number like it's an invitation to get closer. To hold me tighter.

When I'm done, he places his strong hands gently on either side of my face and inspects it.

"You have really nice eyebrows."

Eyebrows? Have my fake eyelashes relocated?

"And lips," he says, then leans in and kisses me.

CHAPTER 13

My doorman, Felipe, stands at attention outside my cab.

"Good evening," he says through tight lips and opens the car door.

I gently lift TJ's sleepy head off my lap and slip out of the cab. As I walk past Felipe, I feel like I've been pulled over by a cop and he's watching my every move.

Walking in a straight line requires all my concentration. *Way too much cheap beer in the sun.* My feet may be straight, but I can feel the rest of me sway around as though on a ship. My dress and hair dried on the way home, but my ropy platforms haven't survived the typhoon. It's like walking on crumbled-up newspaper.

I walk in and throw myself on the bed. My legs are dangling off, so I feel my way around, finding the cardboard box in its new spot next to the bed. I lay my feet on top of it. Expensive Swedish chandeliers in their boxes make great footstools.

My purse is still on my shoulder, so I slip it off to find my cell phone. There's a voice mail from my dad, which makes me smile. My drunk coordination is slow, and it takes a few tries to press play.

Banana, how are you? It was so nice to see you, and it made me so happy you met someone special. But you didn't mention his name. What does he do for a living? Where did you two meet? Call me when you can.

I squeeze my eyes shut as if they could erase what I've heard. Being reminded of my big fat lie makes me feel pathetic. And emotional.

I pull up my purse and empty the contents onto my chest. Feeling my way for a tissue, I push aside my wallet, sunglasses, and ChapStick and find the Denny's napkin with The List. A wild grunt escapes me at the sight of it.

I pat my eyes with it, but it's so old it's lost all absorption qualities. It feels like plastic on my skin.

I look at my handwriting. My tears haven't smudged the words at all. *Who knew Denny's napkins would be ideal for preservation?*

I imagine Landon is the guy I was telling my dad about. I picture him at Sunday BBQ. He arrives with a nice bottle of wine. My father puts it away and tells him all about the rum he's pouring instead. Landon sneaks a glance at me. His imaginary smile makes the stinging in my eyes double.

So what? Who cares? I don't need him.

At least I know what it's like to be with someone who makes me feel that excitement. That *ahhhrgg* feeling. Number 1 on this list, *Makes me feel butterflies*, is definitely TJ. *Though I'll admit the date lacked any deep, inspiring conversation.*

"Have you met Harrison Ford?" he'd asked as he put his head on my lap during the cab ride home.

"No. How would I have met Harrison Ford?"

"I don't know—you work in TV."

We rode in silence for a while, and then he said groggily, "I love him. *Raiders of the Lost Ark, Star Wars, Blade Runner...*" And he put himself to sleep listing Harrison Ford's credits.

Suddenly an idea bubbles up.

I pat the bed around me, find the notebook of lists by my ear, and turn to a blank page. "Who says I can't have everything on my list? I can," I say out loud, wrestling the pen out of the spiral.

I can have this romance. I can *make* it. It's exactly like editing the perfect scene using multiple takes.

I should make this happen because:

1. I have a strong feeling that if I check off The List, I will feel better.
2. I want to feel better.
3. FACE IT! It's the only way I'll ever know what it's like to be with someone like Landon.
4. Duh, I know, stop yelling!

Note to self, don't drink and list.

I should *not* do this because:

1. Beers. Too many.
2. I am not a man juggler like Gia.
3. Juggling four men would be hard even for her.

All true. But I'm so tired of common sense and overthinking hijacking all my fun. And what about the other list? *What other list?* You know the one I'm talking about. The list that isn't a list because a list of regrets can never be checked off. It never has to be written. It stays embedded in your brain. *Oh, that list.*

The trip to Rio for Carnival I didn't take with Gia because of one lousy exam. Saying no to a date with the captain of our college soccer team. It was right after my breakup with Sam and it would have been a healthy distraction, but I wanted to remain single in case Sam changed his mind.

And what about work? There have been so many thrilling, mind-blowing (and free) activities at the locations where we film, but I have never tried any of them. BASE jumping, hang gliding, sea-snake diving. *Okay, none of those sound like a good idea right now either, but everyone on our crew survived.*

I'm tired of doing the sensible thing. New plan. We're checking off this list one way or another.

I open TJ's last text. I smile a drunk, droopy-eyed smile just thinking about him.

Today was

I exhale loudly and send off multiple messages.

wet

and hot

Let's again soon

I mean, do it again soon

I spread out my arms like a starfish and scream, then catch myself and whisper, "Sorry, neighbor. Sorry for you." I open my voice mail and play Philip's recording.

"Ana, hello, Phil Oberon here. Hope this message finds you well..."

As he speaks, I squint and move my face and arms around as though I'm conducting a symphony.

I suck my lips in and open my eyes wide to try to seem composed in my text. *And sober.* It takes me a very long time to type it out.

Thank you very, very much for the invitation to see your studio this week. I'm looking very much forward to it.

Next I find Fernando's text. I double-check that I'm not responding to an old group chat with Gia we haven't used in years.

Favorite summertime poem? Blake, of course. O Summer, go ahead and pitch here thy golden tent. Or something like that. Let's discuss in person on Monday.

I feel eerily calm. This is good. I want this.

One more. I find the number I'm looking for in my contacts. I text as though in a trance, and before I know it, I've hit send.

CHAPTER 14

I feel numb. I rode the subway to work in a daze and had to take my time with every step out of the station and down the street. The heat doesn't help. I walk up to the elevator and find Richard standing there. The up button has already been pressed, but I press it again a few more times absentmindedly.

"Does that work?" Richard asks, snapping me out of my stupor.

"What?"

"When you see that someone has already called the elevator, but you press it again anyway. Does that make the elevator come quicker?"

"Yes. Yes, it does."

The doors open and we step inside, along with a production assistant from our office. He hits 7, and then Richard presses the same button a bunch of times with his finger, like a woodpecker.

"Thank you. I really appreciate that because I'm in a hurry," I say calmly.

"Anytime," he says, playing along.

I'm actually happy to be at work today. Happy to focus on something other than the texts I sent out Saturday night. I spent the entire day yesterday with my phone turned off while I hunted for the perfect screw to hang my chandelier. The last screw I had found was too narrow. The one before that had— get this—too short a thread length. I've learned more about screws than I ever wanted to know. So I tried out a few retro boutique hardware shops in SoHo. *No luck.*

Just before I went to bed, I turned my cell on. I had responses to all four texts. My emotions were all over the place as I read them. I went from excitement to joy to fear and then finally to nausea.

Thirty minutes into the workday, I'm not sure it will help at all. So far all I've managed to do is stare at the four texts on my cell, fluctuating between numbness and panic. And contemplating a brand-new life. One that is free of electronic devices.

"Here, let's switch." Richard gets up from where he's watching a scene we've been working on and walks right up to me.

"What?"

"Switch seats with me."

"Why?"

"I like to watch from a different spot sometimes."

"Are you being serious?"

"Yes. It helps to see it from a different angle. Gives you a fresh perspective. Trust me."

"O . . . kay," I say, getting up. "Fine. I'll go aaaall the way over here to your seat." His spot is literally three feet away from mine. "Maybe we should light up some sage while we're at it?"

Richard ignores me. He has these weird quirks, but I guess there's a part of me that appreciates that he treats our show with the same artistic care he gives his documentaries.

He switches the light off so we can watch the scene in the dark. Another one of his quirks. "Why are you all dressed up today?" he asks when he can no longer see what I'm wearing.

"I'm not dressed up."

"No? Well, you seem different."

"Different? Is that bad? I like to change things up."

"No, that's good."

"It's good to switch things up, you know? Like you, watching this scene from different seats," I defend myself.

"Yep, got it. Noted."

But he's not wrong. I'm wearing a beige summer dress with a pink belt around my waist and tan open-toed pumps Gia gave me for Christmas last year. I've curled my hair, and I'm even wearing coral-colored lipstick. I wanted to feel graceful and feminine for my date tonight. *So maybe I shouldn't be slouching way down in Richard's seat.*

The scene stops playing, and Richard turns on the light. "So, what do you think?"

"It's getting there." I get up and navigate around him in the tight space.

"Yeah, I think so too."

He was right. It did help to see it from another angle. *But there's no way I'm admitting it.*

"Could always use more cymbals," I tease and throw an empty paper cup in the trash. The weight of the cup makes the liner slip off the rim and slump down into the can, so I get up to fix it.

"This bag is way too small. I hate when they don't order the right size."

Richard turns around and watches me try to wrangle the bag into place on the trash can. "It's fine," he says calmly.

I lift the bag back up, but it slips off the rim again. I squat down, and after a few moments of coaxing, I manage to get two sides to stay put, but they're perilously close to falling off again. A castoff paper clip would do the trick. "This is the opposite of fine."

"It doesn't matter," Richard says, sounding even more at peace.

His relaxed tone makes me more annoyed. Like we're on a seesaw and only one of us can feel good at a time.

"I just think things should work the way they're supposed to." I sit back down, and my knee starts to nervously bounce up and down. "A drawstring would fix it. Why has no one come up with that?"

"Oh, I almost forgot. I have something for you." Richard digs into his satchel.

I lean back in the chair, feeling dumbfounded and a little creeped out. The only thing I can imagine is that he's about to pull out a trash bag with a drawstring. Like he's clairvoyantly invented one ahead of time.

Instead, he pulls out a wooden bowl and places it on the edge of my desk. He then takes out a small brown paper bag and pours the contents into the bowl.

"What's this?"

"Trail mix."

The bowl is overflowing with different-colored, oddly shaped items. It looks like what you'd find if you emptied out a child's pockets. Sticky nuts, thick twigs, little pink balls, and long white slivers of what might be coconut.

"Those are raspberry-yogurt-covered macadamias," he explains, probably because I look confused.

"Oh, okay."

"I made it."

"You *made* trail mix?"

"Yeah. It's all organic. I also make granola, if you have any interest."

"Thanks," I say, but it comes out sounding more like a question.

"Sure, you know, I figured since it's almost eleven. First the trash bag, and now you're doing that thing with your leg," he says, and I instantly stop bouncing my knee. "Around this time you always get peckish and a little..." He stops himself as though he's worried he's about to say the wrong thing.

"A little what, Richard? What are you trying to say?"

I grab a pink ball.

"Testy," he finally says.

"I don't get... mmm." The sound escapes me. The yogurt melts in my mouth, and then with just a little nibble, the nut melts away too. "Okay, you're not wrong. Sometimes I get a little hangry."

"A little? You hung up on that poor woman the other day."

"If I can't order a tuna on rye in this great city a little earlier than usual, that's a problem."

"I think it was, like, ten thirty a.m."

"It's not my fault. I think it's my metabolism or something to do with my blood sugar," I protest, grabbing a few nuts.

"Those are cashews glazed in smoked avocado oil with salt flakes from Newfoundland."

I'm about to laugh at the ridiculous list of ingredients. My spice rack consists of salt, pepper, and dried parsley. But instead I let out a moan. And not just any moan. A sensual-sounding moan. I can't help it. *Damn, these cashews are good. And they're still warm.* Did he toast these nuts this morning?

"The cashews are my favorite," he says in a friendly tone.

"Okay. I *need* to have lunch on the early side."

"Freakishly early."

"Fine." I let out a laugh. "Freakishly early."

"I thought this could help tide you over to a more socially appropriate mealtime."

"Thank you. I appreciate it."

And I genuinely do. This definitely beats the snacks I typically get at the closest deli: too-ripe bananas, sugary fruit cups, stale bags of chips.

"Try blending the hickory barbecue pretzel sticks with the strands of coconut," Richard says and gets back to work.

I comply and pick out the items like I'm making a tiny bouquet. The wild burst of flavors is incredible. Thankfully,

Richard is playing the scene back, and my lewd whimper is muffled by the music.

I'm feeling more level already. Can't believe how badly I needed nourishment. *And that Richard noticed before I did.* The fact is, I also need to eat when I'm stressed. And right now I am beyond nervous. My date tonight is a big mistake.

Why did I drunk-text the other night? I wish my cell phone had a breathalyzer. One puff and it would have locked me out for twelve hours.

————

A few hours later, I'm standing in front of the Morgan Library on Thirty-Sixth and Madison. The little guy lights up, telling me it's time to cross the street, but my feet are glued to the ground. *What am I doing?*

I can still turn this ship around. Cancel all the plans I made when I wasn't thinking straight. I consider it, but somehow the feeling of disappointment is worse than the fear of going through with it. *I just want to know what it's like. Is that so wrong?*

With just a few steps, I'm transported. I've gone from the haute couture shops of Fifth Avenue to a quaint English country square in the late 1700s. There's a quartet of violins and a flute playing at the end of the lobby and a dozen couples dressed up in eighteenth-century-style clothing performing a country dance in the center of the room.

The Morgan Library is having a special exhibition on Jane Austen. Tonight is the last night of the exhibit, hence the quartet and the dancers.

"Is your dance card full?" I hear the familiar voice behind me and flip through the small blank pages of the booklet I was handed on the way in, realizing it *is* an actual dance card.

"I think I can pencil you in." When I turn around, Fernando is bowing graciously like a pro. When he straightens back up, I see he's wearing a tasteful dark-brown three-piece suit. Something about him tonight reminds me of Gia. I tense up, thinking about her. She may have wanted me to marry her brother in college, but if she knew what I was up to, she would *not* approve. "Not to worry, I'm just using your brother to check off a list." *It's just one date. Relax.* I asked Fernando not to say anything to his sister, and I was a little surprised when he agreed, saying, "It's probably for the best."

"You look beautiful." His James Dean frown crops up slowly. "Thanks for letting me make the plans for tonight. I haven't been here since they built this space connecting J. P. Morgan's home with his library. It's really elegant, and I like how it doesn't distract from the original buildings."

"I see what you mean. I love it."

We stop near the musicians, and Fernando closes his eyes intensely and moves his head around like he's hearing a strange language only he understands.

The song ends, and as the applause dies down, one of the professional dancers steps forward. "In Regency England, dances were an integral part of courtship. Tonight we're going to teach you a dance meant to be the last dance of an evening. But that also meant it was the time for any unspoken declaration."

Fernando eyes me, and I smile nervously.

We're divided into two rows and told to face our partners.

Fernando pays careful attention to the instructor, and it's easy to see he's way more comfortable than most of the men who have been dragged here by their girlfriends. A husky guy next to him has his arms folded tightly across his chest and darts quick glances from the instructor to the floor and back.

I knew Fernando would be perfect. He's the obvious choice for the "hopeless romantic" on my list. If you need someone to spin you around a piazza, Fernando is your man. He catches me looking at him and smiles. The violins kick in, and a playful song begins.

The dance isn't too complicated. They've clearly simplified it for us. All we have to do is approach each other and then back up again, then step forward again and take turns skipping down the center. *Surprisingly, my skipping feels on point. Skirt bouncing beautifully. Who needs a piazza?*

The song ends, and we all clap politely. Fernando looks like he has something to say.

"What?" I ask him.

"Nothing," he says with a grin.

"Why are you looking at me like that?"

"I was just wondering what made you have a change of heart," he says, squinting. "After all this time."

I have no idea how to answer. I must look as frazzled as I feel because he quickly lets me off the hook. "Shall we take a turn about the library?" We walk into the library and find a table displaying an original Austen manuscript.

"Look, you can see the words she scratched out." He gets so close to the glass, I'm afraid he's going to leave a smudge. "I think it says 'seriously' or, no wait, it's 'savagely.'"

As he studies the manuscript, I study him. I mull over all the things Gia has said about him over the years:

"My brother has discovered a passion for silk-screening."

"He's not selfish; he's just wrapped up in himself."

"He can't be pressured into making any big decisions right now."

"He's not quitting music. He's just exploring a new side of himself."

"He says if you don't learn Russian you shouldn't be allowed to read Russian literature."

"Ares't thou hungry?" Fernando sounds more Shakespearean than Austen, but I think it's cute.

"Why, yes, I am," I say, making him smile. *He does have a great smile.*

The closing-night tickets include a buffet dinner of historically accurate Jane Austen cuisine, so we make our way to the buffet and stop in front of the serving trays. There's a table with some sort of large bird under a heat lamp. Pheasant? Whatever it is, the thing still has way too many of its parts intact. Beak, feathers, feet.

"I know a great spot nearby, or did you have your heart set on goose?"

"Oh no, I'm definitely up for something else."

Fernando holds the door open for me, and we step out into the real world of Madison Avenue and honking taxis.

We're only a few blocks away when he says, "And here we are," pointing to the Celtic Organ, an unassuming Irish pub I've walked by so many times but have never been to. The door has a thick layer of grime so you can't see through the glass panes. It's always seemed a bit gross to me.

We walk inside, and it's so dark my eyes have to adjust. Only a few weathered stragglers sit at the bar, and an old piano is tucked into a corner.

"Cheeseburger, brandy?" he asks as he moves two barstools closer together for us.

"Sounds perfect."

Our bartender is balding and unkempt and nothing like the ones I normally see on this block: trendy mixologists with tight-fitted button-down shirts and suspenders. Our drinks arrive in small, thick glasses.

"To the power of poetry," he says, clinking my glass. We both drink without taking our eyes off each other. "I've been waiting a long time for this," he says and carefully sets his glass down on the bar. "When Sam hurt you back in college, I wanted to kick his face in. Remember, I was taking tae kwon do and you were worried I would follow up on my threats?"

I nod, but it's a lie. I was never worried. Gia and I had watched Fernando flunk all his kicking tests. Including one involving balsa wood.

"Cheating is pathetic. It's a sign of a weak character," he says, making me shuffle in my seat.

"Another round?" I ask the bartender, trying to change the subject, but it doesn't work.

"I love thee to the depth and breadth and height my soul can reach." Fernando takes his time to overenunciate every single word. "Shakespeare."

"Right."

"That was about one person. He didn't write 'I love thee but not all the time.' Sam two-timing you was unacceptable."

"Mm-hm. Yep." *I wonder what Shakespeare would say about four-timing?*

"So why didn't you write anything?" He can tell I have no idea what he's talking about, so he adds, "On the little piece of paper at the party."

"The wish paper we burned at Gia's? I don't know." The question throws me and makes me think of Landon.

Why *hadn't* I written anything? I never let an opportunity for a wish pass me by. I always throw coins in fountains, think really hard before blowing out birthday candles, and never leave a fortune cookie unopened. But that night I felt no desire to make a wish. There was no point. Landon was across the table, but he may as well have been across the Atlantic.

"I thought maybe it was because you were afraid I would see it," he says, and I think it's sweet he's given this any thought.

"I guess that's true," I say. Because, technically, he's right.

"In a way, I completely understood." He's so close, I can smell the brandy on his breath. "I think it's difficult to express in words what we desire."

He excuses himself and heads to the bathroom. I look around the place. In here, it's so different from what's just outside. That's the thing about Manhattan. Every block has so many layers. Just next door there's a high-tech do-it-yourself wine bar that allows you to serve your own wine from all around the world using sleek, stainless-steel vending machines. In here, everything is worn-out and soft. The wood on the bar is dark and dirty, and there's a three-tiered serving tray of hard-boiled eggs on the counter.

Someone starts playing a slow song on the piano. It's a melancholic tune but also beautiful and a bit out of place in this crusty bar. I scan the room, and there's Fernando, sitting at the old piano like it's his job to play for us tonight.

The song sounds similar to the Regency music we've just heard at the museum, but in his hands, it's refined and haunting. He plays so beautifully. I haven't heard him play since college, and now I can't understand why he isn't performing with an orchestra like he'd always wanted. Everyone in the bar is transfixed.

It's darker in that part of the room, and the light around the piano catches on the tiny particles of old bar dust floating around, making it all seem like a dream. He's playing for me, and it looks like it's snowing in here. If I were producing this moment, it could never be as magical as it is right now. Even my lighting guy couldn't achieve an effect like this.

CHAPTER 15

Bianca and Nina's edit room door is open as I walk by. They're making the sounds of two people getting along. Chitter-chatter. Laughter. I walk into my edit room and shut the door, but the sound bleeds through the wall between us.

"How come we never laugh like that?" Richard asks without turning around. I want to say something snarky about the lilac scarf he's wearing today, but my cell phone rings before I can come up with anything clever. My throat clenches. It's Gia. Since we last spoke, her brother's tongue has been in my mouth.

Last night was so surprising. I didn't expect to feel so comfortable with Fernando.

My only regret was letting him walk me home. He kissed me good night in front of my building, and I kept one eye open, watching my doorman, who was standing there watching us the entire time.

In all the years I've known Gia, I've only lied to her once. A tiny lie regarding a pair of red pants I borrowed without asking when we were in college. I bent down to tie my shoe, and they ripped right down the back. I had the dry cleaners sew them back up and was so relieved they'd done such a good job.

"Did you borrow my red pants, rip them up, and put them back in the closet?"

"No."

"Why are you lying?"

I can't keep things from Gia. She *knows* everything.

And this is a way bigger lie.

"What are you up to, young lady?" she says in a cute, parental way.

"Um, nothing. Why?" I must *sound* guilty.

"Why didn't you come to Bloody Mary Monday at Pico's?"

"I had to . . . work late yesterday." I suck at lying.

Richard spins around in his chair, his eyes wide open.

"Yep, it's um . . . I was really busy with all the editing for this episode." Richard puts his feet up on the desk and shakes his head disapprovingly.

"So have you slept with the old man yet?" Gia's voice echoes out of my cell phone so loudly Richard may have heard. Why is it so quiet in here all of a sudden? Even Bianca and Nina's laughter has died down next door.

"What? No. I'm just visiting his studio after work."

Richard scratches his beard and stares right at me, so I focus on the book sitting on his desk instead. It's a thick one, but I can't read the cover because it's facedown. According to the bookmark, he's halfway through it. I picture him reading it on the subway to and from Brooklyn.

I hang up as quickly as I can and look up at the screen at a shot of Elizabeth's breasts popping out of her dress. "Can you change that shot? It's really distracting," I say calmly, trying to steer Richard back to work.

"Who did you just lie to about working late last night?" he asks without turning around.

"None of your business."

"If *you* had to work late editing, then *I* had to work late; therefore, you just implicated me in your lie, so it is my business. Literally." The book on his desk must be about one of those brilliant young lawyers taking on some government conspiracy.

"My friend Gia."

"And why did you lie to her?" He eggs me on lightheartedly.

"I don't want her to know who I went out with last night."

"Because he's twelve?"

My face burns up. "No. He's of age. And not that I need to justify anything to you, because I don't, but I've never dated *anyone* under twenty-two. Maybe twenty-one. At worst twenty-one."

Richard spins around, calmly presses a few buttons, and we watch as Steven and Elizabeth walk into a restaurant. He pulls the chair out for her, and she sits down. Then there's the same shot of her and her bulging breasts.

"You didn't cut the shot out."

"That's because there isn't anything wrong with it."

Laughter seeps in from the next room. Richard drops his head, which almost makes me laugh, and then he swivels around, so I stop.

"I've been meaning to say that you have a very eclectic selection of slacks."

"Eh, thanks," I say, unsure that was a compliment. I'm surprised he's even noticed. They're nothing special. Just a pair of beige linen wide-legged pants I've cinched high at the waist with a thick brown leather belt. I was trying to go with something age-appropriate for when I see Philip Oberon tonight. I thought they were Jackie O meets Katharine Hepburn. But I'm still questioning the need for such wide legs. These pant legs are really wide. Four legs could fit in each one.

"My grandmother used to say, 'Richie, an eclectic selection of pants will take you places.'"

Now I know he's joking.

"I saw this documentary about the use of clothing around the world." Richard leans in like he's about to say something compelling. "It shattered a lot of myths about why humans dress the way they do. How it's not so much an expression of who we are but who we *want* to be."

"Oh yeah, I saw that." But I'm not 100 percent sure we're talking about the same thing. I don't think we have similar viewing habits. The one I watched connected culottes to King Louis XIV.

"More often than not, headdresses and jewelry," he says, nodding toward my chest, "are used for protection. To give others something shiny to look at while keeping the true self out of sight. Kind of like a fishing lure."

"I don't remember that part," I say and touch my necklace self-consciously. I rarely do jewelry, but today I'm wearing a thick, triple-wrapped chain choker. But Richard couldn't be more wrong. I've got nothing to hide. The only reason I have this heavy thing on is to make my simple silk top look more sophisticated. *Plus, am I getting fashion feedback from Sir Scarfalot?*

"I think this is the first time I've seen you wear a necklace."

"Me? I wear them all the time. On weekends. Nights and weekends mostly."

Richard nods suspiciously and gets back to work, leaving me flustered. And thinking about where I can buy a lot of necklaces for very little money.

Besides, what do Richard's wardrobe choices say about him? His jeans today are super fitted all the way down; they're probably water-tight. *Why is it I can never hit him with a good comeback quickly enough?*

———

Eight hours later, I'm standing in front of a wall covered with paintings all the way up to the ceiling.

"I've always loved this one. To me, it's about love." I catch myself playing with my necklace and stop. "It's like two people coming together and experiencing something powerful. Am I even close?" No one responds, so I turn around and realize I'm alone. I'm embarrassed but also relieved Philip missed my theorizing.

The entire room is overwhelming. It's more of a gallery than a studio, and it's also a bit of a mess. There are paintings stacked in front of other paintings, and only one small corner of the studio appears to be used for any actual work. Philip asked me to meet him here, which was always the original plan, but as soon as I arrived, I realized his studio is *inside* his apartment.

"Follow me." Philip appears in the doorway, and we walk down a wide hallway covered with photographs of him with political figures and celebrities. In one he's got his arms around Bill Clinton and Morgan Freeman having a big ol' laugh like they're a geriatric rat pack.

We walk into a large living room that spills into another living space and then into a large dining room. *Here's a new way to know if someone is wealthy in Manhattan: count the number of couches that fit into their apartment.* We're only a few rooms into the living quarters of Philip's Fifth Avenue apartment, and I've already walked past nine couches. And we're talking big, full-length, comfy sofas.

I never imagined there were apartments this big in New York. It takes up an entire floor of this building. The elevator door opens up right into his apartment like you see in the movies, but even those elevators never opened up to this many couches.

We step out onto his terrace through a pair of double French doors to a view of Central Park in all its glory. Sure, it's nice when you're down there in it, but from the thirty-fourth floor you can take it all in at once. A green sea of tranquility nestled safely inside a perfectly manicured rectangle of towering buildings. The sun is setting and bathing the city in gold. It's breathtaking.

His terrace is about four times the size of my apartment. There's an elegant outdoor dining table and a pair of luxurious chaise lounges. *(Yes, they technically count, so we're up to eleven couches.)*

"I was in Scotland when I got your text," he says casually as he walks over to a tray that has been set on the table. "Do you like whiskey?"

"Yes. Sure."

He takes a pair of reading glasses out of his shirt pocket and puts them on to inspect the bottle. When he hands me a glass with a beautiful golden rim, I decide to spin the small amount of whiskey around in the glass like it's wine.

"It's over a hundred years old," he says just as I've put all of it into my mouth. *One hundred years old? Probably not supposed to drink this all in one shot.* So I let the liquid slip out of my mouth and back into the glass, which is still at my lips, and take a sophisticated sip instead, but it ends up being more like a slurp. *Ugh. Why, yes, I always drink century-old whiskey like it's hot soup. Doesn't everyone?*

"Good stuff." I have no idea what makes whiskey good. I don't even know what makes whiskey.

"Yes, good stuff." He laughs like I meant to be funny.

I take a seat on the chaise, and before I know it, he's right next to me.

I want to move over a few inches but don't know how to do that without offending him. But I am *not* ready to be this close to Philip Oberon. I thought I could ease into it. Get to know him. Maybe give myself some time to be comfortable with his age. What if he makes a move right now on this chaise? It's technically a bed! *Why didn't I sit at the dinner table or on the balcony ledge? Anything would feel safer than this glorified futon with hanging tassels.*

"Cheers." He looks into my eyes as we clink our golden

glasses together. "To you," he adds just as the glass is at my lips, causing me to take in another ungraceful slurp of whiskey.

Can I pull this off? *What am I trying to do again?* I think of my perfect man list. I guess when I wrote "talented artist," I never imagined I'd find one that was *this* talented or *this* big of an artist.

Come on, Ana. It's all good. You can do this. Gia always says that when you want something big, you have to take big steps. *Ugh. Gia. She would know how to pull this off.*

"I like your watch," I say to keep the conversation going. And also because I genuinely like it. It doesn't look fancy or expensive. It's just a nice, normal-looking watch.

"Thanks. It actually belonged to Albert Einstein."

I almost drop my golden goblet. I set it down on the fancy outdoor coffee table for safekeeping while I compose myself. *New way to tell if someone is truly wealthy: Rolex out. Einstein in.*

I consider asking him about how he finds inspiration. But what if he's tired of people asking him stupid questions about his work? I'm his date, not the president of his fan club, so I decide to keep it cool instead.

"Tell me about you," he says, and I feel his knee softly tap mine. "What do you do all day?"

I prepare myself for the fallout of my response. Sometimes when I tell someone "I'm a reality TV producer," they look like they just stepped in poop.

"Television. I work in television."

"I've always wanted to make short film installations," he says, and I'm relieved he's changed the subject.

"What about?" I ask and watch as he stands up to refill my glass. Eureka! An empty glass is the answer. If I drink quicker, I'll keep him busy refilling my glass.

"I don't know. Sex. Drugs. Brazil." He takes his time with each word like he is intimately familiar with them. Like he was there when they were invented.

"Brazil? I've never been to Brazil."

"It's an incredible place. Wild, raw, vivid. Every corner is completely alive. Feels like I lived a whole other life there."

My eyes are wide open as Philip tells me about how he met his first wife on a beach in Brazil. While he speaks, I see flashes of his paintings:

Brazil #3 (A painting of white tousled sheets on a bed)
Brazil #12 (A taupe tousled beach blanket)
Brazil #26 (A white fuzzy rug near a window)

Over the next hour I have him refill my whiskey glass continuously as he tells me about some of the people he's met over the years. Janis Joplin, JFK, Picasso. I'm sitting with the artist of the century who seems to have been in the right place at the right time, like Forrest Gump with a paintbrush. And he's so nonchalant about it all, it doesn't sound pretentious. On the contrary, it sounds like he's talking about someone else.

"I want to show you something," he says, walking toward the other side of the terrace.

As soon as I stand up, it's clear I've had too much whiskey.

"I find I'm a little nervous to show these to you."

He finally stops and turns toward me. Behind him is a row

of tall metal sculptures lining the wall. I'm trying to focus on them, but I notice something sticking out of his ear.

"No one knows about this," Philip says, looking off at the sculptures.

There's a long gray hair poking out of his ear. A really thick gray hair. I scan his face for other strays and notice he's more handsome than you'd expect for a man his age. And he's in really good shape. But then I see the hair again. It seems to be coming from deep *inside* his ear.

"This is the reason I haven't been painting the last few years. I haven't told anyone else. You are looking at something that doesn't officially exist."

I try to take in the bright-red metal sculptures, but the gray hair coming out of his ear comes back into view. The whiskey's made my face numb, but it's given my eyes razor-like focus.

"I know it's the last thing anyone expects from me. To go in such a new direction."

I can see the sculptures are curvy, and each base is different. One is wooden, and one is made of smooth marble. But the hair is there again, waving around with the breeze. It's at least an inch long. How has he not noticed it?

"Well, I imagine the creative process can't be controlled," I say, mesmerized by the hair.

"My agent wouldn't know what to do if he saw these... OWW!"

I'm holding the gray ear hair between my fingers. I've yanked the thing out from the root with my bare hand.

———

The driver I've been sent home with has beaten Felipe to the car door. My poor doorman looks confused. I can tell he's racking his brain, trying to figure out who's about to step out of the imposing, dark-tinted windowed luxury car.

The elevator's been shut off for repairs, so I have to walk up the four flights of stairs. I reach my apartment out of breath and feeling like a complete idiot. An idiot with one small couch. *And technically it's a love seat.*

I'm sober enough now to understand I was standing in front of priceless sculptures that no one in the world has seen, and what do I do? And my apology was so lame.

"I'm so sorry! Did I actually do that? I thought I only yanked it out in my mind."

I'm thinking I'll never hear from him again, when I get a text on my phone.

I'm being honored at an event in Vienna soon. Join me for the weekend?

I lie on the couch, feet dangling over the side, and try to figure out why in the world I want to say yes.

1. I've never been to Vienna.
2. I've always wanted to say, "I'm going to Europe for the weekend."
3. Gotta love a guy who doesn't hold a grudge when someone pulls a hair out of his ear.

CHAPTER 16

She is the most (sniffle) beautiful woman in the world. My everything (sniffle, sniffle), she's my best friend."

A certain New York Knicks point guard has lost his composure. We're halfway through taping Steven and Elizabeth's episode, and as his big proposal day gets closer, he's more agitated. Today we're interviewing him in the living room of his bachelor pad. It's a massive multilevel commingling of manly wooden beams and modern steel fixtures. Basketball memorabilia is tastefully displayed here and there, and the tile floor in the foyer has his jersey number laser etched into it.

Above the fireplace is a giant life-size photograph of Steven during a game. He's suspended in midair, and his hands have just released the ball, which is now floating above him, heading toward the hoop. The ball still has a way to go, but it's clear the thing is going to make it in. You can tell by comparing the look on his face with the one on his opponent nearby. Steven is calm and focused, while the guy on the other team is all horror and devastation. That ball is going in.

On the court, Steven is in control. But right now he's completely disarmed. And he doesn't seem to care that people will see him like this when the show airs. He rubs his eyes and fidgets in his seat, takes a deep breath, and looks up at me, eager for the next question.

But I'm having a difficult time focusing. I'm distracted by things like:

Maybe tonight's date will surprise me? Philip's definitely did.

What's Vienna like this time of year?

What should one wear when one's date is being honored?

Will I have to give a speech? *I should prepare one just in case.*

I hadn't responded to Philip's text, so this morning I woke up to another one from him.

Don't worry, there's more to do than honor me. I hear they've also got some opera. And you'd have your own room, of course.

For almost a decade I've spent my days editing proposals in a dark room and going home to a tiny apartment and takeout. In just the past few days, I've been serenaded *(romance: check),* I've danced in a storm with the sexiest man/boy alive *(butter-flies: mmm yes, check),* and soon I'll be traveling around the world with one of the most important painters of our time *(talented artist: couldn't be more literally checked).*

It's all been going somewhat smoothly. And tonight's date checks off the last one. Someone who makes me laugh.

But there's nothing funny about how I feel right now. At the same time, there's something stronger than my fears driving me to see this through.

At this moment this is all perfectly sane and logical, and I don't know what's happening. I barely recognize myself. Well, even Steven Davis barely recognized me when I arrived today. Our call time wasn't until noon, so this morning I went to the salon across the street from my house and dramatically changed my look. Hello, bangs!

I'm wearing my hair up in a ponytail and my new bangs are framing the top of my eyes. The hairstylist was able to coerce my new bangs to lie nice and flat like a silk sheet across my forehead. TJ was surprised when he saw me today too.

I was standing by the snack table we set up in Steven's enormous kitchen, adding some sugar into my coffee in a manner that was all dainty and such because I now have *bangs*. Hello, I have *bangs* over here, and people with *bangs* stir their coffee like this. And I love the way he looked at me. Like *I* was the snack table. Covered in free soda and chocolate-covered pretzels.

While we stood there, he sent me a text.

Meet me in the basketball closet after the interview?

My phone buzzes with another text, and I open it, still thinking about TJ's sexy proposition.

You inspired me.

It's from Fernando, and he's attached a photo. I open it, worried *but also excited* that I could possibly be getting my first penis pic. I can't make out what it is. It looks like the chicken scratchings of a lunatic. I bring the phone up to my face and realize they're musical notes on composition paper.

"Ana, we're still rolling," says my cameraman Dan, snapping me back. I look up, and Steven is wiping his eyes with the back of his hand.

"Have you ever written her a song? Or taken her to Vienna?"

"What?"

"How did you know she was the perfect girl for you?"

"You asked me that already."

"Oh, right."

I'll admit, the rest of the interview was not my best work.

Afterward, I sneak into the basketball closet and find TJ standing inside the tight space by a wall of balls, some brand-new and still in their boxes. *This is so unprofessional. But the smell of new leather intermingling with TJ's eau de ocean is so sexy.*

"Hey," he says.

"Hi," I say and lock the door behind me.

TJ isn't moving. His eyes are doing all the walking. *Up and down my body.* So I move closer and stop a few inches from his face. Suddenly, he turns me around, pins me against the metal shelves, and starts to kiss my neck. I imagine the basketballs falling all around us. *If they fell in slow motion, that would be kinda cool.* I'd also like to replace the overhead lighting to something less harsh. He's probably seen this move in the movies, but my forehead is pressed against a shelf, and it's starting to hurt.

He pulls at my shirt so his lips can work their way over to my shoulder. I don't even mind that it's a new top and he's stretching the cotton.

TJ's soft hands slip under my shirt and start to tug at my bra.

Who says I can't develop a hit show? I'm basically producing my perfect guy. And a whole new life. Am I also making up for lost time? After starring for so long on the show *Ana: The Prudish Years*, am I really ready to star in *Ana: The Slutty Slut*?

"We should go," I whisper. "You go first, and then I'll walk out in a minute."

"Whatever you say." He leans in and gives me another kiss before walking outside and shutting the door.

After counting to twenty, I step out and look at myself in a hallway mirror, tucking my top into my pants as discreetly as I can. My bangs are disheveled too. They're starting to curl. *Why can't I be like a regular Cinderella and not come apart before midnight?* If I wet them, my new bangs will turn into a frizzy piñata of hair sticking out of my forehead. I sigh and consider canceling my date tonight. *He better be as funny as I remember.*

I was fifteen minutes early, so I've been sitting in this tapas restaurant in Battery Park for way too long without a drink. The waitress comes back around, so I order a glass of wine to calm my nerves.

A burly guy walks in, followed by his date. A businessman wearing dark sunglasses walks in and looks around. He spots his friend at the bar and heads over to him. I watch the door open and close a few more times until I realize I haven't blinked in a while. Ugh. Where's that wine?

"Here you go." The waitress is about to set the glass on the table, but I grab it from her and take one long sip.

A few days ago, my man math was adding up, but right now

I feel sick as I sit here waiting for the guy who is the missing piece of my perfect man pie.

1. Gives me butterflies: TJ
2. Talented artist: Philip
3. True romantic: Fernando
4. Makes me laugh: _____

I feel a dizzying sense of déjà vu. Which makes sense because he loves tapas. When I set the glass down and look back up at the door, he's standing there.

Sam. *A.k.a. Sam I Scam.*

I haven't seen him since our college graduation twelve years ago.

He hasn't spotted me yet, so I get another second to check him out. He looks good. He's wearing a black T-shirt, black blazer, and dark jeans. He looks like he doesn't have a care in the world. Like he's ready to embrace any situation.

"We are here to suck the joy out of life. And I mean really suck it till there's nothing left but a bunch of flappy, lifeless teats," he said the night we met. We were both in line at one of the cafeterias on our campus. We ended up having dinner together, and afterward we walked over to the other cafeteria on campus to compare the mac and cheese. I agreed with everything he said that night. And he was right, the first one was "mac and cheesier." He was so carefree, so spontaneous.

"I think you just like to hear yourself say the word 'teat.'"

"You're right. I think you might be the only person in the

world that gets me." *This was before he met the sexy Bosnian student doing a semester abroad who "really, really got him."*

I watch him as he looks around the restaurant. He sees me, and his whole face lights up. Even his eyes are smiling as he walks up to me.

"Hey there," he says, kisses me on the cheek, and sits down.

"Hey, yourse—" I'm interrupted by our waitress handing us menus.

"Oh, we won't need those. We'll have an order of meatballs, a cheese and ham plate thing, with five cheeses, not three. Oh, and two orders of bacon-covered dates."

Sam always orders like it's his last meal. Sucking the teat out of life means eating everything that can kill you at every sitting.

"She'll have another one of those"—he points to my still half-full glass of wine—"and I'll take Johnnie Walker Blue on the rocks. Please. And a couple of slices of Spanish omelet," he says with a wink, like it's their inside joke.

He leans back into his chair and stretches his legs out under the table. "What took you so long?" I feel his shoe tap my leg.

"Well, I—"

"Doesn't matter. I'm just glad you finally came to your senses." He exhales like he's made a great point. *Have I come to my senses? Or have I given them all up for Lent?* "I watched that show you were working on a couple of years ago. And not just for material, I swear."

"I'm still working on that show." Sam looks confused, so I add, "On *Marry Me, You Fool!*"

"Really?" He sounds surprised. "I thought you were running that place by now."

The compliment makes my cheeks burn, but the rest of me prickles. His unwavering faith is touching, but he's also clearly disappointed I haven't moved on, and it hits a nerve.

Our waitress is back and smiling at Sam as she delivers a large wooden slab of prosciutto to the two girls sitting at the table next to us. Like most places in New York, the tables in here are only a few centimeters apart.

"Let me know if you ladies need any help with your ham. Not that I don't think you can handle it—it's just, you shouldn't have to." The girls giggle and offer Sam some of their prosciutto.

My cell phone buzzes on the table, and it's Gia calling again. I jam the phone into my purse. She would *not* approve of this. When Gia heard Sam had moved to Harlem a few years ago, she was worried I'd reach out. I assured her I would *never* do that, and at the time, I meant it.

Gia told me that she heard he was dating some Russian model, and I said I didn't care. But she could tell it had upset me. And she was right. Hearing about him, even all these years later, had taken me back to the night he broke up with me.

"I'm so glad we're doing this," he had said that night. He was looking at me in a way he'd never looked at me before. We had been going out for six months, and by taking me to a fancy tapas place, I was sure it meant he wanted to take things to the next level.

I was delirious that night. I had this premonition that he was going to give me a promise ring. Like an "I promise to propose to you one day" ring. And I had decided I was going to promise to get him a promise ring too.

"Listen, I'm going to be honest with you," he said instead. "There's this girl. We met a few weeks ago. I don't want to stop seeing you, but she and I are going to move in together over the summer."

I felt like such a fool. One moment I was having tapas with my first love, and the next thing I knew, some girl had swept in under my nose and moved in with him before the fried cheese had arrived. Sam hadn't taken me to a fancy tapas place because he was ready to get serious. He brought me there because he had commitment issues and couldn't decide on any one dish. *Why should he when he could have lots of little dishes?*

Maybe that's why I'm not telling Gia about this. Putting Sam into this equation is dangerous in a way the others aren't. The main reason being he's already broken my heart.

Here's the deal. TJ's way too young and Philip is way too old and Fernando is too—well, too *Fernando*—but Sam's problem is that he's a huge flirt, and I was wrong to trust him with 100 percent of my heart. *But what if I were only trusting him with a smaller percentage? Say 25?*

Besides, now I'm the one who's brought him to a tapas restaurant. I'm the one craving lots of small dishes.

I watch Sam leaning in closer to the other table as he chews. The girls are waiting attentively for a verdict, as though he may actually collapse and die from their prosciutto. He savors the ham theatrically, swallows, and waits for a moment.

"All good," he says, holding up both of his thumbs. The girls laugh and finally start to eat their meal.

"How about you?" I ask. "How's the stand-up?"

"Sucks. Big-time. Everyone's a critic. But at least I'm not bored."

Our waitress is back and takes forever trying to make space for all the food on our small table. He's so excited it's arrived that he starts to do the robot, making me laugh so hard I nearly spit out my wine. He's the worst at the robot.

"I see your robot has only gotten sloppier."

"How. Can you. Say that?" he says in a lazy robot voice and wags his head from side to side.

"Robots do not move like that."

"On a serious note, have you ever noticed how other people's ham tastes better than your own?" he says, which makes me laugh but also makes me want to kick his legs super hard under the table.

"To other people's ham." He lifts his glass more toward the girls next to us than to me. I scowl at him, so he revises it. "And to *you.*" Our eyes lock for a moment, and my heartbeat picks up.

He looks in his glass as he swirls the liquid around before setting it down on the table. "You know, I've grown up a lot since we were together."

"Really?"

"Yes. I've changed."

"Do you still yell at people if they talk during the trailers before a movie?"

"Of course. That's still unacceptable behavior. I've paid for those previews. They're the appetizer before the movie. The complimentary amuse-bouche the chef has carefully selected and sent over."

"Do you still have a tantrum when you have to fold laundry?"

"Never."

"What if someone doesn't like the Grateful Dead?"

"I now limit myself to five-minute rebuttals. Seriously. But hold on, you thought there was something wrong with all of this?" We smile at each other, or more accurately, we both try hard *not* to smile at each other.

"I *really* have changed," he says in a slow, earnest tone.

What exactly is he trying to say has changed? Is he good boyfriend material now? Is he no longer interested in women from the Eastern Bloc?

"There's only one way to find out if that's true."

"I agree." He leans in across the table.

"I'll have to come by your place . . . on laundry day."

He laughs and leans back in his seat. I love when I make him laugh. I can feel myself letting my guard down. I can also feel his legs wrapping themselves around mine under the table. Half my heart is singing and the other half is yelling, *Retreat! Retreat!*

Sure, he has a track record of infidelity. But at this moment, I think I can be okay with it. *What I'm not okay with is how lenient our country has become about Russian models coming here and taking womanizing flirts away from perfectly okay-looking Americans.*

He takes me home on a vintage, baby-blue moped, and Felipe is already holding the door as we pull up. Thankfully, Sam's helmet covers most of his face, so maybe my doorman can't tell who this is. For all he knows, it could be the guy who kissed me on Monday or the boy passed out in the back seat of the cab over the weekend or the guy who owns the chauffeured Cadillac.

But then Sam takes his helmet off and dismounts.

"Wait," he commands, and wraps his arms around me. He's holding me so tight, it takes me back. I remember these hugs. Sam hugs like he means it. *Maybe he still has feelings for me?* His smell is familiar. And so different from TJ and Fernando and Philip. *Kinda like the smell of danger.*

"What's so funny?" he asks. The idea that maybe I can have fun with Sam again but this time *without* risking my heart makes me giddy. I can just live in this moment and see what happens while I eat all the ham I want and suck all the teats before me. *Metaphorically speaking, of course.*

"Nothing."

"Don't hold out on me, woman."

"I was just thinking about tapas."

"Yeah, right. Me too." Sam can be really sexy. "Come here," he says, and I get another long Sam-really-means-it hug that I never want to end.

CHAPTER 17

I'm walking a little quicker than normal, even by New York City standards. I'm chock-full of nervous energy. Seeing Sam last night was like stepping into a time warp, and this morning everything's a little out of place.

The closer I get to work, the busier the sidewalks. Trying to navigate around everyone walking in different directions at shifting speeds is like performing a ballet with consequences. It can be graceful if your head is in the game, but one false move and you'd be surprised how excruciating a straight-on shoulder-to-shoulder collision can be.

My pace is off today, but it also feels like I'm floating a few inches above the pavement.

I catch a familiar-looking head bobbing along directly in front of me. I'd know the back of that head anywhere. If I needed any confirmation, the canary-yellow scarf around his neck seals the deal.

It's off-putting seeing Richard out in the wild like this, away from our cave-like edit room. We're so close, I really should say something, but instead, I take a giant step to the right and nearly fall over an enormous double child stroller.

I've decided that I'm not going to say anything. The sight of Richard is a total buzzkill. Just seeing the back of his head has brought me down to earth. Besides, I'd hate for a coworker to disrupt the final moments of "me time" just before we have to sit in a room together all day.

These final moments of peace before the workday begins could be really precious to him, too. I'll just act surprised when we both arrive at the office at the same time.

He reaches the main entrance of our office, but then keeps walking. *Where is he going?* As I walk in, I catch Richard turning down the narrow alleyway next to our building. *What the . . . ?*

———

"What do you have there?" I say when Richard finally arrives at work.

"Hot tea."

"Where'd you get it?"

He sits down and studies me for a moment, like he's trying to understand where this line of questioning is coming from.

"Downstairs," he says, and then, sounding mischievous, "at the coffee shop in our building."

"There isn't a coffee shop inside our building."

"Yes, there is."

"No, there is not."

"You can only get in through the back alley."

I let out a laugh, like *You can't fool me, buddy*. "There's no coffee shop back there." *I've only worked here eight years. I would know if there was a coffee shop in my own building.*

"How about we head down there? You can buy me a cinnamon bun."

I'm curious about how far he's willing to take this dumb joke. "Perfect. And when I prove you wrong, you can get me a scone from the bakery down the street. The line should be wrapped around the block right around now."

"Deal."

All the way down the elevator and out of the building, we give each other disdainful looks.

"Don't forget the clotted cream for my scone. And some strawberry jam," I say as we turn into the dark alley made even darker because it's covered in scaffolding.

Richard shakes his head. "You smell the cinnamon buns yet?"

"Not unless they smell like sewer."

"You know what, this is so much fun," he says with a straight face.

We reach the end of the alley, turn right, and start to pass the tiny stores that line the back of our building. There's a cramped dry cleaner, a one-chair yet professional-looking shoeshine operation, and then we stop in front of a narrow shop with a bag of coffee beans painted on the window.

What the . . . ?

Richard pulls the door open with flair, and the smell of strong coffee drifts outside.

"We'll take two cinnamon buns. On her," Richard says to

no one in particular as we walk in and stand at the end of a short line.

I've never considered myself headstrong. Maybe I should rethink that. *Then again, one could blame Richard and his incessant need to be right all the time.*

He seems even taller than usual in here. Then again, the place is extremely small. There's just enough room for a barista, a narrow counter with a pastry case, and a cute little window box with a small bench. The walls are lined with postcards from Australia and large, sepia-toned posters of old-time rugby teams.

"Wait till you try these cinnamon buns. They bake them right here. In this coffee shop inside our building."

I can't help but laugh a little. And let my guard down. *But hopefully he hasn't noticed.*

"Can I just say, proving you wrong is quickly becoming one of my—"

"How long has this been here?" I say, cutting him off.

"Doesn't matter," he says in a lower, more provocative tone.

"Yes, it does." I've narrowed my eyes at him, trying to hold back a grin.

"No, it doesn't."

"Excuse me." We haven't quite reached the counter, so I'm only pretending to ask the barista.

"Fine." He takes a step, blocking my view with his body. "They opened last week." He sighs. "But even so, I heard about it before you did."

"Congratulations," I say dryly to his smirk.

"Thank you."

Even with Richard pretending he's just beaten me at the game of life, I feel surprisingly calm. It's nice in here. And it smells so good. Like warm butter and espresso.

We step up to the counter, and I check out the coffee menu written on a chalkboard behind the barista.

I feel myself decompress. There's a strange peace to this moment. I must have needed to relax. My whole body has been on edge since seeing Sam. Not necessarily in a bad way. Just more alive and awake. *With shaky heart palpitations.*

"Two cinnamon buns, please," I order, all businesslike.

"For here or to go?"

"For here," Richard says.

"To go," I say at the same time. "Oh, we can stay…" I look around, and my gaze lands on the tiny bench in the ridiculously sweet window seat.

"It's okay." He doesn't sound convinced. "You're right. We have a lot to do."

"Yeah." I glance back at the window seat. There are books lined up against the glass, strands of ivy hanging from above, and a small vase with a single patch of baby's breath in it. *It's downright romantic.* "Well, I guess we can stay for a little bit."

We walk over, and Richard motions for me to go first. I start to scooch in, but the space between the table and the bench is so narrow, I have to sidestep while ungracefully bent over.

"Nice form," says Richard once I'm seated. He nudges the table forward a few inches, steps in, and sits down. I stare him down with an evil eye, but he pretends not to notice. Instead, he hums as he easily pulls the table back toward us and peels into his cinnamon bun without a care in the world.

Meanwhile, I feel like I've been turned to stone. There's absolutely no room between Richard and me. Our legs are touching from our ankles to our hip bones.

Come on, Ana, you're mature enough to handle this. We're just a couple of coworkers grabbing a bite on a tiny bench. I fiddle with my cinnamon roll for a moment before breaking away a small piece to try. *Damn.* This is the best perfectly gooey, not-too-sweet cinnamon roll I've ever had, but I refuse to give Richard the satisfaction.

He tilts his head toward me. "Admit it. You like my buns."

I cough awkwardly.

"Are you okay?"

"Yeah, I'm fine," I say in a shaky voice.

"Hold on." He examines the area around us. "Check this out," he says as he leans across the table and grabs a weathered deck of trivia game cards from a shelf on the wall. He shuffles them skillfully and selects a card at random.

"All right, here we go. Are you ready?"

"Sure." Why not? Focusing on a game will take my mind off how toasty it's gotten in here. It's as though his right leg and my left have become one. Neither of us has moved them since we sat down, and all those points of contact are generating heat.

"In which country do most people believe elves are real?" Richard's TV game show voice is kinda sweet. "Uh, the answer better be 'every single country,'" he says and holds the answer against his chest.

"Easy. It's Ireland," I say with certainty.

He flips the card over. "So close. It's Iceland."

"No, that's not right."

Richard smiles in an almost flirty way, which makes me sit up straighter.

"What?" I say defensively.

"Of course," he says, tapping the card on the table. "The game is wrong. You're one of *those* people."

"Why? What kind of person are *you*?"

"The kind who believes the card. Always."

"What if it's an old version of the game, and the information just hasn't been updated?" I puff up my chest.

"Right. Good point. Elven statistics *do* vary from time to time."

I can't help but laugh with my whole body.

"Do you want to know what I think?" Richard leans in until his face is only a few inches away from mine.

"Nope. Not at all."

"From what I've gathered—"

"Oh, you've been gathering information?" I finish off my cinnamon bun with a grin. It's fun having Richard's attention focused on me like this.

"You like to be in control." His expression changes subtly to something more heartfelt. "But it's okay to be wrong. It's okay to let go."

"Are you hearing yourself? You like to be right all the time."

"I'm being serious."

"And I'm insulted. You just said I'm controlling." I mean, he isn't wrong, but what he doesn't know is I'm already working on this. And making huge strides. *Sorta.*

"Okay. Do you *really* think this card is wrong?" Richard

holds the card up like it's exhibit A, I'm on trial, and everything he's just said will be proven right if I say yes.

I purse my lips, and his eyebrows rise with expectation. *I could lie.* But I have a feeling he'd be able to tell.

I can't hold back any longer, so I fire off, "I really think it's wrong. It *has* to be wrong. It's clearly a typo. It can't be Iceland. It's Ireland. In Ireland they believe in fairies and all that stuff."

As though completely worn-out, he drops his head with a deep sigh.

A few hours later, I'm watching the back of Richard's head. Up on our edit room screens, Steven and Elizabeth are cleaning up a Jersey beach with her at-risk students.

I guess he's my work friend now. *Though not a very good one because he's the kind who likes to point out my flaws.*

I'll admit it, though, Richard is a great editor. We're in the midst of trying to take eight hours' worth of dull material and turn it into three minutes of something entertaining. He's finding the tiniest moments where the kids are actually helping and having a good time with Steven and is somehow avoiding their constant texting, selfie-taking, and seagull harassment.

I'm a pretty good editor, too. I had the best time last night, but I did have to edit out every time Sam checked his phone during dinner. *Twelve!* He said he was sorry and swore it was for work. He explained he was trying to get a gig in Los Angeles and "you know, it's three hours earlier there." *As if I don't understand how the sun works.*

I also edited out all the bad moments from my *other* dates

this week. Like when TJ dragged me to the rowdy mosh pit at PS1 and a teenage girl slammed into my chin so hard I chipped a molar. Or when Philip pulled out an embroidered handkerchief from his jacket and said, "Here, I noticed you have the sniffles." I felt like my grandfather had just said, "Okay, now blow." Or how after playing the piano at the bar, Fernando was so overwhelmed he just sat there. We all applauded, and I stood, waiting for him to rejoin me. He just stayed at the piano, eyes closed for what was probably a few minutes but felt a lot longer. So I sat back down and tried really hard not to check my email.

Sure, it took all week, four different guys, and some editing. But it had happened. *To me.* I close my eyes, and I feel him start to come to life. The right guy.

He flies me around the world, makes me want to gnaw on him like a warm buttery corn on the cob while I inspire symphonies out of him . . . and finally, Sam. Sam made me laugh so hard last night, my cheeks hurt. I wonder if he regrets dumping me back in college. *Maybe we just needed a fifteen-year break?*

"Ready?" Richard has stood up and is waiting by the door.

Our production meeting was pushed to the end of the day because Bianca had some special announcements about her two new shows. Before we even walk in, I overhear her raving to everyone about how much she loves "working with mobsters." Bianca's wearing a loose pink top that falls over to one side, completely revealing her left shoulder. As we take our seats, I'm pretty sure she adjusts in her seat so she can aim the thing right at Richard.

"The taping for my other show is going smoothly," she

announces as soon as the last person enters the room. "The bride is getting plastic surgery to look just like Reese Wither-spoon on her wedding day. I mean, she even wants her underbite." Bianca pops her nude shoulder up like it's an exclamation point at the end of her sentence and moves her bouncy red hair against it as she talks.

"Edith, is it okay if I make the other announcement?" Bianca asks, rolling her milky white shoulder forward.

"Sure."

"Well, the network loved the selects from our first day of taping so much they've already committed to airing the pilots." She pauses for dramatic effect and then adds, "For *both* series."

Everyone starts to clap. One of the interns lets out a "Wow!" If the networks are going to air the pilots, they will most probably order both series.

"And . . ." Edith pauses and shoots me a foreboding glance. "I need to announce some other news."

Let me guess. Bianca has gotten the head of development position that I want, and the Emmys called. They're going to pre-award her for both shows because the selects from the first day of taping are so damn good.

"*Marry Me, You Fool!* [long painful pause that makes the room feel ten degrees cooler] was given the green light for a tenth season."

Everything slows down, and I feel a huge sense of relief. I can hear the eager production associates clapping around us and turn to Richard to see he's giving me a look that says *not bad*.

"But the bad news is . . ." Edith pauses, still looking at me.

Wait, what? She never said there was bad news. Usually, you prep a person by saying there's one of each. *And* you're supposed to ask in what order we'd prefer to hear them. What if we wanted the bad news out of the way first?

". . . this will be the final season of *Marry Me*."

One of the assistants behind me gasps. Richard looks at me with genuine concern.

"And everyone, if you haven't met Richard yet, he's been [long pause] helping out *Marry Me*," Edith announces to the group and then says to Richard, "And hopefully [short pause] we can lure you to stick around afterward."

"Thanks." Richard looks directly at me. "Well, if all of your producers are as talented as Ana, then I'll consider it."

For a second I think he's talking about someone else. But I'm assured it's me by the look on Bianca's face. *Like she just ate a bad clam.*

After the meeting wraps, Richard and Bianca are standing outside the conference room. As I walk past them, Richard looks like he wants to tell me something, but Bianca beats him to it.

"Well, Ana," she says, "since you won't have a show to do much longer, maybe you can help with one of mine. I mean, I'd have to check with Edith first, but—"

"Great." I try to sound as confident as I can and keep walking, leaving them both alone. I can only hear bits of what she's telling him as I walk away.

"You know . . . a sinking ship . . ."

I head straight to the bathroom and lock myself in one of the stalls.

Final season.

I want to scream. I pull the toilet paper out of the dispenser and scream into the roll. Little bits stick to the insides of my mouth.

I walk up to the row of sinks and rinse. I look up at the mirror. *This can be good.* Maybe this is just the push I need to set out and do something new. Who wants to make surprise proposal shows for the rest of their lives anyway?

CHAPTER 18

<u>Weekend To-Do List:</u>

1. Keep mind off work by playing air hockey downtown with TJ, followed by a private Murakami exhibit with Philip on the Upper East Side.
2. Buy sexy air hockey outfit (something airy?).
3. Find out who Murakami is.
4. Call fancy Swedish lamp company and (calmly this time) ask them to send me the correct screw so I can attach the very expensive lamp I bought from them up on the *#^@! ceiling where it *#^@! belongs.
5. *Don't forget to ask them why they don't comply with international screw-size standards so I can just find the missing screw in America. And when they tell me there is no such thing as an international screw-size standard, I will politely let them know that is exactly why they should have*

included the very special Swedish screw in the #&@#$
box in the first place.*

I pick up the phone to dial Sweden, but there's a familiar
voice already on the line.

"What are you up to, young lady?" It's Gia.

"What do you mean?"

"You're being so weird. You're always up to something
when you don't return my calls."

"No, I'm not."

"What about that cult? You never wanted to talk."

"It was a one-week meditation retreat. I wasn't *allowed*
to talk."

"Whatever. Come over. Matt's making breakfast. We got a
waffle machine from our wedding registry, and *somebody* just
couldn't wait to open it." She chides Matt like he's a little boy.
"Oh well, at least he looks hot in an apron."

The image of Matt making waffles takes me back to that
day in college when Gia and I sat at Denny's and wrote out
our lists of what we wanted in a man. I remember Gia ripping
up a waffle with her hands and dunking it in a pool of syrup
on her plate.

*"And he has to know how to make me waffles. From
scratch."*

"You already wrote four things."

"So?"

Gia always breaks the rules. Even when she had *just made
up* the rules a minute ago. She said we could pick four things
that we wanted in a guy and then she added a fifth thing. And

now she was with a guy that checked off everything on her list. *Even the waffles.*

"That looks way too watery." I hear Gia critiquing Matt's batter over the phone. "Just get over here!" she says sweetly, and it makes me feel guilty.

I should go. I've been avoiding her, and her wedding is less than two months away. While I'm there, we can get some actual wedding planning done. Maybe we can even video chat with the twins in Brazil and check in on their progress. Plus, there are always mimosas flowing at their house on the weekend. That has to be better than yelling at someone in Sweden.

Gia opens the door, looking furious. "I can't fucking believe you didn't tell me!" My chest tightens. "You got bangs? And you didn't call me? What the hell?"

I need to relax. She won't find out I'm dating her brother—*and three other guys.* What's the point of doing all this if I'm not going to enjoy it! Besides, I've always followed the rules, and where has it gotten me?

It's nice to see Gia and Matt bathed in pre-wedding bliss. She nuzzles behind him when we get to the kitchen. The doorbell rings just as I sit on one of the counter stools.

I open the door and...if my life were a reality show, this would be a great time to cut to commercial.

"Hi," Fernando says, sounding taken aback.

He's standing there wearing an oversize off-white shirt and holding a bushel of bananas.

"The bananas are here! Let's get these waffles on the road!" Matt yells from the kitchen and begins to whip the batter with inspired vigor to the rhythm of the bossa nova music playing throughout the apartment.

Fernando and I walk slowly over to the kitchen. I can tell he wasn't expecting to see me either.

"How was your date with Philip?" Gia opens a bottle of champagne, and it starts to overflow, so she brings it over to the sink.

I can feel Fernando tense up next to me. "It wasn't a date. It was just a tour of his studio."

"Well, don't give up," Matt chimes in as he cuts up bananas. "He's agreed to show his work at the gallery, so you need to keep him happy."

I can't tell what Fernando is thinking right now. He doesn't even appear to be blinking.

"It's not what you guys think. Really. He invited me to his studio, that's all."

"Well, don't knock it till you try it, right?" Matt nudges Fernando.

This is a nightmare. Plus, Fernando's now looking right at me. He's not even trying to be discreet.

I'm afraid Gia's going to notice, so I decide to do something. I get up and stand *really* close to the waffle maker. Fernando's gaze follows me, so I bend down near the hot machine and pretend to be interested in its design. Now they'll think he's looking at the waffle maker too. The heat is beginning to get to me when the timer goes off and Matt pushes me out of the way.

"Matt, do you still have that keyboard?" Fernando says with a slight crack in his voice.

Matt and Gia simultaneously look rattled.

"Uh, yeah, sure thing. It's in the bedroom, by my computer."

When her brother gets up and walks away, Gia throws her head on Matt's shoulder and covers her mouth with her hands. She looks like she's about to cry.

"What's going on?" I can't remember the last time Gia teared up about anything.

Fernando has found the keyboard, and we can hear his playing from the other room. Gia gets all quiet and closes her eyes. *Why is she so emotional?*

"This is the first time he's played the piano in years. Since our nana died." Gia keeps her voice low so Fernando won't hear.

"What? Why?" My voice pitch is way too high, and I hope Gia doesn't read into it. *As in, that's odd because he played for me and a bunch of strangers a few days ago on our secret date.*

"Because Nana's the one who taught him how to play, and he didn't audition for the symphony when he had the chance, so he felt he had let her down. That's when he started taking sommelier classes."

Great. I pulled the man out of a piano-playing hiatus and I should feel pretty awesome about it, but I don't. Gia's been worried about her brother, and I could have eased her mind a week ago.

The sounds coming from the other room are symphony worthy. Gia walks to the bedroom, dragging Matt with her. Fernando plays so intensely. He's sitting at the desk, his body curved over the instrument, eyes closed. The song is slow, romantic, and dripping with sweetness. His hands fly across the keys effortlessly. Gia watches him, enthralled.

I don't know how, but I can tell this is the song he wrote for me. And I can tell this song is his way of telling me how he feels. *And it's clear he feels a lot.*

Every once in a while he looks up at me. What if Gia notices? He's being *so* obvious. You wouldn't know it by looking at her, but Gia is *way* stronger than I am. If she knew what was going on, she would drag me out of the house but not before she put my face in the waffle maker.

Finally, he plays the last notes of the song, looks at me through one of those squinty frowns of his, and says, "Eu te amo."

I've heard Gia say those words enough times to countless guys over the past decade to know he just said "I love you" in Portuguese. Fernando isn't just a romantic; he's a spontaneously combustive romantic. The room goes quiet, and I brace myself for the wrath of Gia.

"Nana loves you too," Gia responds gently. After a moment, we start to clap.

I've gulped three flutes of champagne and stuffed two huge waffles down my throat, but I still haven't calmed down. How can I possibly get through this unscathed? And how is Gia okay with getting absolutely nothing done today by way of wedding planning?

After breakfast, Gia hugs her brother goodbye like he's going off to war. As we step inside the elevator together, he finally speaks. "Why don't I walk you home across the park?" He seems cheerful.

"Sure."

"If you tell me there's nothing going on between you and that guy Gia mentioned, I'll believe you."

"There's nothing going on," I say, and he takes hold of my hand.

Now that we're not in front of Gia, I'm breathing a little better too. It's too hot for a walk in the park, but I'm glad to be alone with him. Suddenly, he makes us stop, tugs at me gently, and points up to a tree. Perched on a high branch is a white owl.

"I've never seen an owl in the park," he whispers.

"Me neither," I whisper back, as though the sounds of the city haven't made it budge but our voices could spook it away forever.

"It's beautiful."

We watch the owl for a moment in awe.

"What did you think of the song?" Fernando turns toward me and takes both my hands.

"It was beautiful." *If I hadn't been afraid of your sister finding out about us, I would have enjoyed it more.*

"It's yours. I wrote it for you."

"Really? I loved it."

"I'm ready to tell my sister about us."

"Uh, but I'm not. Not yet. I mean—"

"Being in a room with you and not being able to tell the world is too difficult."

"Well, sure, I agree. Really. But I just think we should wait a few weeks. She has the wedding to worry about. And so many arrangements still to do and family coming in. What if things don't work out between us and she gets all excited for nothing?" *I am super impressed with my response. All good reasons.*

"What about the *other* scenario?" *He does have a great smile.*

"What other scenario?"

"The one where it *does* work out between us."

"Let's wait until *after* the wedding," I say, mostly because I don't want to accept for a moment that I will ever have to come clean to Gia about this. There's gotta be a way out of this that doesn't involve me telling her about Fernando and me. Even if we end up getting married. Does she really have to know?

"Okay. I trust you." I can see that having a time frame is calming him down. He looks back up at the owl. "I think he's trying to tell me something."

"Really? Since when can you communicate telepathically with owls?"

"It's a gift."

"So, what is he saying?"

"He wants me to play your song."

"Ah . . . of course he does. So, how are you going to do that?"

"Well." Fernando carefully rolls the sleeves of my T-shirt up over my shoulders. "First, I must prepare my instrument." *What's he doing?* He lifts my arms like I'm a living scarecrow and whispers, "Now don't move." He closes his eyes and begins to "play the piano" on my bare arms.

His fingers delicately play the imaginary keys up one arm, crossing my shoulders over to the other. The soft feel of his fingers on my skin is so nice.

But is he going to play the whole thing? It was such a long song. Especially when you don't actually get to hear it.

My arms are starting to ache, and beads of sweat are forming on my nose. *Must forget about itchy chin and focus instead on Fernando and the adorable way he squints his eyes when he pretends to play the piano.* If this were happening on my show, the New York Philharmonic would join in. Nothing fancy, just a few dozen violins and a couple of cellos surrounding us in the park. And a brilliant (and lithe) flute player hanging upside down from a tree.

We finally arrive at my apartment, and Felipe immediately steps outside to hold the door. He's doing this thing lately where he holds his head up and juts his chin out like he's guarding Buckingham Palace.

"All guests must sign in," he says without looking at me. Another new quirk of his. He's gone from personally delivering packages to my door to being a by-the-book professional prison warden.

"That's not necessary, Felipe. He's not coming up."

Fernando clearly deflates a little at the thought of not coming up. But I need to keep things moving because I have plans with someone else in an hour. And he will definitely be coming up. *I hope.*

CHAPTER 19

<u>To Do:</u>

1. Connect with inner artist.
2. Take crash course in reading music.
3. Take improv class. Again. This time don't duck out during the break.
4. Get highlights? Shorten bangs? *What's more youthful?* Get shorter, highlighted bangs.

"The switch is in the back," I shout toward the kitchen. "But check that it has enough water first." I consider getting up, but TJ demanded I stay put because he wants to make me breakfast in bed. I know he's trying to be sweet, but right now I feel like it's Mother's Day and my young son is making a mess in the kitchen and about to break my high-end espresso machine.

Felipe buzzed TJ up only an hour after he saw me make out with Fernando. Before TJ arrived, I had considered prepping

Felipe somehow. "My young cousin will be visiting me tonight. He will *not* have any suitcases, and he may be back again *another* night this week. But you know how unpredictable cousins can be..." *Ugh, why do I care what my doorman thinks?*

TJ said my mushroom meat loaf was the best he'd ever had in his life. The thing was so overcooked, I had a hard time cutting through the top layer with a steak knife. He was also impressed I own my apartment. And my forks match my spoons.

I have never slept next to anyone so hot. It was a bit overwhelming. All that access to soft, tight skin. Every inch of his body is perfect. I woke up in the middle of the night and just stared at him while he slept. It would have freaked him out had he woken up and seen me looking at him like that. But I couldn't help it.

Full disclosure though, we didn't have sex. It was more of a bizarre ritual of confectionary cleansing. I felt like he'd been saving up every fantasy he'd ever had involving an older woman: sugar, whipped cream, candle wax.

After dinner, he walked into the kitchen as I loaded the dishwasher and put his arms around my waist. He kissed my neck, leaned in close to my ear, and said, "There's something I want to do to you." And though I was nervous and not done with the dishes, I nodded yes, yes, yes.

Unfortunately, the "something" he wanted to do was strip me down and scrub my body with milk, sugar, and honey. This sounds a lot sexier than it was. He had me stand in the bathtub for my scrub down, and there is absolutely *nothing* sexy about a grown woman standing naked in a tub under the harsh bathroom lights after eating meat loaf.

I kept hoping for a blackout or that he wouldn't be so damn thorough. Did I really look like I needed to be scrubbed down this hard, and why did I ever switch to raw organic sugar?

While I was wincing, TJ was in heaven, and he wouldn't let me just rinse myself afterward. He wanted to do it in a way he thought would be more stimulating. He found a small tin cup in the kitchen and poured warm water over me a million times so it was impossible to get all the honey and sugar out of every crevice of my body.

When it was finally over, we got into bed, and he wanted to give me a foot massage with warm olive oil. "Uh, okay," I said and laid myself out naked on the bed. He microwaved a bowl of olive oil and then rubbed each toe sooo slowly with the warm goo that I passed out before the little piggy got to the damn market.

This morning, my first thought when I woke was "He's gotta be done with me." Because:

1. He saw me naked.
2. He could've had sex with me but didn't.

But the way he's behaving this morning with the coffee and breakfast in bed, I'm very confused. He walks over to me holding a tray with coffee and an egg sandwich.

"We're all out of sugar," he says.

"Of course we are." I could always scrape some off the bathroom tiles, and I'm sure there's at least a teaspoon between my butt cheeks.

The scrambled eggs are runny and the toast has a few holes in it, but it's all very sweet. He sits down next to me to watch me eat, and when I take a bite, the egg drips down through the hole in the toast and lands on my thigh. TJ quickly bends over and eats the egg off my leg, and I almost knock the whole tray over. *This is the best Mother's Day ever.*

"You know what?" he says as he pulls up his jeans. "You have great tits for your age."

I take a sip of bitter, unsweetened coffee and edit him in my mind. I hit rewind and play it again: "You have great tits." *Which is clearly what he meant to say.*

––––––

When I arrive at Elizabeth's school for our final shoot today, TJ is guiding one of our production trucks as it backs into a parking spot. He's slurping a soda from a giant Styrofoam cup, and when he sees me, he waves as he bites down the straw between his teeth. He's adorable, but I wish he wouldn't wear the hood from his sweatshirt *over* his head. It makes him seem even younger. *Like he attends this junior high.*

I make my way into the gymnasium, where our entire crew has been setting up all weekend. We've taken over the locker room and turned it into production central. We had to double the crew today to handle Steven and Elizabeth's big proposal, but now I'm feeling a little anxious with all these people to oversee. I'm still shell-shocked from the last proposal. For a moment, I imagine Jorge on a street somewhere drinking a beer out of a brown paper bag, his life ruined.

I find my seat in front of the wall of large TV screens and take a deep breath.

On the right-hand corner of the center screen is a clock counting down to when filming will begin. I feel a tightness in my stomach, thinking about another invisible clock that's also ticking down. The one that reminds me there is now a limited number of these shows in my future. I've been doing this for so long, it's hard to believe after this proposal, we'll be down to just one more season of *Marry Me*. The final season.

I need to do something about it soon. Start looking for a new job. Or come up with an idea for a life-altering series that becomes a huge hit with multiple spinoffs and catapults me to illustrious development producer status. The kind that can afford a true one-bedroom apartment in Manhattan.

The good news is I'm clearly open to trying new things. *New, inappropriately young things. Even various things all at once.*

"Here's what it looks like in the gym." The director takes me through the different cameras we have set up. "And here are the hidden cameras we have in the classroom." He presses a button, and on the monitor I see Elizabeth at work with her students. "We made sure the blinds were up to let in natural light."

"That looks good." I watch Elizabeth walk around the room gracefully and perfectly poised as she talks to the students, unaware we can see and hear everything.

I feel a cold nip at my neck. I reach for it, thinking I've been bitten by something, but I find a tiny wad of wet paper. I look up and see TJ with a straw in his mouth. He blows out, and another wad hits me on the cheek, making him crack up. *Is this really happening?* Is he spitballing me in front of the entire production team?

TJ seems to be regressing in age by the minute, like that Brad Pitt movie. Soon he'll be a small baby and then unborn. Do I pretend to laugh? I don't want to encourage him. I should reprimand him, but that might also send the wrong message. I smile awkwardly and scan the room to see if anyone has noticed. At the edge of the locker room, standing by one of the doors, is Richard. How long has he been standing there?

"What are you doing here?" I ask as he walks over and sits down next to me. I glance up at TJ, and he's just standing by the wall, slurping his soda. *Please let him be out of paper.*

"It's nice to see you too," Richard says, checking out the monitors. "Wow, she looks good today. You sure she doesn't know he's going to propose?" There's an edge to his voice I haven't heard before.

"Positive. She thinks he's out of town filming a commercial. But seriously, why are you here?"

"You've never had an editor actually care about the show? I want to make sure we have all the right coverage," he says. "Make sure everything looks, you know, well lit and *professional.*" What is he getting at? And why is he wearing a white scarf and a denim shirt? It's eighty degrees out.

My production coordinator, Jackie, walks into the room dressed entirely in black and wearing a sturdy new belt to hold up her walkie-talkies. She looks like she's in the Secret Service. I imagine TJ trying to hit me with another spitball right now and Jackie jumping out in front, taking a tiny wet wad in the chest for me.

"The principal is ready to send in the students, so just give me the word and I'll let him know," she says a little too loudly, like a drill sergeant. She takes in Richard sitting next to me and looks visibly perplexed. "What is it that's happening at nine again? Because I thought you wanted the lighting delivered at noon." I notice a slight arch in Richard's eyebrows. *Oh no.* Her codes are so obvious. Richard is sitting at my nine o'clock, and TJ is standing directly in front of me at noon.

"Nope. We don't need any more lights. It's fine," I say, hoping she'll leave and take TJ with her. "Tell Mr. Gonzalez we'll be ready in two minutes."

"Roger. Roger. Copy that. No lights at noon." Jackie walks across the locker room and talks to TJ, who quickly nods, and they both head out.

I click on my walkie-talkie. "All right, everyone, we are ready to start the pep rally." *I really wish Richard wasn't here watching my every move.*

"Roll cameras." Our assistant director's calm voice comes over everyone's headsets.

The gymnasium slowly fills up with students, and on the monitors I see the cheerleaders arrive and start to do their thing on the court. I can also see Elizabeth and her students leave their classroom, walk down the halls, and enter the gym. They sit right where the principal told us they would. Thanks to the preassigned pep rally seating, our cameras now have great shots of her.

The cheerleaders finish their cheer, and the whole gymnasium quiets down. Each second is more uncomfortable, and people look around, waiting for the principal to take the microphone and do what he normally does at a pep rally—get everybody pepped. But nothing's happening. Next to me, Richard makes a snoring sound, pretending he's so bored, he's fallen asleep. I look at him deadpan and click on my walkie-talkie, feeling more confident. *Hold on to your scarf, Richie.*

"All right, Jackie, send them in three, two, one." The gymnasium doors slam open, and the students go wild. The New York Knicks run inside as they dribble basketballs and high-five the kids in their seats. Everyone in the gym stands up and cheers as the team lines up in the middle of the court. The director cuts to a shot of Elizabeth, who looks completely perplexed.

"I thought you said this was going to be a laid-back proposal?" Richard says mockingly.

This is not the reaction I was hoping for. But there's *no way* he isn't going to be blown away by what happens next.

"Camera four, remember to stay on the spotlight," I say over the walkie. "Get ready to kill the lights in three, two, one."

On my command, all the lights in the gym are shut down, and a spotlight appears high up on the bleachers. Everyone quiets down and turns to look up at the light. A man in a fedora is standing under the bright spotlight, holding a microphone. Suddenly, he belts out a sound of pain. But it's an incredibly beautiful and perfectly pitched sound of pain. The kids go berserk, and it's fun to cut to a shot of the Knicks looking surprised as well, but I wish I had a camera on Richard's face right now.

The man on the bleachers tips the hat off his head and catches it with his hands, twirls around, and lets out another long moan, *"Ohhhhhh."*

"Is that"—Richard leans over to me—"Usher?"

Grammy-award-winning-artist Usher waits for the students to calm down for a moment and then asks them, "Have you ever been in love? How do you know when it's real?" He takes a few, graceful steps down the bleachers. "Well, I know someone who can tell us all about that." He takes another step and puts his hand on the shoulder of a lone figure who has been sitting up there all along. Steven.

I love working with artists. Usher is delivering every line beautifully. He is a real professional. Unlike Richard, who now has his head in his hands and is shaking it in disbelief.

Our assistant director comes on over the walkie. "Hit the lights in three, two, one." And with that, the entire gymnasium appears to be floating in the clouds. We've set up a dreamlike sky effect projecting on every surface, every wall, including the court and the ceiling. Richard murmurs something under his breath that I can't make out.

"*When you feel it in your body you found somebody who makes you change your ways . . .*" Usher sings his song "U Got It Bad" a cappella as he and Steven walk down the bleachers together. We have a camera on Elizabeth, who is mouth-wide-open baffled like she's still trying to figure out what's going on.

Usher is singing the song to Steven as if they're old buddies and he's giving him advice. *"Tell her, I'm your man, you're my girl."*

This is going to be a great premiere episode! I don't even care what Richard thinks. Richard is so annoying. He knows this can't get any better. Celebrity performance, professional athletes, the kids going crazy, standing up and singing along, and the bride-to-be is starting to cry. *Happy tears! This is going to happen just as I planned. No one is running out on me this time.*

It was relatively easy to get Usher. He's a big fan of the Knicks and of Steven's, who is now just bobbing his head in agreement while Usher sings. Having this tall basketball player walking with Usher while he sings to him looks kinda silly, but it's also really sweet.

They arrive where Elizabeth is standing just as Usher sings the lines "I'm fortunate to have you, girl, I want you to know I really adore you."

"Perfect timing, Usher, thank you!" I say to myself.

Next to me, Richard folds his arms and lets out a sigh of resignation. Steven then takes her by the hand and walks her over to the court, where the players are set up in free-throw formation. Usher finishes his song, and the crowd breaks into applause. One of the players throws Usher a basketball, who then hands it over to Steven.

"Come on, Steven, nothing but net for your girl," he says into the microphone. The crowd quiets down to complete silence. Elizabeth looks so proud and steps away from Steven to give him some room.

Richard leans in, blocking the monitors in front of me. "I hope he misses." What a jerk. Of course he's not going to miss. Steven Davis holds the record for consecutive free throws. That's the whole point—he *never* misses. *I guess there's always a chance. No, there's no way that's going to happen.*

Steven goes for the throw. And misses.

I can hear disappointment pass through the gymnasium like a wave.

"No problem, Steven," I walkie quickly into his earpiece. "Just go again. We'll edit that one out." I try to sound as peppy as I can for poor Steven, who looks crushed on the monitors.

"What? No way, that's amazing! We're keeping it in." Richard is just trying to annoy me now. But I've had enough of his "real life is greater than thou" attitude.

"We are taking that out!"

"It's staying in," he says, looking up at my forehead. *What's he looking at?* Hasn't he ever seen bangs before?

"Out!"

Our faces are right next to each other, so we almost miss it when Elizabeth runs up to Steven, takes the ball away from him, and says, "Yes!"

"Aw, babe." Steven picks her up in a tight embrace.

What? No ball in the basket? No actual proposal? *I'm* going to start crying now if I don't hear Steven say the words "Will you marry me?" Doesn't anyone know how proposals work anymore?

"Wait." Steven gets down on his knee and opens a small red box, revealing a ring with a diamond so big we don't even need to cut to close-up to see it sparkle under the lights.

"Babes, I can't believe I missed that shot." Steven wipes some sweat away. "I was so nervous. That felt like the most important shot of my life, bigger than the championships. Will you marry me? Make me feel like a winner every day of my life," he says, choking up.

"Yes," Elizabeth says softly with a dreamlike haze in her eyes.

Steven gets up and kisses her. The kids flip out, the basketball team applauds, happily yelling out "Woot, woot," and the captain picks up Usher to help him dunk the ball. But Steven and Elizabeth haven't noticed. They just keep kissing. Steven missed the shot, but this is cute too. *I guess.*

Richard is leaning in so close to me, I can feel his breath in my ear. "In," he says, all smug. "Oh, and there's a spitball stuck in your bangs."

There's a thick layer of heat under the catering tent where we've set up lunch for the crew. It's like a greenhouse in here with the midday sun blazing through the fabric and the steam rising from the warming trays.

I'm still upset. Richard can be such an ass. After the proposal, I went to the bathroom and checked for more spitballs in my hair. I had a student double-check too. Not a high point for me. Having to ask a teen to check my hair for "You know, like, wads of tiny wet paper."

I see Richard at the far end of the tent, making himself a plate. After we were done filming, I told him he should stay and enjoy the free meal. I felt I had to. Just common courtesy. Besides, on our last day of filming, we splurge and order from three different places. There's no reason anyone should have to miss out on pizza, fajitas, *and* an expansive roast beef station. As I get to the pizza, I notice Richard is already gone.

I walk around a corner and find him sitting at a lone picnic table under a breezy canopy-covered area of the school.

I can't turn around now. He's seen me. As I approach, he looks bothered so I skip the spot directly in front of him and sit at the far end of the table. As soon as I sit down, I regret it. It's childish to sit diagonally across from him like this.

"Here." Richard stands abruptly and hands me a metal accordion-like plate holding three small tacos tidily upright. "Have one." He sounds curt but holds the tray with care. "I noticed you skipped the Mexican section altogether."

My stomach clenches. Mostly because it's oddly sweet that Richard's gruff but still trying to share his food with me.

"In case you were wondering, I wasn't avoiding you," I say, matching his tone. "And thanks."

"Two are veggie and one's grilled fish," he says when he sees me inspecting them.

"Oh good." I place a taco on my plate. "Here." I stand up and pass three sliders in a small, oval plastic basket. "Since you didn't make it to the roast beef."

His eyes light up as he peeks inside the basket. "I don't know how I missed those," he says, a little less testy.

"Napkin?" I offer, just as he takes a messy bite.

I grab my taco, and he tosses me a packet of spicy sauce.

"Thank you." I crack a smile. We've never had lunch together, but we've obviously been paying attention to how the other one eats. In no time, we've divvied up everything on our trays.

A balmy breeze swings by, and I close my eyes to enjoy it. I'm relieved TJ's still inside, breaking down the gear. I'd prefer to avoid any more awkward moments between us. No need for Richard to be jumping to conclusions . . . *or facts*.

When I open my eyes, Richard is holding his sparkling water in the air toward me. "Cheers. To another episode in the can."

"Yeah, I guess." I reach my coffee cup across the table, tap his drink, then place it back down on the table.

Richard watches me thoughtfully. "You still have one more season to go. You should celebrate the wins till then."

He's read my mind. And he's right. We did just have a successful proposal that went off without a glitch. *Except for Steven wrecking his free-throw reputation.*

"I just wasn't feeling it today. On the last day of filming an episode, I usually have the crew stand in a circle and hold hands while everyone makes their own proposal. You know, like a vow to do something they've always wanted to do."

"That's cute," he says just loud enough for me to hear.

There's my stomach clenching again. Not that I need Richard's approval, but it's nice to feel backed up at the moment.

I think back to all the episodes that have ended this way. *The ones before Maria and Jorge.* Some of the crew thought the little ritual was cheesy, but I could tell they were into it by the time we were done.

We'd all be high off the proposal that had just taken place, and I loved how everyone would cheer in unison for all our silent vows. I started it because I wanted to make the magic something we could all experience. I can't believe I completely forgot about it today. Then again, it seems kinda pathetic now that the show has been canceled.

Richard squints, his interest piqued. "Let's do it," he says, suddenly rising from his bench.

"Really? But it's just us here."

"So." He holds out his hands, beckoning for mine. "Come on," he says in a sweet, parental tone.

I take a deep breath. At the moment, breaking my tradition seems to make the show ending more dismal.

"Okay," I say as I rise, dropping my hands into his.

His fingers intertwine tightly with mine, and I stifle a nervous laugh. He seems to stiffen up too. *This is not how we do it with the crew.*

"Well, close your eyes." I try to sound professional, but my voice is jittery. "Uh, so this is what I normally say: 'Everyone, close your eyes. Make your proposals, and make them count. On three, we'll send them off.'" I sneak a one-eyed peek at Richard obediently playing along. I try to consider what I want, but it's hard to think. *Richard's hands feel nice. Like I've slipped on a warm pair of gloves.*

"And then I count," I say to move things along, but I can't think of a single thing to make a vow about. I feel Richard tighten his grip on my hands. *To develop my own show,* emerges in my thoughts. "And three, two, one..." We open our eyes.

We stare at each other for a few vulnerable seconds before he lets go of my hands and sits back down. "That was nice," he says calmly.

"Mm-hm. Thanks." I feel like I'm recovering from a dizzy spell.

"You know, they didn't have much pizza." Richard sounds

different. He's testy again and suspicious. "Do you need to go get some for anyone? You know, maybe to set aside for someone in particular?"

"No." I huff like I have no idea who he's talking about. "I don't need to do that."

He raises an extremely skeptical and judgmental eyebrow and chugs the rest of his water.

CHAPTER 20

There's still a good chance Richard doesn't know I'm dating TJ. One little spitball in my hair is totally inconclusive evidence. What could that prove?

Still, he hasn't said much the past few days. Except this morning, to tell me he has to leave a little early to go to a concert. "Hot new Brooklyn polka band?" I joked, but he only chuckled halfheartedly and turned back around.

I've been watching the back of his head for a sign, and the only thing I've gathered is that he's tense and uncomfortable. His thin gray cotton scarf is making *my* neck itch.

His legs are stretched out lazily under the table, like he doesn't want to be here. I'm pretty sure he's upset with me and it has something to do with the proposal shoot. I just want things to go back to when he was mad at me for no reason.

Plus, our trail mix bowl is dangerously low for the first time. Don't know how to say, "Hey, buddy, don't forget to keep the nuts coming," without sounding like an ass.

We've made steady progress editing the proposal, but every time Richard sees Usher on the screen, he shakes his head or shuffles in his seat. He taps the keyboard slowly like it physically hurts. It's hard to watch. *Can keystrokes lead to actual strokes?*

It's been especially tricky to edit the performance. It's tough getting the pacing right. Richard says it's because we have too many cameras to choose from. Which makes him the only editor in the world to complain about having too much coverage. I personally love the view from the basketball hoop. *But totally agree we could live without Usher Fedora Cam.*

Ultimately, it's taken four days to edit a three-minute song. We've heard "U Got It Bad" so many times, I'm pretty sure I could pick up an electric guitar and nail the solo.

Richard rewinds the source material, stops at an image and lets it play. Usher makes a smooth 360-degree spin on his heels at the top of the bleachers.

"That's a nice shot." I try to sound upbeat.

Richard nods slightly. He slowly taps on the keyboard and brings up a sequence he put together of student reactions. A couple of guys singing along, one of a girl who looks over at her friend and screams, and another one of a young student who fumbles with his backpack, finds his phone, and starts to record what's going on. With a few more key taps, Richard has placed the students' reactions after Usher.

"What if we slow-mo the spin?" I make an extra effort to sound non-commanding.

Richard's response is a side-to-side head wag.

Some slightly harder typing on the keyboard alters Usher's speed. It all comes together. Now the kids seem to be reacting to Usher's ability to defy gravity. Just as the last kid is fumbling with his cell phone, the screen goes gray and a small message appears in the center.

The message of doom.

It's rare, but every once in a while the editing system will freeze for no particular reason and devour all the work you've done since it last saved. The computer is supposed to autosave every few minutes, but inevitably, whatever made the system freeze will also have affected its ability to autosave for the past few hours.

You'll call the software company and a tech person will walk you through all the things you need to do, and when none of that works, they'll tell you to turn the computer off and on.

The editing system will come back to life and run smoothly again like it never had a care in the world and didn't just spit out hours of your toil and creativity. Like a spaceship that's thrown out the trash, your edited masterpiece is floating away forever somewhere in the ether.

"Should I call tech support?" I ask in as soothing a tone as I can muster.

"No need."

"You sure?"

Richard doesn't respond. Instead, he just clicks away at the computer. I'm bracing myself for a reaction. A system crash brings out the worst in an editor. I've seen it all. Keyboards slammed toward the wall or yanked out entirely. Nina once yelled a nonstop row of curses at a software tech. There were so many, it was almost comical. The next day, she sent them a spa coupon for a massage.

Typically, I manage this curveball pretty well. It's my role to stay positive and get things back on track.

But at the moment I feel something welling up inside. Defeat. I had everything pretty much worked out a second ago. This episode. My life. But it feels like someone has pricked my balloon.

Mostly, what's coming up is Gia. I'm seeing her after work, and I know she and I have been off-kilter lately, but each day that goes by and I don't tell her I'm seeing her brother, I feel more awful.

She rang on my way to work, and when I told her about the network canceling *Marry Me* after one more season, she was so supportive. She said she'd always be there for me and that I just need to start believing in myself.

I watch Richard methodically go through every single step to recover the edited scene.

I'm surprised by his composure. I'm convinced people show you who they really are when faced with infuriating or awful circumstances. *So far, I like Crisis Mode Richard.*

I hear a few more clicks and then the familiar low boom sound of the computer shutting down. After a few seconds, Richard turns the system back on and opens the folder that should contain the proposal scene. Nothing. The folder is empty.

"Oh well." Richard sounds weirdly calm. "I can redo it. I remember what we did."

"I have the number right here." I search for the technician hotline on my cell as quickly as I can.

Richard turns toward me. "It's okay. There's nothing they

can say that I didn't already try." He doesn't even sound upset anymore. I've heard him but continue looking for the number.

He comes closer and places both hands gently on the edge of my desk. His fingers are stretched out like he's trying to settle an earthquake. "We lost it. So what? Reworking it can lead to better ideas, right?"

"Yeah, that's true."

His hands on my desk have a soothing effect. They're like a weighted blanket comforting the table and everything touching it, including me.

He's right, and I slowly feel some relief. I also know what I need to do to let the rest of my tension go. I need to confess to Gia.

Keeping the most exhilarating thing I've ever done from her makes it all feel like it's not really happening. I need to come clean to my best friend. Just how clean, I'm still not sure. *Maybe not squeaky clean.*

I sit up straight and place my cell down a few inches away from Richard's hand. "Should I be worried?"

"What do you mean?" He lifts his hands to grab some nuts from the trail mix bowl.

"Are you holding in all your frustration only to explode on me one day when I ask you to change something?"

"You never know," he says and turns toward his computer. After a moment, he looks at me over his shoulder. "But it's best not to test it."

———

"Thank you! Thank you!" I yell at my doorman as I sprint out the front door of my apartment building, balancing the giant wedding dress bag over my arms. It's so heavy, my biceps are burning.

I slide onto the middle seat of the cab and negotiate the long puffy white thing on my lap. I have to fold it over twice and can barely see where we're going. And it smells like someone's been smoking a cigar in here. Gia's going to flip out. I'm going to be late to her fitting, *and* her dress is going to stink. I try to open the windows, but the wind makes the bag go berserk. I hold it down and take a deep breath.

"Finally!" Gia says to my reflection coming through the door as she checks herself out in the grand triple mirrors.

A few minutes later, she's back on the pedestal, this time in her wedding dress. A consultant with hair slicked tightly back into a bun is darting around her, making minute adjustments. The gown is skintight down to her knees and then flares out like a mermaid in a dozen layers of delicate lace. On top is an extremely low-cut bust that makes her boobs jut out like they're coming up for air.

This is the fourth time I've seen Gia in her wedding dress, and it blows me away every time. The first time was when she picked it out, the second time was when her mom was in town, and then again for her actual fitting. That should have been her *final* fitting, which is why I took the dang thing to my apartment. But now the custom veil has arrived, and she wanted to see how it looked with the dress.

"What is going on with you? I've been worried."

"Just busy," I say after a moment.

"I know how you get sometimes. You don't let anyone in when you're down."

"I'm not down." I stand up hastily from the fuchsia upholstered bench I've been sitting on and walk around the pedestal for a better view. In the mirror, Gia's eyeing me doubtfully. "Just because I'm not returning calls right away doesn't mean I'm down. I'm up, actually. Way up!"

"Sorry. I'm just looking out for you."

"Well, you don't have to worry," I snap.

"Great," she says with a hint of worry.

"Great!"

"So . . ." Gia snaps a few photos of herself with her phone. "Are you bringing a date to the wedding? You know, like whoever it is you've been spending all your time with lately?"

Gia knows things. Sometimes I think she inserted a tracking chip behind my ear.

"No, I'm not bringing anyone."

"Here we are." The fitting specialist returns from the back room holding the veil across her arms like it's an ancient relic. She attaches it to Gia's head, and with a few skillful flicks of her wrists, the thing fluffs out, fulfilling all its potential. As soon as she steps away, Gia lets out a happy squeal. The veil has hundreds of tiny sparkles all over it, making her go from unbelievably sexy bride to *glowing* unbelievably sexy bride.

"Each one of these crystals is sewn on by hand," boasts the consultant.

"What do you think?" Gia asks me. She knows she looks amazing. No one on earth has ever looked this good in a wedding dress.

"It's incredible," I say as I step behind her and look in the mirror.

"Thanks for bringing the dress." She reaches out and squeezes my hand. "And for being my family here. I know Fernando moved back, but"—I try not to flinch or look away—"you've always helped me miss them less."

"Of course." I feel a wave of gratitude. I'm grateful she's grateful for me, and I'm grateful I get to be here for her. "Love you." I give her hand a little squeeze and let go.

"With fondue?" she says sweetly.

"Of course. Globs and globs."

This is exactly what I had hoped wedding planning would feel like all along. But instead, it's been a stressful couple of months dealing with her cousins' lack of organization and simultaneously being disappointed that Gia's still flirting with other men.

But I do feel bad she's been worried about me. Especially when that's the last thing she should feel. *I'm flying to Vienna next weekend!*

Now is the perfect time to tell her about the four guys. I'm sure she'll be impressed. *I just won't mention any names.*

"I'm actually seeing a couple of guys right now."

"Really?"

"Yes." What a relief. I'm so excited to tell her everything that I can't get my thoughts in order quickly enough. "I found that list and—"

She cuts me off. "No, stop. Not this again."

"No, you don't understand, not just any list. *The* list. Remember the one we wrote back in college?"

"No."

"*The* list. You said we should write what we wanted in a guy. But we could only write four things. And Matt, by the way, is exactly what you wanted because I remember your list. Isn't that crazy?"

"What are you talking about?"

"You said you wanted a guy like Brad Pitt, and Matt looks like Ryan Gosling and Ryan is today's Brad Pitt, so you got that. He had to be rich, about six two, and worship you. And then at the last minute you added waffles. I mean how crazy is that?" *This is a relief. It feels so nice to be honest with Gia again.* "So right now I'm checking off *my* list. With four different guys, but whatever. I started out giving up on the list altogether, but . . . I mean, the plan has evolved, and now . . ."

"Here, take some pictures." Gia cuts me off, handing me her cell.

I step back and start to take pictures as Gia strikes different poses. *Didn't she hear me? Why doesn't she sound happy for me? Or proud?*

"Matt is five eleven."

"Really?"

"Who are these guys?"

"Oh, you don't know any of them," I lie and hand her the phone.

Gia watches me through the mirror. Instinctively, I rub my earlobe, searching for tracking devices. She scrolls through the photos I've taken and sends off a couple of texts.

"You should have told me." She sounds defensive. "Was it because you knew I would have talked you out of it?"

"I'm just having fun," I say, ignoring her question.

"Just know that while you waste your time with the wrong ones, you could be missing your chance with the right one."

I shrug halfheartedly.

Gia takes my hand and holds it up to her heart. The gesture catches me completely off guard. "And you don't need to keep anything from me," she says, looking into my eyes. "It makes me feel like I'm not a part of your life anymore."

Her bluntness makes my mind muddy. Gia's so good at them, but I'm terrible at confrontations. Even peaceful, hand-on-your-heart ones.

"You're right. I'm s—"

"Here, hold this for me." She hands me her cell and walks into the dressing room.

The moment I look at the phone, a text comes in from someone named Mr. Dave and then another from an unknown number.

Damn, you look hot!

Marry me instead.

Gia's flirting with other men using photos of herself in her wedding dress, and she has the nerve to lecture me? I'm the single one here! Talk about a double standard. Why am I not allowed to flirt with a bunch of guys? *Sure, one of them is her brother. And she would flip if she knew about Sam. When he dumped me, she had to console me for months.*

"Matt invited Philip to the wedding. Maybe *he* can be your date?" Gia teases from behind the dressing room door.

Philip is coming to the wedding? Philip *and* Fernando will

be in the same place? And Landon? The wedding is only a month away. I suddenly feel sick.

On the way out of the shop, Gia picks up a sparkly headpiece and tries it on. "What do you think?" She looks at me and poses like I'm supposed to be taking her picture.

"I don't know. It might be overdoing it with the sparkly veil and the—"

"I'll take it!" And $2,147 later, the thing is painstakingly wrapped in a thousand layers of light-pink tissue paper and placed in an enormous box that comes home with me. Along with the marshmallow dress.

CHAPTER 21

Fernando squeezes my hand as he leads us up the steps and into the Cathedral of Saint John the Divine on 112th Street.

"It's an evening of Bach's organ sonatas. Surprise!" Fernando says, leaning into me.

"Really? You know me so well," I say, trying to sound sincere.

"You think so?"

"Absolutely."

Too bad his sister doesn't know me after all these years. What I'm most upset about is she didn't even acknowledge her list and how she's gotten everything she ever wanted. *Typical of people who have it all.*

As soon as we sit down, I catch Fernando eyeing me. He gives me a flirty look that brings me back to the moment.

The cathedral's large stained-glass windows don't allow much light in, causing the place to feel musty. A recorded announcement plays over the speakers asking everyone to turn off their cell phones, and I notice the audience is made up of mostly senior citizens who are moving like molasses with their canes and walkers.

"I read that parts of the organ were recovered from an old mansion upstate. Can you imagine having that thing in your home?" Only Fernando can be this excited about an organ.

I take in the massive pipe instrument built high into the walls surrounding the altar.

"You've clearly never been up to my apartment."

"Yet."

Music bellows out of the enormous instrument. The sound is severe and full of pomp and circumstance. The beginning of the song made me feel like we were at a graduation, but now it sounds like we're watching a silent movie and someone's getting tied to a train track.

The musician is clearly accomplished. He must be one of a handful of people in the world who can play an organ that size because of the way his feet manage the twenty or so pedals. But after an hour and a half, *my* organs are exhausted. The music has reverberated its way into all of us.

"Rumor is that Bach wrote that last piece for a young student he was in love with." Fernando leans in so close, I can smell his cologne. It's not patchouli, but it's definitely something herbal.

"So what happened?" I ask, noticing a small scar just under his chin for the first time.

"I think he wasn't wealthy enough for her or young enough or cool enough."

"Sounds like she was difficult to please," I tease.

"Certainly, but 'tis better to have loved and lost, don't you think?" he says with his signature frown. "Oh, I almost forgot. I have another surprise for you." He reaches into the front pocket of his jacket and pulls out a beautiful gilded leather book.

"Whoa," I say, impressed as he places the heavy book in my hands. I flip through the pages carefully. "Thank you," I say, genuinely moved. It's a blank journal except the first few pages have already been written in.

"Don't read it now. It's a . . ." He pauses for a moment as an elderly couple slowly squeezes past us.

"It's a poem," he finally says. "I had an idea. Since we both love poetry, I was thinking you could write a poem in response to mine. And then give it back to me." He has such an innocent look on his face, and it makes me feel a little guilty.

The only thing more romantic than someone writing you a poem is someone wanting to create a *poem correspondence* with you. Sure, I haven't written any poems since college, and those were forced rhymes about feminism and free speech. I've always wanted to pick it up again. This will be fun. *But hopefully it won't require too much time and effort.*

"I love it. What a great idea." I rest my head on his shoulder.

"There's something I want to tell you," he says, prompting me to look at him again. "No! I'll say what I need to say best in the next poem. And then you can respond to it that way."

"Okay." *Great, now I'm behind two response poems.*

I'm eager to get home and read the poem Fernando has written for me. As soon as I walk in, I sit on the bed and open the leather-bound book. I close my eyes for a moment just to bask in the romance of it. *No one has ever written me a poem.*

I'm interrupted when my phone vibrates with a text. It's a photo of a penis. TJ has sent me a picture of his private parts. It's a bit intimidating. Like a flagless pole demanding allegiance.

What am I supposed to do now? Respond with "Thanks!" or "Way to go!" *Or worse, did I just get more homework?* Gia would know. She always knows, and it's so freaking annoying. Well, what matters is I've received my first penis pic! From a ridiculously hot guy. I'll respond in whatever way feels right *to me.* Maybe after reading Fernando's poem, I'll find some inspiration.

in a fortnight it all begins
just a fortnight till angels sing
a choir song of glorious news
that can only begin and end with you

It goes on like that for twenty-four stanzas.

I shut the poetry correspondence book and respond to TJ with a thumbs-up emoji.

———

Two days later, I'm sitting across from TJ, trying not to think of his flagpole. "Mine's not prickly," he says sweetly. "Wanna switch seats?"

"I'm okay, thanks."

His text said he wanted to take me to the "tp chow n ny under triborough," but I'm not going to tell him that this is technically the Robert F. Kennedy Bridge or that a family of rats just tramped by a few feet away. We're sitting on refurbished forklift crates and the tp chow is barbecue pork doughnut sandwiches.

But I really don't mind. TJ makes me feel so sexy. My hair is flying around with the wind, so I let some strands linger on my face once in a while because I'm certain it makes me look like a seductive penis pic–receiving goddess.

TJ is seriously gorgeous. The sun kisses his skin, and his eyes literally sparkle. He takes a big, sloppy bite of his sandwich and looks at me longingly. He wants to repeat our first night together with a new round of sweets and confections, and sometimes the most random words will turn him on.

1. Licorice
2. Milk
3. Tapioca
4. Sunday
5. Dish
6. Crème de la crème

"So, can we talk about your mom? When did she pass away?"
Wait, I was ready to talk about tapioca.
"Um, it's been about twelve years."
"How did you get through it?"
I'm supposed to be telling him about the blueberry sauce I got for

him to wash my hair with. But his tone is so direct, I can't help but do as I'm told. It's only a few minutes later when I hear my voice cracking.

"And then my dad remarried a year later. Sometimes I think he might have been seeing her before my mom was gone." I've never told *anyone* about this. Even Gia. And TJ's the last person I thought I'd open up to. I expect to feel some relief, but saying it out loud gives my father's potential betrayal more *potential.* It feels like someone's tightening a belt around my chest.

"Sounds like you went through the hardest time in your life and you were all alone."

My heart feels like it's caving in on itself. *Who is this kid? How does he know what to say?*

"It's like you went through a war you had to fight."

We should be talking about blueberry sauce. Cheese blintzes. Climbing flagpoles. Anything but this.

"But you had to go through it alone . . ."

He's deep in his thoughts and looking at me lovingly and with . . . *maturity.*

". . . because your father wasn't there for you."

And that's it.

A dam breaks inside me, and I start to cry. I don't even know why. It's not like I still believe my father did anything wrong. There's just this sense of betrayal. It's overwhelming. I'm sitting on a bunch of crates under a bridge and I'm bawling. It's not a pretty cry, either. It's big, uncontrollable wailing.

Afterward, we walk to my place with our arms around each

other like a bona fide couple. No sex. Just a blueberry mess that clogged my drain. I'm starting to get the feeling he wants to wait for sex. Like you do when you aren't just fooling around with someone. Which makes me feel so incredibly special. *And like the idea may be worth looking into.*

CHAPTER 22

It's been a week since we lost the original edits, and I'm back to feeling like Richard is a tool. He huffed all day long as he edited a scene where a helicopter lands and Steven and some of his basketball buddies hop out. They've arrived at the top of the Harry Winston building to find an engagement ring for Elizabeth. I thought he would enjoy editing it. It was such a fun scene to film. *Though there were moments of panic due to the height of the men and the speed of the helicopter blades.*

But instead, he did nothing but mumble to himself that the whole thing was "way over the top." *Like that's a bad thing.*

For a moment, things did get spicy.

"Helicopters provide more harmful pollutants than you would imagine." Richard has this way of speaking that makes it clear he believes he's the better human in the room. "A more rational way to express your love is to leave the world a better place."

"You do understand that we have to film actual scenes, right? What would you have us do?"

"This is why I don't work on reality shows."

"Well, you're working on one now."

His reaction was subtly maniacal. Part laugh, part grunt.

Richard's probably never going to propose to his girlfriend Maxi, who calls him about ten times a day. He'll probably just throw an unpolished ring made of recycled trash cans at her and say something like "Think quick."

After such a long day, I definitely need a pick-me-up. Thankfully, it's Wednesday, and that means it's Sam Night. Sam is so Wednesday-appropriate. He's spontaneous, exciting, and light—perfect for overcoming any hump.

And I loved his text this morning.

you + me + annie hall

We used to watch marathons of Woody Allen movies back in college. He'd come over to my dorm, and when I opened the door, he'd be standing there doing the sloppy robot holding takeout bags.

But instead of a movie night, he's brought me to Coney Island on the subway.

"There's no way you're getting me on that thing."

"Come on, we have to. Because of Annie Hall when Alvy says, 'I was brought up underneath the roller coaster.'"

"I do remember that, but I'm still not riding it."

"At the end of your life, do you really want to look back and regret not trying this?"

"I think I'd be fine with that."

"Let's go." He casually grabs me around the waist and

guides me onto the rickety worn-out wooden coaster, and my body gives in.

Sam is a lot like this roller coaster. Perilous yet full of thrills.

Using the same mortality argument, he gets me to consume a sticky cloud of pink cotton candy, a very dry corn dog, and three strong vodka tonics.

But that's the thing. I feel so free with Sam. I don't care what anyone thinks or what makes sense. I'm never as silly as I am when I'm with him. And I just know that neither is he. We really could be good together. And yet I can't help but feel that with Sam, it's a case of wanting what I can't have. *But why do I feel I can't have him? He's here, isn't he?*

On our way back on the crowded subway, we're sitting closer than before. The heat is still on everyone around us from an afternoon in the sun.

"'I think crime pays. The hours are good, you meet a lot of interesting people, you travel a lot.' What movie?" Sam thinks he does a dead-on Woody Allen imitation, but he's terrible. He stutters and shakes his head around. It's almost as bad as his robot.

"I should know that!"

"*Take the Money and Run.* Come on, that was an easy one. Your turn."

"'I would never want to belong to a club that would have me as a member.'"

"You're insulting me now. *Annie Hall,*" he says and nudges me as if to say I need to try harder at this game he's just invented. "'Last time I was inside a woman was when I visited the Statue of Liberty.'"

"*Crimes and Misdemeanors!*" I yell out too loudly, and his reaction is to put his arm around my waist.

We play this guessing game all the way home. His turns are impressive, sometimes reciting both parts of an entire conversation, while I squeak by misquoting obvious one-liners.

Not much talent in quoting a movie. Just a stubborn commitment to the fruitless task of memorizing his favorite screenplays. *And yet...* this back and forth (of mostly my failing and his expertise) is escalating the tension between us. By the time we get to Union Square, the game is feeling an awful lot like foreplay.

We need to switch to our respective trains now, and it's my turn again. I rack my brain for quotes, looking around the station for some spark of inspiration. Sam is watching me, loving it that I can't think of anything.

"Concede already. I promise I won't think any less of you."

"Never!"

"Okay, but your train is coming."

He's standing so close to me, I can't think straight. I scan all the films I can think of. We've already used every line I can remember. And then it hits me. It's from *Deconstructing Harry*. They're making a movie within the movie, and the director notices the main character is out of focus. But what's the character's name? My train is almost done pulling up, and I still can't remember. I'll just make up a name and maybe Sam won't notice.

"Richard looks a little soft, doesn't he?" I finally say proudly.

He starts to laugh, and as the train stops and the doors open, he takes a step closer and whispers erotically in my ear, "It's Mel that's out of focus, not Richard."

Suddenly hearing Richard's name makes me uncomfortable. But before I can process the reason, the most unexpected thing happens. Sam kisses me.

Moments later, I step into the subway car and stand right by the door as it closes. I watch Sam watching me as I roll away. I replay it all in my head. At first he was hugging me goodbye. Then his lips kissed my neck. Then my cheek. Then he hopped from my cheek to my lips. I feel buzzed. *And completely unsettled.*

————

At work the next day, I'm still thinking about Sam's kiss. How it hopped like a little kangaroo. Neck. Cheek. Lips. I'm replaying it again when our phone rings. Richard turns around with a surprised look on his face. The edit room has a landline, but no one ever uses it anymore. He finally finds it on the edge of his desk.

"Hello? Oh sure. I'll let her know." And then to me, "There's a package for you at the front desk."

As I approach the main lobby, I see an enormous bouquet of white flowers. Peonies, tulips, orchids, and the vase is dragging a long white satin bow. Our receptionist has a huge smile on her face as she sees me. "They came with this," she says, handing me an envelope. I tuck it under my chin and grab the arrangement with both hands.

I set the flowers down on my desk, and Richard doesn't say a word. He only looks at them and nods approvingly for an uncomfortably long time before he finally returns to work.

I'm about to open the envelope and then stop. *Who do I want them to be from? Sam? Fernando?* A name drops from somewhere deep in my subconscious...Landon. I've been purposely not thinking of him, yet even now it's his name I want to see inside.

I peel open the envelope and pull out the card.

Inside is an embossed invitation to Philip's event in Vienna.

———

The following day, I'm as high as the clouds. *Well, I'm about to be.*

I step out of the taxi at JFK wearing a light-blue blouse and a navy blazer. I bought a weekend's worth of new outfits that say, "I am a globe-trotting gal who shops exclusively at the fancier Ralph Lauren shop in SoHo."

I am definitely owning this outfit. *Well, from the waist up at least.*

These riding pants with suede inseam strips didn't feel this tight at the store. And the knee-high brown leather boots are so stiff. Bending my knees takes a gargantuan effort. I try to look natural, but I feel like the only thing missing right now is Gia's riding whip.

I find my seat in first class and sink into the plush lounger with ease. The flight attendant is probably in his sixties but very handsome. Before we've taken off, I've said yes to the complimentary champagne, yes to the hot towel, and yes to the free pre-flight light bites.

I get through customs feeling dehydrated but also extremely

collected. I'm excited to spend the weekend with Philip. I have no idea what he has planned, but every single thing will be something I've never done before.

The driver Philip arranged drops me off at a hotel that looks like it may once have been a private mansion.

"I'll be back for you at four thirty," he says and hands me a note.

I open it and follow the valet carrying my bag into a tiny yet gorgeously ornate elevator. The note is written on the hotel's stationery:

> Ana,
>
> Welcome to Vienna. I recommend the crepes in brown sauce at the hotel.
> See you at my little shindig.
>
> P

By "my little shindig," he's referring to an event at the Austrian Parliament, where this artist is being honored for his life's work.

The good news is I won't know anyone here other than Philip. The bad news is my new strapless gingham gown and these stockings are creating static and making the dress ride up my calves, so I have to keep tugging it down every few steps.

The hall at the parliament building is filled with elegant

guests, reporters, and photographers. And me. I should be used to all the cameras, but I'm worried they'll photograph me at a moment when my dress is static-clinging around my waist.

An important man is easy to spot. He stands out in a room because everyone else is watching *his* every move. The busy room wraps around Philip, and he's the eye of the storm. He looks so relieved when he sees me, like there was a chance I could back out. I send him a smile, feeling a swell of pride that I could have any effect on him.

A few minutes later, Philip and I are drinking champagne as he leads me to one of the rooms filled with his work. "You look beautiful," he says.

"Why, thank you," I say, trying to sound okay about all of this. He's quiet for a moment, but I can feel him just staring at me, so I tug my skirt down as I take a few steps closer to a black-and-white striped painting called *New York*.

"I need to do it tonight." He's right next to me again.

"What?" I almost spit champagne onto his painting.

"When we get back to the hotel. I need to paint you. Tonight."

"Paint me?" We've stopped at an enormous work of green splotches. I look at it and then at its artist. "I thought you didn't do portraits."

"I haven't. But, Ana, you are meeting me as I boldly go in new directions." He looks around and whispers, "Much like the pieces you saw in my home."

"Right. Of course." But I barely registered his bold new work. All I managed to see was ear hair. "Okay," I say through clenched teeth, my face in a frozen smile. The idea of being painted by Philip makes me feel as exposed as I did when TJ scrubbed me down with sugar in the bathtub. Lights on.

Back at the hotel, it's all been set up. I have no idea who has done this for him or when he passed the information along, but when we walk in, the suite has been turned into an artist's studio. The whole thing reminds me of our interview sets for *Marry Me*, but the lighting is much warmer and there's a light gray paper covering the back wall and rolled out across most of the floor. At the center is a lone metal stool.

"Let's take a look." Philip motions for me to sit down.

It's impossible to back out now. I know it. The stool knows it.

I walk past a mirror and stop for a moment to inspect myself. Nothing in teeth. Hair looks reasonable.

I sit down and cross my legs. The stool is very uncomfortable.

Philip sits down in front of the easel and then stands back up. He walks behind me and turns off one of the lights. The room is so quiet, I can hear him breathing.

Suddenly, he's bending down in front of me. "Move slightly to the left and lift your hand. Higher." I obey his commands and lift my arm like I'm asking the teacher for a hall pass. "No, no, place it on your shoulder." None of this feels natural to me. Who rests their hand on their shoulder? I sit up straight. Uncross my legs. Cross them again.

"Move your head to the left a little. Now down. Okay, that's great right there. No smiling."

He starts to work quickly and looks up at me every couple

of nanoseconds. He smiles from time to time, and it makes me feel like he's in on a secret about me.

After a while, I truly take in the magnitude of this moment. Philip Oberon is painting my portrait. *The Philip Oberon.*

"It must be incredible seeing so much of your work in one place like that." I know there's been an unwritten rule not to talk about his art, but his event was so impressive. I think it's gotta be okay to bring it up this one time.

"I suppose," he says after a long pause like it's no big deal. The EU. A Lifetime Achievement Award. No big deal.

"Are you really *never* impressed?" I say, sounding a little coy.

He studies the canvas as if it holds the answer. "Once." He dabs more paint onto the brush and continues painting. "In Osaka. An investor bought some big pieces for his restaurant, so I went out there for opening night." Philip looks at me for a moment and then goes back to work on the painting.

"He said he was sending me a gift to the hotel. So that night there was a knock at my door. Two beautiful women are standing there. You can imagine what was going through my mind. And then this older gentleman walks in, and I was *even more* worried." Philip smiles, and I can see a glimpse of the young mischievous painter inside. "Turns out they were there to take my measurements and bring me a custom suit the next morning before I got on my flight."

"A suit? That's the one thing that has ever impressed you?"

"It wasn't just *any* suit. A custom suit."

"How did it turn out?"

"Perfect. Nothing has ever fit me better. And the inside of the suit was even more beautiful than the outside. There was a whole other suit no one got to see or feel but for me." He's got this big grin on his face, and I smile back. "Don't smile," he says, which makes me laugh, but then I quickly go back to not smiling.

Another hour goes by before he speaks again.

"What do you say we skip out on the rest of the festivities here this weekend and head to the Coast?"

"Okay. Sure!" I instantly feel so impressed with myself and how far I've come with the whole idea of making things happen for myself and dating multiple men, including a wealthy older art— *What the?* Philip has completely lost it. It's like he's having some sort of seizure.

He's throwing paint on the canvas wildly, thrusting his body back and forth. He dabs more paint and thrusts again and again. It gets even more intense as he begins to grunt with each thrust. I look down and see that even though I'm sitting about twelve feet away from him, a big glop of yellow has landed on my new Ralph Lauren pointed-toe pump.

CHAPTER 23

I think we should cut around Usher and lose him altogether."
Richard sounds serious, but he must be joking.

"What do you mean 'cut around Usher'?"

On the screen is a close-up of Usher singing his heart
out into the microphone. We have one more week to finish
editing Steven and Elizabeth's episode.

It's been two weeks since I got back from Vienna, and
neither of us has brought up the fact that Richard is leaving the company in a few days. I only found out when I
received a company-wide email announcing "Goodbye drinks
for Richard" this Friday at a bar a few blocks away.

I had opened the invite carelessly, believing it was about
Richard in Legal. When I realized it was about the guy who
has been sitting a few feet away from me all summer, the
room felt immediately warmer. How did I not know that
Richard is leaving the company? I simultaneously wanted
to throw my tower of Post-its at the back of his head and

contemplate what I would wear to guarantee a reaction from him. *Lime-colored V-neck bodysuit, my tightest black jeans, woven leather mule pumps.*

"Trust me, it would be so much better without him," Richard says firmly.

Better *without* Usher? What's better without Usher?

"There's no way we're losing Usher. That's not even an option."

I've started a list of things I'd like to do with Richard's scarf collection:

1. Burn them in a beach bonfire.
2. Sew them all together so he has to wear one enormous scarf.
3. Use them to tie him to his editing chair.

"It's too ridiculous. It should just be about Steven and Elizabeth, not Usher. What's he even doing there?" Richard is sounding quite frustrated. "Just hear me out. I've thought it through, and I can totally edit Usher out of this entire proposal. The team would appear, and *hello*, it's Steven's team, so at least that would be logical. He shoots. He misses. They kiss. You wouldn't even miss Usher. And it would make sense."

Why would any of this need to make sense?

"The network signed a contract with Usher's label, so there's no way we can back out of it now."

Richard makes a deflated sound and gets back to work. For a moment I actually feel bad for him having to work on something he doesn't believe in. I'm about to apologize or something along those lines when I get a text.

Chomp, chomp, chomp.

It instantly takes me back to the dark and dingy comedy club on the Lower East Side where I saw Sam perform a few days ago.

"Everybody's always got an idea for a new app," he said while adjusting the microphone stand. "They're like 'My new app tells me when the moon is full.' Or 'I have an app that tells me when I'm in a good mood.' Here's an idea for an app. I want an app that *eats* all your other apps when you're not looking. That's it. That's what it does. Chomp, chomp, chomp."

The crowd really loved him that night. He's so good at appearing as if he doesn't need their applause, and I think that's why they give it to him.

"It'd be like Pac-Man. Chomp, chomp, chomp." He walked across the stage, pretending to eat apps. "That's right. I'll say it. I want an app with an *app*-etite." He cracked himself up, which made me laugh too. Mostly because I love when Sam laughs at his own jokes.

Then his eyes found me in the audience, and he pointed the microphone at me, as if to say, "I wrote this one for you." I start laughing, so Richard brings up the volume on Usher's performance of "U Got It Bad."

The song fills the edit room. *You got it bad when you're out with someone but you keep on thinking about somebody else.*

I can't stop thinking about the last few weeks with Philip, TJ, Sam, and Fernando. It's been so . . . *busy.*

<u>Things NOT to do:</u>

1. See Fernando after Sam (my playfully mocking mood with Sam is clearly too harsh for Mr. Sensitive).

2. Go on a date with Philip after lounging in sweats all day with TJ (waffle fries, then wine, you will NOT be fine).

3. Call guys by the wrong nicknames (am now dating three Boos, two of whom are also sometimes Bunny, and one Bunny Boo).

I've even started editing a "best of" moments montage in my mind.

It all starts with a shot of me diving into a cool, blue sea in Italy. When Philip had said let's go to the Coast, he meant the *Amalfi* Coast, where he chartered a yacht after he got me an overpriced black bikini in Positano.

Then we'd cut to Sam and me screaming as the Coney Island roller coaster races down its steepest drop. He leans in and pretends he's going to throw up on me, which makes me laugh just as the coaster drops again, so now I'm laughing *and* screaming.

Cut to Fernando reciting his latest from our book of poems on a picnic blanket in the park.

Cut to Philip thrusting his hips as he splashes paint on the canvas. The camera pans to me sitting there fascinated by his lack of inhibition.

Cut to TJ dipping my big toe in duck sauce. And then cut to me laughing in pleasure/discomfort.

Cut to Fernando playing a baby grand piano for me.

Intense. Romantic. The camera widens out and reveals that we're inside Bergdorf Goodman.

Cut to TJ pouring syrup on his French toast at a diner and then looking at me mischievously like he's getting ideas.

Cut to Philip as he pushes in a bookshelf in his apartment, revealing a secret room. "This is my collection of Japanese watercolors." The camera pans to me in visible awe of being one of a select few to see these delicate works under the soft, protective light.

Cut to Sam and me doing the sloppy robot on the roller coaster...

And then to Fernando dancing with me around the Lincoln Center fountain just as it lights up...

And then me dripping with sweat as I jump up and down uninhibitedly with TJ at a free hip-hop concert in the park...

Then back to Sam, who pins me in the tight hallway back-stage at the comedy club and kisses me.

Of course, there's another kind of montage that could be edited. *The bad kind.* The one with all the moments you wish didn't happen.

Like when I was kissing Fernando on his couch and he kept getting up every time the song ended to change the record because he owns nothing but singles.

"Singles have better sound integrity."

Perhaps. But having to get up every three minutes to turn a record around sure ruins a mood. I also edit out every night I have to stay up late working on one of his response poems. *So many!* And I'm still way behind.

And when TJ spent $200 on a pair of headphones at a fancy electronics store. I pay for most of our meals, but he can afford enormous neon blue headphones?

Or when Philip jumped off the yacht to join me and slipped at the last minute, whacking his knee. He was underwater for a really long time, and all I could think was, *Nice. You've killed Philip Oberon.* Thankfully, he popped up for air eventually, but his knee was swollen like a watermelon for the rest of the weekend.

The montage would also include every time Sam checked his cell phone. *A lot.*

As I head out to grab lunch, I convince myself it's okay to focus on the good. The moments that do make the cut. I can even edit together the perfect sentence.

Sam: You're the funnest,

Philip: most charming,

Fernando: sensitive woman...

TJ: with great tits ~~for your age~~.

When I get back from lunch, there's a note on my desk.

"I've been meaning to ask you. What's the policy on inter-office dating here?" Richard asks without turning toward me in his chair.

"I don't know. Why?"

Please tell me TJ didn't come by and leave this note while I was at lunch. His texts lately are strictly limited to "I want to dunk _____ (a part of my body) into _____ (a kind of sauce)."

"Besides, why do you want to know? You have a girlfriend," I say, holding the note tightly in my hand.

"I don't have a girlfriend."

Really? So, Richard dumped Maxi. *Typical.* He was always so rude to her. So now he wants to go out with someone from the office? Is it Bianca? I read the note while still trying to figure out what Richard is up to.

Ana,

Give me a ring when you can.

Landon

When I was little, I flew off a swing once and landed flat on my back. I was completely out of breath for what felt like hours.

Right now I feel the same way. This note. Has completely. Knocked. The wind. Out of me. Landon. Here.

"Oh yeah," Richard says casually, "that's right. Some guy came by. What was his name? Something out of a soap opera...Bradford. Brandon. Langley."

I can hear Richard, but he sounds far away. And I'm even farther away, in a land where Landon leaves me notes.

"Landon." My voice is deep and breathy. His handwriting is just as it should be. Tall, elegant letters.

"That's right. Preppy guy. I told him you'd be right back, but he said he had to go shop for more preppy clothes." Richard is mocking Landon's style? The guy who wears scarves in August? And who brought a teacup from home today? A teacup *and* a saucer. A porcelain teacup with a bunch of blue koi fish painted on it. Add that to the list:

38. Men who bring teacups to work

I remember that Landon was supposed to be back in town a week before the wedding. But why come by my office? Maybe he wants to ask if there are any best man duties he can help with. It doesn't make any sense. Why not just ask Gia for my number?

Gia always says, "Tune him out and you'll turn him on." Her theory is that men can sense when you're entertaining other options. *Maybe she's right?*

CHAPTER 24

Are you okay?" Richard sounds genuinely worried.

"Oh, I'm fine, thanks." But the truth is I feel a lump in my throat that for some reason just got lumpier because he noticed there's something wrong with me.

It's been two days and I still haven't responded to Landon. *What if he wants to ask me out? And how am I going to manage juggling Fernando and Philip at the wedding without letting Gia find out that her maid of honor has been dating her brother?*

A knock on the door makes my heart stop. Richard sees I'm not moving, so he gets up and opens it. It's TJ and he's standing next to a couple, both with extremely broad shoulders. The man probably played football in college, and if there was a female wrestling team, this lady was the captain.

"Hi!" I say a bit too loudly because I'm relieved it isn't Landon.

"Hey . . . I wanted you to meet my parents."

"Ah." The sound comes out before I have a chance to block

it. I'm not sure what it must look like to them, but I feel my face recoil.

I take a closer look at the man and woman standing next to TJ. They're in such great shape. *And so young.*

"Nice to meet you," I say in the tone of someone who has never eaten s'mores off their son's belly button.

"Hi, yes." TJ's mom kisses me on the cheek. I try not to read into the fact that she doesn't return with an "It's nice to meet you too."

She looks around the room suspiciously. *Does she think I'm hiding the real age-appropriate Ana somewhere?*

"And this is one of the editors," TJ says excitedly.

"Richard." He shakes their hands politely and sits back down. "Your son is quite the go-getter around—"

"When did you get in?" I cut Richard off.

His mom looks me up and down but doesn't respond.

"Just now," TJ's dad cuts in. "But we've heard so much about TJ's girlfriend, we just had to make this our first stop."

The room is dead silent. The sound of Richard pouring himself another cup of tea from his thermos is deafening. He's just sitting there watching us like Sherlock Holmes at teatime. *Girlfriend?*

I look at TJ, hoping for a rebuttal like, "Dad, we're just friends," but he's completely oblivious.

Sensing the tension, Richard puts his teacup down. "Yep, this is where the magic happens. Here, let me show you how it all works."

Just when I thought things couldn't get any worse, TJ's mom takes a seat in Richard's chair, slips off her blazer, and hands it to her husband. She is wearing a gray silk blouse with small white polka dots. The exact same one I'm wearing.

———

"I just want you to know these last few months have been..." Sam looks right into my eyes. "I dunno, awesome."

Thankfully, I already had plans with Sam after work, so I had an excuse when TJ's father invited me to dinner.

Sam's phone dings, and he replies to a text. I look away and try to focus instead on what he's just said. The narrow streets of Chinatown are packed with both tourists and locals, but we were able to get a table by a strictly sweet and sour food truck. It's so hot out that the fish and fruit vendors have moved most of the products inside.

"I feel like I can tell you anything." Sam suddenly looks a bit anxious. "When I'm with you, my brain gets, like, kicked into another gear, and it's so nice to be with someone I can have that with." I try to get a word in, but he doesn't give me the chance. "Someone that you have so much in common with..."

I feel like an announcement is imminent. Like he's about to profess that he's fallen in love with me. Finally. After all these years.

"You know what I mean? It's the perfect balance," he says, and *ding*. Stupid cell phone. He responds to it and I try to relax, but the truth is I'm dying to hear what he's about to say.

"My girlfriend got out of work early, so she's on her way."

His girlfriend?

It's not so much *what* he's just said but *how* that I'm having a problem with.

He's never even mentioned a girlfriend before. I thought he was about to say he wanted me to give him another chance at a real relationship. *Now there's a girlfriend and she's joining us!* And he's told me about it like it's not a big deal at all.

"Okay," I manage to say after a few moments.

"It's like, what can I do? I can't help it, you know? I mean, it's like, ooh, she drives me crazy!"

I'm speechless. In an instant, I'm back at college. This has gone *exactly* the same way.

A tall brunette with model good looks walks toward us. Sam's back is to her, so he doesn't see her approaching us the way I do. She's wearing a thin sundress and is sucking on a Popsicle as she strolls toward us.

She walks like a lioness. The queen of the jungle in a translucent dress. She approaches Sam from behind and holds the bright-red phallic-looking Popsicle in her mouth so she can wrap her long fingers around his eyes. She sees me and just smiles. She doesn't seem to care that I'm sitting here with her man. *Why would she?* She's a lioness. And I'm just a slow-witted zebra that has strayed from the pack.

"Whoa! Hey!" Sam smiles.

"Hey!" she says, taking the Popsicle out of her mouth.

It's only one syllable, and there was a Popsicle in her mouth for most of it, but I could tell that "Hey" was dressed in a Russian accent.

"What's that?" Sam asks, still not introducing her to me.

"It's pomegranate."

Finally, Sam motions to me. "This is an old friend of mine, Ana. Ana, Tasha."

"Wonderful. Hi! So nice to meet you." I'm overcompensating. "That looks delicious," I say too loudly.

"It's fresh. Taste." She's shoved the thing into my hands.

But how does one share a *Popsicle?* There's no germ-free way to do this. Who knows where that mouth has been? Well, at least one place comes to mind, and I've been there too. She uses her now free hands to hug Sam, and the two of them embrace tightly while waiting to see what I think of this stupid Popsicle.

I put the thing in my mouth and quickly pull it out. "Mmm, that is good!" I hand it back to her, but the only thing I taste is shame.

It's all Sam's fault, but I feel guilty that this generous immigrant model just let me try her pop. I should have known better. I should have asked Sam if he was seeing someone.

"What time is the show?" she asks Sam.

"Nine. We still have some time." Sam scratches his neck. "I've got a gig in Midtown. You should come." But I can tell he's just inviting me to be polite.

"Yes, come. I never laugh. Maybe you will," Tasha says. She's leaning over Sam like she's absolutely tired of being beautiful. Her body drapes over his shoulder as though her spine has stopped working.

"Well, I . . ." And that's when I notice it. The ring on her left hand. *They're engaged.* "I . . . There's something I have to do."

I have to get away from here.

I throw my hand out to shake theirs goodbye, but Tasha

gives me three quick kisses and then, after a brief pause, Sam gives me an awkward goodbye hug.

I walk quickly and in a daze as Chinatown morphs into Little Italy. I'm feeling so many things, but the main one is *used*. I was clearly part of Sam's pie chart. *Sure, he was a part of mine.* But it still hurts. Especially because in his pie Tasha was clearly the buttery, flaky crust and I was the bumpy innards.

CHAPTER 25

I'm done with Sam. This time for good. He hasn't even texted to see how I'm doing. I woke up today understanding there's a reason things didn't work out the first time. I just need to focus on work now.

Richard has finished editing the Steven and Elizabeth episode, and for the next few days we'll look for minor changes (that we can agree on) to make it better. This is the premiere, so it has to be perfect. That's why I got Usher. So it would be amazing. There's just one problem. *It isn't.*

I mean, Richard's very talented. He's done a great job. The problem is that even with Usher and the New York Knicks, this proposal leaves you feeling a bit bleh at the end.

"It's just not a Maria and Jorge kinda love," I say out loud without realizing it. And it's true. There's something about Steven and Elizabeth's relationship that isn't very deep. Now that it's cut down to twenty-four minutes, their perfect love story feels a little too good to be true.

"Oh yeah, I know what you mean. *Not*. Who the heck are Maria and Jorge?" Richard asks. Dainty teacup in hand, check. Lilac-colored scarf, check.

"It's the episode I worked on before you started."

"I thought she didn't say yes?"

"She didn't..." And I'm quiet for a moment.

"Then their love wasn't so deep."

"No. You're wrong. I'm sure they loved each other in a way these two wouldn't understand," I say, defending Maria and Jorge and pointing to the screen where Elizabeth and Steven are frozen in time. Elizabeth is smiling, Steven down on his knee.

"Why would things work out for them and not for Maria and Jorge?" I say more to myself than to Richard.

"Maybe she didn't really love him," Richard says calmly.

"You don't know her."

"She was probably dating the wrong guy on purpose."

"What? Why would she do that?"

"Sometimes people do crazy things. You know, because the wrong person can't hurt you. But then when things get serious, like, oh I don't know...maybe when a guy introduces you to his parents, it's hard to keep up the facade."

He stretches out the word "facade," which is annoying. Plus, he's clearly referring to TJ, and I had hoped we'd squeak by our last few days together pretending that whole thing never happened.

"Maria *did* love him. In fact, I'm sure she still does."

"Aww," he says annoyingly, "but if she really loved him, we never would have had the chance to work together."

"You don't understand," I say, ignoring him. "If you had seen them together, you would get it."

"Believe me, I do understand." He sounds a bit flustered. "I was engaged once."

Richard has dropped this little nugget of information as if he's just said, "I got a bad haircut once."

I don't say anything. I don't have to. My face is doing all the talking with a look that is a crystal-clear *Say whaaa?*

"Yeah. Three years ago, for a whole week," he says with mild sarcasm. "She called it off because she thought she was still in love with her ex." Each word comes out of his mouth at a slightly higher pitch.

"Ouch. That must have hurt," I blubber out, immediately wishing I had a more thoughtful response filter. It's just a lot to take in:

1. Richard has a past.
2. Richard is opening up about his past.
3. Richard's past sounds intense.

"Yeah, it did, but you can't let something like that hold you back. When it's time to move on, you move on. You know, two people can be perfect for each other, but that doesn't stop them from being imperfect humans. With issues. With history."

4. Richard is either a cold fish or has genuinely made peace with the past.

I want to know everything. What the heck happened? Did things work out with his ex and her ex? Did he ever hear from her again? But something stops me from prying. He's back to taking calls from Maxi the past few days, so they've clearly patched things up. And from the sound of it, he's ready to move in with her or something. Maybe he's even ready to propose?

In the spirit of sharing, I decide to open up. "For a long time, my friend Gia thought I was still hung up on my ex, too. She wouldn't drop it." As I say the words, I realize this is actually a terrible example. I have a flash of Sam and his fiancée, and I feel a chill all over my body.

"Was your friend right to worry?"

"No, not at all." *Yes, absolutely. Everyone should have been worried. Including me. But it's been over a decade. I thought falling so hard for Landon meant Sam was completely out of my heart. But he was still in there. Freeloading. I guess if Richard the Stoneheart can move on, so can I.*

My phone buzzes with a text, and I quickly pick it up. I feel instant dejection when I see that it's from my stepmom. *Clearly not 100 percent ready to move on. Had hoped it was an apology text from Sam.*

But I'll get there. I have this feeling that simply realizing I was stuck on Sam is a step in the right direction.

Jam-Hands: Anita, I can't believe I haven't sent you the lovebirds' honeymoon photos.

Dana and her husband took a weeklong honeymoon cruise around the Caribbean, and though I have no idea what could make Jam-Hands think I'd want to see these, I find myself in-specting every image. They're drinking mai tais on the beach. Parasailing. In one picture, she's feeding him lobster. *Even they look more in love than Elizabeth and Steven.*

"Here Comes the Bride" starts to play on my cell phone. It's Gia. She must have loaded her ringtone onto my phone when I wasn't looking. *Why doesn't she harness this energy into planning her actual wedding?* I don't pick up because I know she wants me to be part of a video conference she's having right now with her cousins in Brazil about the wedding. But our last call went like this:

Me: Hi, Emilia, hey, Esther. Now, which one of you is working on the schedule for the shuttle buses back to the hotel after the wedding?

Gia: Have you seen my new rehearsal dinner dress? It's so much better than the other one.

Emilia: *Rolls eyes at Gia*

Esther: *Curses in Portuguese*

Me: It's fine. I'll just add the shuttle bus schedule to my list.

The wedding is this weekend, and Gia is unperturbed. The twins need to get their act together. They're the ones planning this thing, but somehow my to-do list is the longest.

1. Update wedding website with directions to Aura, sight-seeing ideas, and weather information.
2. Create rehearsal-day schedule.

3. Create wedding-day schedule.
4. Update hotel list.
5. Create bus pickup schedule to and from ceremony.
6. I know I'm forgetting something. Remember what it is, and do it.

I wish I hadn't volunteered to do all of these things. Though in a way it will be nice to have a distraction from Philip, Fernando, TJ's parents, and Sam's fiancée.

I bolt out of my chair. "Be right back." I'm out of the room and down the hallway before I can talk myself out of what I'm about to do.

I'm determined to call Landon today. Before too many days go by. Just find out what he wants. If it's a date, great. If not, at least we're talking, right?

I find an empty edit room and shut the door. I've programmed the number into my phone, but his name looks so foreign among my contacts. *Not going to overthink what I'm going to say. Just gonna wing it.* It rings. And rings. And rings. His voice mail comes on, and as quickly as my brain can send a message to my hand, I've hung up.

———

"Why don't they make edible toenail polish?" At the moment, TJ is on my bed. Completely naked.

"I'm not sure, but that's a really good idea." I decided I would call Landon after my date with TJ. I know I'll feel more confident once I've received one of TJ's special mani/pedis.

He's getting more paint on the toes than the nails, but the look of concentration on his face is really sweet.

"I wish we could go away for the weekend. Somewhere I could show off this amazing pedicure." I give him a wink, but TJ's lost in his own thoughts and applying polish over and over on the same nail.

"I can't really afford to travel right now," he says without taking his eyes off the polish.

"It could be anywhere really. Anywhere other than Gia's wedding."

TJ moans softly. "How come you didn't ask me to go with you to that?"

My foot flinches at the thought of TJ at the wedding, making him drag the color under a toe. "Crap, sorry." I wipe the polish off. "It's going to be stuffy and no fun at all. Plus, you'd need a tux."

He nods steadily, taking this in.

"I just want us to stay here. Forever," I say to lift the mood. "Like on that episode of *The Twilight Zone* where—"

"I don't know what that is."

"*The Twilight Zone*? Really?"

"Really," he snaps.

"I mean, I never watched it much," I backtrack. "It was a little creepy."

"You know what?" He sits up abruptly. "We need to talk about the elephant in the room."

What elephant? There's an elephant? He's probably too young to know what that expression means.

"What are you talking about?"

"I don't think I can do this anymore...because of the elephant," he says, grabbing his shirt off the floor.

"What elephant?" I say louder than I expected.

"You know, the age difference." The age difference? I thought that was supposed to be *my* issue with *him*. He starts to walk around the apartment, picking up his clothes. "I'm just glad we never had sex."

"And why is that?"

"It's kinda obvious. If we had sex, you wouldn't have handled it well. Because of your age and all."

"What are you talking about?"

"I mean, you're amazing, and it felt like we could have something. But my mom warned me. She said that because of how old you are, you could get too attached, so I should be careful with you."

"I see." His mom told him to be *careful* with me? *Like I'm a fragile, handle-with-care box of expired explosives?*

"I mean, I was willing to go there, but—"

"You were *willing*?"

"That's not what I meant." He zips his jeans and then slumps onto the couch.

I watch his smoothly sculpted face and try to match the genuinely disappointed look in his eyes. The manic energy that was just in the room dissolves.

"What can I offer you, anyway?" TJ clears his throat. "I don't know half the things you do, and you'd always have to pay for us to be able to travel anywhere. I don't even have a tux."

"Well, no one really owns a tux—"

"I have to go."

"No, listen—"

"I hope we'll still be friends." He's done dressing and is standing by the door.

"Sure. Yes."

"See you on Friday?"

"Huh?"

"At your editor's goodbye drinks." He turns around to look at me.

"Right. Yes, okay," I say, but I know I won't be there. I'll be on my way to Gia's wedding. "See you then."

After he leaves, I sit on my bed, stunned. I don't know what I was expecting, but it wasn't this. I have no idea what just happened. The only thing I know is that I know nothing about relationships. Or how to date. Or how to break up. Plus, I've never felt older in my life. Like all the aging molecules in my body were holding on for dear life and they've just decided to give up all at once.

———

I stay up until 4:00 a.m. working on Gia's wedding website. The cover page is their official engagement photo, which consists of Gia pole dancing at a strip club while Matt throws hundred-dollar bills at her.

It takes me forever, but I finally figure out how to add interactive tabs to the photograph. Now, if you click on the pole, you get a list of fun things to do in Aura (apple picking, oldest wooden firehouse). If you click on the hundred-dollar bills flying toward Gia, you get directions to the wedding, and if you click on Gia's face, the shuttle bus sign-up page appears. I send the link for the new and improved website to Gia so she can approve it before I pass it on to all 133 guests. Right away, I get a text back from her.

Matt says Philip is coming to the wedding with his wifey. Didn't know he had one! Oh well, maybe you can be my brother's date? lol JK.

I don't know how to respond to her text. Philip is married? Is he in an open relationship? Call me hypocritical, but I don't want any part of that.

I feel like each piece of my dream guy is evaporating right before my eyes. Leaving me numb, old, and pieless. The only slice that's left is Fernando. As much as I've enjoyed getting to know him better, I should probably end things with him before I break his heart. I go to bed with a terrible feeling that Gia is going to kill me. No matter how many hours I've just spent on her wedding website.

CHAPTER 26

Can't you take a later train?" Richard asks.

"I wish I could, but I need to pick up a fifteen-passenger van when I arrive, and the place closes early. It's a long story."

It's Richard's last day, and I'm going to miss his goodbye party after work. I feel disappointed, and I can't quite figure out why it's hitting me so hard. I just can't believe he's leaving. Not just me, but the company. There isn't even a chance I'll run into him in the elevator anymore.

I put on a good face as we automatically approach each other for an obligatory goodbye hug. We've spent too many months working together in a confined space for a mere handshake.

It's a quick embrace with an even quicker release, but a lot happens in between. My arms wrap easily across his solid back, his hand presses on my waist and the other lands affectionately on the back of my head. Then we both pull away at the same time.

I want to say something, but I have no idea what.

Remembering I'm in a hurry, I turn to grab my bag and fling it on my shoulder. He steps away and leans back against his desk.

"Well, thanks," I say, digging in my bag for my cell. "You were awesome, you know, in spite of being so difficult."

He flashes one of his smirks. "Ditto."

"So, what are you working on next?"

"My brother and I are opening up our own production company."

"Wow. That's great. Congratulations."

"Thanks."

I had no idea Richard was moving on to such a big endeavor. He's a scarf-wearing, tea-drinking documentary geek. I never would have pegged him as an enterprising businessman.

He crosses his arms and then uncrosses them. "Hey, remember that first time in the elevator?" he asks abruptly. I purse my lips doubtfully, making him clarify. "When we first met," he says, pretending to be all prim and proper.

My neck tenses up. I feel I've been put on the spot. This whole time we've been working together, I thought he hadn't made the connection.

"I might have been a bit rude," he says, looking down at his hands.

"You *were* rude. You made fun of my outfit."

"Strictly as retaliation, but I actually liked what you were wearing."

"Unbelievable," I say, pretending I'm upset. "I haven't worn any of that since."

"I had thought as much."

"And noticing *that* is rude, too."

He throws his hands up, cocks his head, and smiles. Surprisingly, it feels nice to leave things on a good note. A note that's friendly and not about work. "Good luck. With the company."

"You too. With everything."

I wave a hand goodbye and walk out, leaving him there wrapping up his things.

Two hours later, I've traveled to the quaint town of Aura. After renting a van—which I scraped against another van while maneuvering out of the parking lot—and checking into the hotel, I pass out early, feeling sorry for myself. Mostly because I won't be able to tell Richard about this on Monday, and I still can't believe I was too chicken to leave Landon a message.

I had a horrible dream last night. I was in Central Park at night by the Bethesda Fountain. There was a bright spotlight on me, and black goo was dripping down the statue of the angel. I was wearing Christmas pajamas and standing right where Jorge had proposed to Maria.

An angry howl came from under the bridge. A shape was walking toward me. It was stumbling as though drunk. As it got closer, I could make out that half its body was taller than the other, and it was dragging one leg behind it like the hunchback of Notre Dame. When it stepped out into the light, I let out a scream (in my dream and probably in real life too).

It was a man. *Well, sort of.* He had TJ's face but was wearing

Sam's "I pee in my wet suit" T-shirt. One hand was holding a keyboard, which he was trying to play with his head, while the other hand held a large paintbrush that would whack the other arm from time to time. He was a mutant. *He was all four of them.*

It was really sad to watch. At one point, he collapsed and struggled for a while to get back up. When he reached the X, he knelt down. All at once, dozens of cameras appeared around us and it was suddenly daytime, making the monster even more hideous. He spit near my foot, and I heard something clang onto the ground. It was my engagement ring. I woke up in my hotel bed drenched in sweat. And slightly disappointed that I couldn't remember what the ring looked like.

Now I'm sleep-deprived and sitting alone in the fifteen-passenger van parked in a deserted lot across from the Sushi Garden Restaurant, staking out the joint.

I spent the entire day driving all over town running wedding errands. I even missed the rehearsal because I volunteered to find a jeweler who could enlarge Matt's wedding ring at the last minute.

I would do anything to stay away from Philip and Fernando. But right now they're both sitting inside the Japanese restaurant I'm avoiding.

Gia and Matt and twenty-eight of their closest friends and family members are enjoying the rehearsal dinner. *More like Dinner of Doom.* This is it. It's all going to blow up in my face tonight.

I was worried the wedding would be the moment of truth, where I'd have to face things. But I hadn't considered Matt would invite Philip and his wife to the rehearsal dinner. Will Gia be able to tell something's going on between her brother and me? Will Landon finally tell me why he called? Will Philip's wife stab me with a chopstick?

By now the wedding party has taken over the back patio of the restaurant. I know what items from the menu have been served and what type of sake they should be drinking right now. I also know that in thirty minutes, a mariachi band will appear to surprise Gia. No one loves a mariachi band more than Gia. I'm sure it's because they remind her of herself, a festive, loud thing that's always the life of the party.

I've been in cahoots with Gia's mom, Isabel, about the surprise. Her parents are paying for everything tonight but asked me to organize it all. *Or maybe I volunteered? I can't remember.*

The mariachi band has driven all the way up from the city for this thirty-minute gig, and they're my excuse for being late to dinner. They called me about an hour ago to tell me they were lost, so I've been navigating them into town. They should be close, so I cross the street and wait for them in front of the restaurant.

An old beat-up van pulls up, and the driver manually cranks the window down and extends his hand.

"Ana?"

"Oh good, you found us!"

"Yes, thanks for the directions. I'm Marcus."

"Oh sure, sure. Don't mention it." I see the other men in the back. Marcus is definitely the face of the operation. The two older ones are sitting in the small backseat holding their guitars, while another three men are sitting up against the walls on the floor of the van, holding violins and an accordion. Their sparkly outfits are brand-new, but the men themselves seem pretty worn-out.

"Well. Okay. So. We'll see you in there at"—I look at my watch—"nine thirty."

"Yes. Don't worry, we're ready." Marcus has a nice demeanor. The inside of his van is nice. The elders are sitting there looking so wise. I picture myself joining them and avoiding the rehearsal dinner altogether. We could drive around Aura, drinking tequila. Maybe they can teach me a thing or two about life and love.

"Life is like a bottle of tequila. Some days you get the worm. Some days, no worm," the one with the accordion would say. And at that moment, everything would just make sense.

I scan the men in the van for reassurance. The eldest is starting to look a little worried. If I stay a moment longer, I'll need to crawl in and cry on his lap.

"Okay. Wish me luck. I mean. Good luck!" I say and turn around.

My armpits are sweating. Thank goodness I'm wearing a sleeveless dress. I had no time to get ready, so I just ran into my hotel room, threw on the dress, pulled my hair back into a ponytail, and let my bangs do what they wanted to do (which was clearly curl into ringlets). And I'm hoping the dewy look is in, because my face is definitely glistening.

"I'm with the rehearsal dinner in the back," I say to the lady approaching me with menus.

She nods, and I make my way slowly toward the back

patio. Sparkly light bulbs hang over the long table, and large serving boats filled with sushi are being put out by a handful of servers at the same time. Everyone sitting at the table looks so polished and well dressed. New Yorkers and stunningly beautiful Brazilians are sprinkled with a few of Matt's refined New England family members.

I'm standing by the door that leads to the garden but tucked back by the sushi bar so no one can see me yet. I see Landon sitting at one end. He's chatting with Matt's parents, who are sitting across from him. Next to them is Philip, who is the best-dressed person at the table in a dark gray suit and tie, and the woman sitting next to him looks like she works for French *Vogue*. She's busy talking to the lady next to her, so Philip is just sitting there looking around. He doesn't seem to be having a good time. At the other end of the table are Matt and Gia. Gia looks incredible in a short white dress. Fernando sits next to her, distracted by his cell phone.

I can't believe I don't have a plan. It's 9:04 p.m. Only twenty-six more minutes until the mariachi band walks in and takes over the party. Maybe I can make my escape behind the accordion and get back to the hotel without anyone noticing? Empowered by this kernel of an exit strategy, I open the patio door and step outside.

Gia sees me and jumps up with excitement, making her chair slam to the ground behind her.

"Oh my God, finally!" She runs over to me as fast as she can in her extra-tall black patent-leather heels and gives me a huge hug.

When Gia's drunk, she's still graceful and glorious, but

she's definitely a couple of octaves louder. She takes my hand and guides me along the table, so I can say hello to everyone...beginning with Landon. *Stay calm. Maybe this is a good thing. Get it over with. Rip the Band-Aid off.* He gets up as he sees us approach and gives me a tight hug.

"Hey, good to see you again," he says sweetly.

"Yeah? Thanks. You too. Of course—"

Gia drags me behind her before I can say another word.

"And this is Celine, Philip's wife."

I shake her hand and smile politely, but Philip lights up when he sees me. He's way too obvious. If women have an internal alarm that alerts them when competition is within range, hers is now going *ding, ding, ding.*

"Great to see you," Philip says, a big smile on his face.

Ding, ding, ding, ding.

I'm pulled on by Gia, thankfully. I can now feel Fernando's eyes watching me as we make our way toward him. There's an empty seat between the wedding planning twins. For a moment the girls are like Switzerland. If I can sit between them, I'll be safe.

"Is anyone sitting here?"

"No, no, no! You are sitting by me!" Gia interjects, obliterating Switzerland.

By the time we reach Fernando's end of the table, he's gone. I sit down and grab a bottle of cold sake from the table. They've set out tiny brown ceramic thimbles for the sake, but that's not going to work for me. I pour it into an empty water glass and study Landon at the other end of the table as I chug the white liquid. Ah, Japan's finest unfiltered cold sake. It's actually thirst-quenching. I fill up another glass and gulp it down.

"That's sake you're drinking, not water!" Gia tells me jokingly.

"I know, cheers!"

Just then Fernando sits down next to me. "Hey," he says, looking at me dreamily.

"Hey." I feel very uncomfortable sitting between him and Gia.

I pour another glassful of sake, though I'm already feeling the numbing effects of the first two on my tongue. Fernando reaches under the table, and I jump. He's handed me something. Without looking down, I know it's our poetry correspondence book.

I remember the last poem I wrote in it and feel instantly guilty. Fernando's had been nautical in theme:

I navigate your thighs in the black of night
with mast and sail and cannons fit to fight

It obviously made me think of Landon, and I wrote my response poem as if it were for him, not Fernando. Now I'm worried I've sent Fernando the wrong message.

You sailed away and left me
altered and hungry
for any-you-thing I can have
from a menu of haven't-happened-yet memories

"Your last poem really moved me. The one I've written in response is *very* important," he says calmly.

"Okay. Great." I smile and slip the book into my bag undetected.

Fernando seems to be behaving himself. Maybe I should just relax and give myself time to figure out how to end things with him when we're back in the city. I pour another glass of sake and make a silent toast to relaxing.

I look over at Landon just as he's getting up. He's now walking over toward our end of the table. I chug back the rest of the glass and contemplate what I'm going to say when he gets here. But my cheeks have gone completely numb. *A dentist-could-extract-a-tooth kinda numb.*

And then something inside me *(is that you, sake?)* says *Tell him.* Tell him? Tell him what? *Everything.* Tell him I was dating four men because I couldn't be with one of him? *Exactly.* And then say something like "Guess what? They still came up short!" *Calmly. Tell him calmly.* Okay, sake, you're right. If I tell him what I've done, he'll be flattered.

"I want to tell her tonight." Fernando leans in too close.

"What? Who?" I say and watch Landon stop to talk to Gia.

"Look, she's in such a great mood." He motions to Gia. "She's so drunk. She's used the word 'love' like a hundred times," he says, continuing to make his case. "I think she'll be a little taken aback, but nothing could upset her tonight. Especially not when I tell her how we feel about each other."

Okay, excuse me, sake. I need to be sober for one minute. Sake. Hello? Oh, *now* you're just going to leave me all alone on this one? Sake! I need to tell Fernando how bad an idea this is, but I can't get the words out in the proper order.

"Uhl, no I won't blids for that's, ees nhot toe thimes for nah no." My tongue has been hijacked by sake.

I can't let this happen. I know without a doubt Gia will be extremely hurt if she finds out I've lied to her. Plus, I told her I was seeing a bunch of guys at the same time because of my stupid perfect man list. How would she feel if she found out her little brother was part of that? Out of nowhere Matt squats down between Fernando and me.

"Hey, I really want to thank you . . ." he says to me.

"Hey, oh eeh nolh."

"For Philip."

"Waaah . . . flip?"

"He told me about your trip to Vienna and *the yacht.*" He nudges my arm. I feel large beads of sweat forming under my bangs. "He told me he's smitten and . . ."

The sake won't let go of my tongue, and it's also started to take over my eyes and ears. I can't tell if Fernando can hear this. I can't even see Fernando anymore.

Matt's voice comes in and out. "He said they were technically separated . . . He appreciates our discretion."

Matt finally gets up, leaving a large gap between Fernando and me. His face is out of focus, so I can't tell what he's thinking. I look at the end of the table and see Philip is staring at me too, I think. I turn and watch Landon wrap things up with Gia, and now he's looking at me too. Did he just smile? Oh man.

Everyone needs to slow down and stop being blurry. Food.

I need to eat something. I grab a roll with my hand, dunk it messily into all the different sauces laid out on the table, and shove the thing into my mouth.

Gia grabs her wineglass and taps the side of it loudly with a fork, making everyone at the table hush just as Fernando's hand grips just above my knee under the table.

"*Hello, my loves!*" she yells out and then, switching to a demure voice, says, "I just want to take a moment to thank you all for being here to help us celebrate our love." She puts her arm around Matt, who has stood up on cue. "Now, you know I absolutely adore everyone at this table, but there's one person who was missing, and now that she's here, everything is perfect!" She looks down at me, and I almost choke on the seaweed-covered roll that me and my sake tongue are still trying to break down.

"I love this girl so much." She starts to tear up. "I would take a bullet for you, Ana, you know that?"

I nod and chew.

"I would literally jump in front of a bus or beat up anybody that ever hurt you. Because I love you. Heck, sometimes I wish I could just marry *you* . . . I'm sorry, babe, but I do . . ."

I gag on the sushi.

"Because no one understands how valuable this girl is. I don't know why the right guy hasn't seen it yet," Gia says, her eyes watering up. "But I see it. Here, I had this made for you." She hands me a hot-pink baseball hat that says "MADE OF HONOR" and puts it on my head. "You've done everything to make this day so special for me. And I will never, ever, ever forget it. Ever. Our friendship"—she grabs my hand—"means

more to me than you will ever know. You are my family." She
lifts her glass.

Everyone at the long table raises their glasses to me. I peel
Fernando's hand from my leg so I can get up and hug Gia. I
look her in the eyes, feeling so low.

"La cucaracha, La cucaracha..."

Gia screams when she sees the mariachis. She starts to dance
with Matt. Right away, the band has wiped the Zen-ness out
of the outdoor garden. It sounds like there are more of them.
And they're impressive. *Wish I could say the same about myself.*

It's easy to sneak away. The restaurant is only a few blocks from
the hotel, so I cross the street and stumble in that direction.

I get this crazy feeling someone has followed me outside.
I turn around, and there he is. Standing by the door of the
restaurant. We look at each other for a moment, and then he
walks back inside. It's like a Moby Dick sighting. That was
either Landon or a sake-induced wave cap.

CHAPTER 27

I managed to finish Gia's wedding-day schedule last night. I needed to pour all my anxiety into something productive, and it helped. That and also when I went down to the front desk and yelled at the night attendant when she refused to print out the schedule for me.

"You can use the business center in the morning. It opens at ten a.m."

"Ten? I have to be at the jewelry store at eight to pick up the groom's wedding ring. Do you want to tell me how that's going to work?"

"It's just that I'm not supposed to—"

"What kind of business center opens at ten? Ten isn't business—it's pleasure. What you have here is a pleasure center!"

Ultimately, she printed out twenty copies of the wedding schedule on Aura Inn invoice paper.

This morning, I feel so much better, optimistic even.

Landon following me outside the restaurant last night had to be a good sign.

I check my phone and find a cryptic text from Fernando.

Well?

And a not-so-cryptic one from Philip.

Morning, beautiful. When can we talk?

I ignore both of them and send Gia a message.

Happy wedding day!

So far today I've had everything under control. I made sure the flowers were delivered to the barn. Check. Picked up Matt's ring at the jeweler. Check. And scheduled myself a hair and makeup appointment at a salon in town.

Gia asked me to get ready with her at the bridal cottage at the farm, but I've decided it would be safer to spend as little time as possible around her.

I'm back in my hotel room, standing in front of the mirror in awe. The country-western outfit Gia picked out for my maid of honor look is a strapless corset and a pencil skirt, both different shades of yellow denim. I typically stay away from pencil skirts, but the strong, unstretchable material is working for me. The matching cowboy boots come up to my calves and have a small heel, which give me a little lift but won't be difficult to walk in. I was afraid I'd look like a rodeo clown, but I actually look fantastic.

I wonder what Richard would say. The thought creeps in without warning. I take a step back and really consider this. I hear his voice at last. "It isn't you, but it isn't bad."

———

Bobby, a motherly and heavyset woman, welcomes me to the salon and gets to work setting my hair in large curlers.

"Normally, I would tell you I want the makeup to look natural, but I don't want that today. I want to look extremely unnatural."

"You got it," she says with a laugh.

"You see, there's this guy. He's like Moby Dick. But I'm starting to think he's only Moby Dick in my mind."

"The whale?"

"Yes, exactly, but I'm done feeling like he's not a possibility."

"That's good," she says, and it somehow calms me.

In an hour and a half, I'm completely transformed. My eyes look dark and sexy, and I actually have cheekbones. My hair is long and wavy, and my bangs are lying obediently on my forehead.

"Go catch that whale," Bobby whispers, and I let out a huge sigh.

Appleberry Farms is a classic red barn surrounded by twenty-two acres of apple orchards. In just a few weeks, they will be ready for picking, but right now the rows of trees are covered in bright-red dots, adding a vibrant and cheerful feeling to the wedding. The pre-ceremony cocktail hour is in full swing when I arrive. The sunset is less than an hour away, which is when Gia and Matt will be exchanging their vows.

It looks like most of the guests have gotten into Gia's Wild West Glamour theme. The women are wearing long silk gowns with paisley patterns or buckskin dresses with fancy beading. The men are in tuxedos with string ties, red bandana pocket squares, and cowboy hats.

Haystacks draped in white linen dot the hill where the ceremony will take place. The aisle is marked by two curving rows of cream-colored rose petals that lead up to the altar in front of the apple orchards. I walk inside the barn and see the twins holding a couple of clipboards and having a pre-wedding meeting with the waitstaff. They finally appear to be professional wedding planners while at the same looking like western saloon floozies in sexy, off-shoulder dresses with tall feathers poking out of their hair.

But I have to hand it to them. The barn looks amazing. When I arrived this morning, there were large mounds of flowers everywhere, and now I know why. I look up and all I see is a sky of billowy softness. The entire ceiling is covered in thousands of hanging white roses.

There's also a giant crystal chandelier over the dance floor and dozens of smaller ones hanging over the tables. I can't get one small chandelier to stick to my Manhattan apartment ceiling, but they've somehow managed to hang about twenty in this old barn. The effect is magical. White satin curtains have been wrapped around the old wooden pillars, and elegant orchid and candle centerpieces decorate each of the tables.

I go back outside and try to find Landon on the crowded lawn. I was thinking that since I wasn't there for the rehearsal, I could tell him how important it is that we practice walking down the aisle before the wedding.

So we can make sure we have the right speed down.

So we can get the speed right.

Right down speed?

I've had so many daydreams about Landon. Like when someone in our future asks him when he knew he had met the girl of his dreams, he's supposed to say, "When we walked down the aisle together . . . *the first time.*"

I turn around and see Fernando sitting at the piano we've set up for him just outside the barn. Gia was so happy when he volunteered to play as the guests arrived, but he's just sitting there with his head in his hands like he can't remember any of the songs or how the instrument even works.

I avoid him and head toward the bridal cottage.

On my way there, I prepare myself for an angry Gia. I think about all the lies I could tell her to explain why I wasn't here to help her get ready today, but I decide to simply say my phone died.

I swing open the door and see Landon and Gia sitting right next to each other on a small love seat. They move apart quickly, but their heads were awfully close together a moment ago. My eyes flicker around the room as heat rises up the back of my neck. There's no one else in here. It's unmistakably cozy. Everything is white, and the sun is coming in gently through the linen curtains. Gia looks up at me surprised. I am definitely interrupting something. *What the hell am I interrupting?*

Landon wearing a tuxedo and Gia in her wedding dress makes it seem like these two are the ones getting married today. Landon is the groom who threw away convention because he just had to see his bride before the wedding. I notice he isn't wearing his bow tie though the shirt is all buttoned up and ready for it.

"Oh wow, you look hot!" Gia screams across the room. "I did a good job picking out those dresses."

Landon hasn't noticed how I look because he's looking at Gia. She's stunning in her wedding dress. Veil and tiara are on, and she's ready to go. Her makeup and hair look flawless. I walk over to her and kiss her on the cheek because I really don't know what else to do. I'm in here now. I can't just leave.

"Hi."

"Here, help me up," she says, so I grab her arms and pull her up off the couch.

She turns and admires herself in the large standing mirror in the middle of the room.

"What do you think?" she asks, striking a pose.

"Amazing" is all I can say. I see Landon behind me in the mirror. He looks like someone ran over his dog. And I can't figure out quite how I feel. Sad. Nauseated. Sadly nauseated?

"I'll be right back," Gia says and steps into the bathroom, leaving me alone with Landon.

As soon as the door closes, he gives me this look like I'm the only one who knows how to bring his puppy back to life. He's desperate. His eyes are saying, *Thank goodness you're here. I heard you know puppy CPR.*

"What do I do? I'm in love with her. She can't go through with this," he says, pleading with me. That's the most he's ever said to me. I want to say it hurts, but my brain is too busy with "does not compute" to process any emotion right now.

"Gia...please..." he calls to her through the door. "She knows we're supposed to be together," he says, addressing me again. "She knows this feels right. I've asked her to marry me, but she won't give me an answer," he says and goes back to watching the bathroom door. And then after a pause, "But she hasn't said no, either."

We hear the toilet flushing behind the door.

Only Gia would get proposed to on her wedding day.

The door opens, and she comes out looking glorious and stands in front of the mirror again.

"Will you check the stupid corset? I don't think it's tight enough," she says to me, sounding annoyed and disgusted. I can't move. I realize this is her way of responding to Landon. She's just going to continue to get ready for her wedding and completely ignore him.

The man I thought was so perfect in every possible way is now moping. I walk over to Gia and move aside the sparkly veil to look at the corset. If this thing were any tighter, we'd have to remove a few ribs, but I pretend I'm doing something to the silk ribbons.

I watch Landon through the mirror. I take in the details of his face. His eyebrows. His smooth-shaven skin. The way his suit sits on his shoulders. He's watching and waiting for a sign from Gia. I see myself in the mirror and realize Landon has not and will not ever see me.

"He doesn't deserve you. But if that's what you want, then you deserve each other." Landon gets up and storms out of the room, slamming the door behind him like a spoiled teenager.

"Guess my brother's been promoted to best man." Gia's completely unaffected by what just went down. Meanwhile,

I'm feeling like my insides have been carved out and I'm now just an empty shell.

"Let's make this about *me* again, shall we?" she says, taking an open bottle of champagne out of an ice bucket and handing it to me. I fill up her glass and one for myself.

"To me and this dress!" she says, clinking my glass.

"Yeah," I say, trying to gather excitement from somewhere in my hollow body, but the air is still dense with Landon's anguish. I really want to be happy for my best friend right now. But I'm having a hard time trying to figure out how things got to this point. Did she encourage Landon? Or did he just misread her flirtations?

"Could you make sure the horse looks good? I asked the twins to send me a picture hours ago."

I set the champagne glass down and feel relieved to have a task to focus on. On my way out of the bridal suite, I look around for Landon. I scan the orchards to my left and the road to my right. But there's no sign of him. He's gone.

The enormous black horse is pooping when I walk into the stable. Defecation aside, it's the most elegant animal I've ever seen. Strands of orchids are braided into its mane, and the saddle has been custom-fitted with hanging gardens of white lilies and gardenias, which make the horse look like she's getting married today too.

Unlike other brides, Gia will not be holding a bridal bouquet while she walks down the aisle. She will be riding a horse decked out as one. It all goes back to her "wedding vision" of a horse on a hill in the sunset.

To get a good photograph, I'd need to get really close to the horse and get to the other side of the stable. There's no way I'm doing this. How can Gia be so happy about riding a horse sidesaddle down the aisle in a skintight dress? The horse starts to pee, making me jump back and bump the stall behind me, causing another horse I didn't know was there to stomp, scaring the crap out of me.

"You know, they can tell when someone's afraid of them."

I turn around and see Philip standing by the door.

"No kidding."

Gia's horse exhales through her nostrils loudly, so Philip walks over and pets her head and neck.

He looks comfortable standing by a horse in a tuxedo. Philip doesn't quite fit in anywhere, but he has this way of being completely at ease in any situation.

"Is this how you'll do it?" His voice is low and gentle. "Get married?"

"Oh no, I don't even want to get married," I say casually, but I'm lying. I do want to get married. And I do want a wedding. *No large, four-legged animals.* But a wedding, yes.

"Well, if you're not interested in marriage, maybe you'd be open to other types of unions," he says with a grin.

I smile and shake my head, though I'm not totally certain he's being serious and trying to make me some kind of offer.

Now we're just looking at each other. He puts his hands in his pockets, and I get lost in my thoughts. Why did I just tell him I didn't want to get married? After a few seconds, I have an answer: It's what I thought he wanted to hear.

"Could you take a picture of her?" I ask reaching my cell toward him.

He takes the phone, walks around the horse, and carefully snaps a few pictures.

"I'd like to explain." He hands me the phone and leans calmly against a post.

I'm trying really hard not to fidget. I know I have no right to, but I'm secretly hoping he's going to apologize to me. *Sorry I brought my wife to this wedding. Also, sorry I have a wife.*

"When Matt invited me to the rehearsal dinner, I thought it would be a great opportunity to spend some time with you. With your friends. So I accepted. Then Celine reappeared. We've been...apart for a while." He takes a deep breath and then gives me this indecisive look, like he needs to be sure before he'll continue. I fight the urge to smile encouragingly because I really don't know if I want to hear any more.

"You see, we just found out that our daughter is having a baby. She had been trying for a long time. So, we're finally going to be grandparents. Something we weren't sure if we'd ever get to be." He pushes his shoulders up like he's giving up trying to get all of this to make sense for me. "I know this must sound strange, but it felt like this could be a new beginning...for all of us."

"Oh." I feel surprisingly disappointed—not that I want to break up Philip Oberon's life, especially not now that I know more about it. I've been so busy trying to fit into his world, I didn't really get to know him. "Congratulations," I say mostly as a natural reflex.

He smiles and shifts his weight off the post, like he's

preparing to leave. "I'd like to send you the painting. Would that be all right?"

"Yes. Of course. I can't wait to see it."

"Great. I'd really like for you to have it. I—" He pauses for a moment. "I'll miss our . . . lively conversations."

Gia's horse takes a few steps back and then digs her head into an empty bucket.

"You are splendid, you know that?"

I shrug slightly in response.

"Especially when you're jetlagged," he adds.

I try to smile, but it doesn't quite form.

"I'll see you out there," he says sweetly.

"Okay."

"Thank you," he says when he reaches the door.

It's not an apology. It's not even a clear goodbye. But somehow it's more definitive. When he's gone, I'm left with the sense that I've missed out on something.

I scan through my phone and text Gia the pictures of the horse. I'm in the background in a few of them, looking a bit lost. I step outside of the stables and decide I am in fact feeling lost. *And a bit unhinged.* Philip is gone and Landon has vanished. All this time I imagined Landon was flirting with Gia, but those were just jealousy-fueled visions. I wasn't supposed to be right.

CHAPTER 28

In my handbag I find the wedding-day schedule I created last night. I carefully unfold it and stare at it like it's a relic from another time.

Just stick to the schedule.

Problem is, nowhere on this thing does it say, "Landon proposes to Gia," or "Ana gets dumped by a grandpa."

—AURA INN INVOICE—
Gia and Matt's Wedding Day Schedule
4:00 p.m.: Cocktail Hour ★With a special performance by the bride's brother

This did not happen. Unless you consider sitting and sulking "playing the piano."

4:10 p.m.: Ana and Landon practice walking down the aisle (both feel sparks)

We all know how this turned out, but just to recap: Landon declared his love for Gia. Gia flushed the toilet. Landon skipped town.

> 5:45 p.m.: Guests are ushered to their seats for ceremony

This actually happened on time. Which has turned out to be a bad thing.

I thought I'd find Fernando at the piano, but the instrument has been abandoned. The guests are being ushered to the haystacks, so I head behind the barn to meet the rest of the bridal party. The bridesmaids and groomsmen are being corralled by the twins, but there's no sign of Fernando.

I step inside the barn, using the service entrance. The waitstaff is busy clearing out the cocktail hour and laying out the dinner table settings. I find Fernando sitting alone at one of the tables.

"Hey, we need to get going."

"Did you like the poem?" he asks, still staring off into the distance.

Crap. I completely forgot to read his new poem last night. "Yes! Yes, I loved it. *So good.* It's my favorite one so far."

"Really?" He turns to look at me, his body energized. "It's your favorite? Mine too."

"Yes, absolutely. My absolute favorite. Loved it."

"So . . . what do you think?" he asks with a bit of a crack in his voice. "What's your answer?"

My answer? There was a question in the poem? I don't know what to say.

"Uh...well..."

Fernando's body starts to sink again, and within seconds his eyes are brimming with tears.

Time is ticking. Gia should be getting up on the horse right now. I need to come up with an answer to whatever his question was.

"Come here." I take Fernando's hand and lead him behind one of the columns. "How's *this* for an answer?" I whisper and kiss him. I mean, I *really* kiss him. Anything to calm him down and get him to walk me down the aisle looking happy for his sister, like a good backup best man.

It seems to be working. He hugs me for what seems an eternity.

"Thank you." Fernando sounds drained.

"Sure, thank you...for asking the question."

"I heard I was walking you down the aisle. But without an answer from you, I..." He pauses, shutting his eyes in a deep frown. "I couldn't do it." *Oh jeez. Why the heck didn't I read that poem?*

"We should join the others." I hurry him out of the barn to take our spots in front of the bridal party.

I can't believe I'm going to walk down the aisle with someone other than Landon. And that this someone is squeezing my hand *so* hard. Fernando looks *deliriously* happy. What did I just agree to?

As we walk up the hill toward the altar, Fernando is walking so close to me, I can feel his weight.

At the altar, Matt is looking sharp with a delicate red and white gingham pocket square poking out of his tuxedo jacket.

His eyes are focused on the end of the aisle, waiting for Gia with the same look of desperation Landon had for her back in the cottage.

I have no idea what Matt heard about Landon or why he had to leave. It definitely wasn't the truth because he doesn't seem upset or concerned. Maybe they told him there was some kind of emergency back home?

Fernando and I take our places on either side of the altar.

Two acoustic guitarists sitting on a haystack near the altar begin to play "The Wedding March," giving the guests their cue to rise. A collective gasp lets me know Gia has appeared. I see her turn up the aisle, sitting tall and rocking back and forth gently as she rides sidesaddle. The stark difference between the jet-black horse and her bright white dress makes her glow in the soft light of the setting sun.

The horse walks slowly up the hill, its head held down obediently as if it's been training for this moment its entire life. Walking proudly alongside and holding the reins is Gia's father, Esteban. With his salt-and-pepper hair and well-fitting tuxedo, he looks like the wealthy landowner patriarch from a Brazilian soap opera. It's the most ridiculously beautiful thing I've ever seen.

Gia arrives at the altar, slides off the horse, and lands in Matt's arms. I'm so in awe of the whole thing, I don't even notice when her dad hands me the reins and takes a seat next to Gia's mom. I look around for a horse handler, but there isn't anyone around me. Sure, the flower-covered horse is technically her bouquet, and the maid of honor *always* holds the bride's bouquet during the ceremony, but it's clearly *more* than a bouquet and no one has bothered to find out if the maid of honor is comfortable around horses.

The guitarists continue to play as the ceremony begins and the guests take their seats. "Friends and family, Matt and Gia are honored you are all here to witness their devotion and love for one another." The priest has known Gia since she was a little girl back in Brazil. Matt flew him here just for the wedding, which I thought was a sweet extravagance, but right now I'm wishing he had hired a "during the ceremony horse handler" instead.

"When Gia was a little girl, she dreamed of one day meeting her Prince Charming..." continues the priest.

The horse tugs me toward the nearby apple trees, pulling my arm so hard I have to lean in the opposite direction to keep from toppling over.

"Today she has arrived at this altar on a horse as a symbol of her connection to nature and her gratitude for all of God's gifts on this earth."

Yeah, let's get a horse! And then force it to stand near an apple orchard covered in bright-red delicious things. And to make things interesting, let's have someone who is terrified of horses hold on to it throughout the ceremony. And let's also make sure it's a huge horse with extra-large hooves.

"Today, Matt and Gia are each other's gifts as well."

You know what I'd like as a gift? *Not* to be kicked by this horse. I hold the reins with both hands and feel sweat dripping down my chest. If I let go, they won't be able to ride up the hill right after the ceremony for Gia's stupid hill-sunset-horse moment.

"...and love is the biggest gift of all. One that has to be honored and cherished..."

I'm starting to imagine what my brains will look like when this horse has kicked my skull in.

"And now Matt and Gia will read the vows they have written for each other."

"Look at me—I'm young, successful. You'd think it would have been easy for me to find the right person," Matt begins humbly. "But it wasn't. Not until I met you. And I know I'll never meet another woman like you."

My sweaty hands are starting to slip on the reins. By the time Gia gets through her vows, I feel like I'm going to pass out from exhaustion.

"You may now kiss the bride." Matt and Gia kiss for the first time as husband and wife. Even with the horse beginning to exhale loudly, there's something so special about this moment and their kiss. I realize that despite her bad decisions, all I want is for my friend to be happy.

Matt helps Gia back on her horse, and he gets up on a tall, good-natured chestnut stallion someone has brought out for him. *Confirming horse handlers are always nearby but never when you need them*. With three wedding photographers waiting on cue at all the right angles, they both ride up the hill just as the sun sets behind the orchard.

CHAPTER 29

I take a glass of champagne from a server and make my way toward the back of the room. The twins are nearby, and I listen in as they are congratulated by a steady flow of guests. *What an incredible job. Best wedding ever. Gia is lucky to have you.*

One of the twins breaks away and walks over to me.

"Good luck with your speech," she says, handing me a microphone. "The DJ will introduce you." Stunned, I cradle the microphone with both hands. I feel seasick. *And like I just lost a very serious game of hot potato.*

In what feels like nanoseconds, the music is cut off, the DJ says a few words, everyone settles into their seats, and the barn goes completely silent.

I checked off everything on my list. Everything. I even remembered to get the old-time feather pen for the guest sign-in book that Gia wanted. *How could I forget to write a speech?*

I look across the room and find Gia smiling at me encouragingly from her bride and groom's table.

I can't believe I have to give a speech right now. The bouquet horse has worn me out, and I'm still processing what happened during the ceremony. Matt and Gia's kiss had been magical. It caught me completely off guard. The last thing I expected was to be *moved* by this wedding.

"Real love is..." My voice has begun, though I never really gave it permission to. "You know? It's..." I have no idea where this train is headed. "What I mean is. The real thing. It's out there. Isn't it? But it's just so hard to find. So, so hard. So hard."

I speak slowly. And start to feel like I'm figuring out something important right this second. "Impossibly hard. But when you find someone that you can be yourself around, no matter how ridiculous you want to be..." I think of Gia up on that enormous horse and the way Matt was looking at her. "And they'll only love you more for it and be there to catch you. That's nice. That's gotta be nice."

I've gone blank again. If there's a maid of honor speech manual, I imagine it suggests things like "bring up funny anecdotes." I think of Landon in his tuxedo in Gia's bridal cottage, trying to convince her to run away with him. Someone coughs.

I scan my memories of Gia and me back in college. The guys. The fraternity parties. How she'd always hold my hair back when I threw up.

"Many of you don't know how we met." I've stopped pacing, and my heart has slowed to a more comfortable rhythm. "My roommate and I were sharing a bathroom with the girls next door. I was in there trying to find a spot for my shower caddy."

I notice Gia is smiling and shaking her head.

"In walks this huge ficus in an enormous planter, way more lavish than any college student needs." I'm addressing the guests comfortably, as though I've rehearsed this. "It was Gia carrying this plant, and there's been a lot of debate about what happened next." A few people in the back laugh.

"Gia blames the plant. I say it was her enormous foot that stepped on me and broke my toes. Two of them." I get a few more laughs.

"It was the ficus," Gia yells out.

"I had to wear a boot for two months and use crutches around our campus, which was very old and had hardly any elevators, so Gia carried my backpack around for me. I think it was a pity friendship at first." I get more serious and turn to Gia. "But it was the nights that made our friendship. Gia was an insomniac back then. I was not. But I actually tried to be for her. We'd stay up, and it felt like we were the only people in the world."

I pause because this part of the story is impossible to describe. How do you explain that we talked and laughed about everything and nothing and how in a matter of weeks I was a completely changed person? A happier person.

"I didn't know how much a friend could make you love all the strangest parts about yourself because they loved them too."

The look in Gia's eyes is easy to read. It's pride. She's proud of me. Proud of our friendship. A sense of remorse rises through me. But I push the feeling down and out of the way.

"And, Matt, I know you feel the same way. And that she feels that way about you."

Matt nods and lifts his glass toward me. One of his friends nearby lets out a "Yeah baby!"

"So cheers to you both!" I say way louder than I mean to because I'm so relieved I've made it through.

As I get hugs from Matt and Gia, I'm aware that it's a beautiful moment, but I'm feeling too light-headed to enjoy it. I need to sit down. *By the bar, preferably.* So I walk off in search of something strong still holding the microphone.

"That was great, Ana." Fernando's voice announcing through the speakers stops me in my tracks. My smile drops as I turn around with an uneasy feeling bubbling in my stomach. He's been given another microphone and taken center stage right in front of Matt and Gia's table. "I wasn't expecting to give a speech today, but the best man had to leave, and I'm glad because now I can say how I feel about these two. And about someone else as well."

My throat clenches up. *What did he say?*

"Where is she? Oh, there you are." He spots me halfway to the bar. "Ana, come back over here, please."

My whole body goes feverish and I feel a fake smile plastered on my face.

"Come on. Don't be shy," Fernando says into the microphone, and it gives a little feedback. The guests are shuffling in their seats, so I find myself walking toward him. I'm having one long hot flash that doesn't go away. I join him in the center of the barn and avoid looking at Gia.

"You two have shown me that love is real. It's deep and meaningful and, most of all, it's possible. That's why I can't wait another second to tell you that I've found it too."

Oh. No. Oh no.

"There's no reason to keep this a secret anymore. Ana, I know you already answered this question, but now I want to ask you here, officially, in front of my family and friends."

Note to self. From now on, read poems before responding to them by saying, "How's this for an answer," and then kissing the poet.

"It's time to take the next step, and I'm ready to do that," he says, reaching for his tuxedo jacket pocket.

I mean, really? Why does he have to be such a ridiculous romantic? What's wrong with him? This is insane. We've only been dating for a few months.

"Ana, will you—"

"No, no, *no, stop*! I can't marry you," I say into the microphone because I'm holding on to it for dear life.

"...girlfriend." Fernando realizes what I've said, so he repeats himself as if in a trance. "Be my girlfriend. Wait, marry you? We've only been dating for a few months," he says, still speaking calmly into the microphone.

I look down at his hand, and he's holding the fresh lily that was on his lapel.

Someone drops their champagne glass, and it seems to serve as a cue for the DJ, who abruptly kicks off the first track from the dinner music playlist I emailed him a few days ago.

When I finally have the courage to look in the direction of Gia and Matt's table, there's no one there. Out of the corner of my eye, I catch a glimpse of her long veil dragging out the side door.

A few minutes later, I find Gia with Matt back in the cottage where Landon had proposed to her just a few hours before. It's dark now, so there's no soft sunlight coming in through the curtains. Instead, the ceiling lights are on, and the room feels cold. I enter the room just as Matt heads out without saying a word to me.

"You told me you were seeing a bunch of guys." Gia speaks calmly as she looks at herself in the mirror and applies a fresh coat of lip gloss.

"It's nothing. It's just been, well, it's hard to explain."

"You know what your problem is?" She looks directly at me, and I flinch a little. "You're so afraid of getting hurt that a real option doesn't interest you."

"Landon was real," I say, gaining strength.

"Yeah, a real *ass.*"

I can feel my heart palpitating through my tight dress. "That's only because *you* led him on."

"What?"

"He was *my* list, and you knew that."

"What the hell are you talking about?"

"He was everything I wrote on that list because—"

"Oh, give me a fucking break. You are so immature."

"No, I'm not. Lists aren't for children!" I'm screaming, and my hands are shaking. I've never argued with Gia before, and I can't believe it's taken me this long to speak up for myself. "And since you hadn't noticed, they helped me keep the twins on track to plan *your* wedding—"

"I didn't ask you to do so much," Gia interrupts me calmly. "You offered, remember?"

"While you've been flirting with *my* Landon! And who knows how many other guys."

"What did you say?"

"You heard me. You're allowed to string along guys, but I can't? Why? You're the one who was engaged. *To be married!*"

"I've been trying to protect you from Landon. But even if you didn't know that, nothing gives you the right to lie to me. Or my brother. Does he know about the other guys?"

"No," I squeak. "But you have no idea..." I try to defend myself, but I'm losing gusto. "You always think you know everything, but you don't."

"I know I don't want you here," Gia says firmly.

I walk along the path that cuts through the vineyards to the parking lot. Why is it that when things are bad, we make them worse by adding everything else that's wrong on top?

1. I no longer have a best friend.
2. I'm terrible at my job.
3. I'm too old to find a new career.
4. I paid too much for my microscopic apartment.
5. I can't wear bangs.
6. I don't even have ¼ of a boyfriend.

I walk onto one of the vans rented to shuttle people back to their hotels and sit down in the first row.

"Aura Inn, please."

"I have to wait until we have a few more people." The driver looks at his watch and back at me.

"I know, I'm the one that told you that. Remember? Now I'm telling you it's okay to just take me. Alone. Now."

"Let's just give it a minute."

The Brazilian band begins to jam, so I sit there and watch as people get up to dance and the golden light from the chandeliers spills out of the barn doors.

CHAPTER 30

<u>Must do this week:</u>

1. Get hair growth serum for bangs.
2. Hang chandelier up or throw it out the window.

Monday

The edit room is empty. I'm the only one in here, but I'm an idiot, so I don't count. I'll be working alone for two weeks before I get Nina back. I was stunned when the ratings came in for our premiere episode. It got the biggest numbers of the night and pulled in more male viewers than ever, probably thanks to the New York Knicks.

The words "come by" flash on my computer screen.

I'm being summoned to Edith's office. Maybe I'm just overly sensitive after Gia's wedding this weekend, but as I walk down the hall, I'm really worried about what I'm about to hear.

"Usher's manager called and . . ." Edith begins without waiting for me to sit down, then stuffs a large spoonful of yogurt with berries in her mouth. *Did Usher hate the show? Am I fired?*

"He feels that . . ." she says, and I wait patiently while Edith takes a long sip of her coffee.

"There weren't enough close-ups. We need to reedit the show for the repeats and put more shots of him in there. I felt the same way."

As I walk back to my desk, my eyes water. I have a few dozen reasons to be sad right now, but I can't tell which one is making me want to cry at *this* particular moment. Maybe it's everything? Gia hating me. The way Landon had looked at her. The cold text I received from Fernando last night.

Please leave the poetry book with your doorman.

When I get back to my desk, I try to focus on Usher. Maybe Richard would be interested in coming in for a day next week to work on this reedit with me? At the very least, we'd have a good laugh about Usher demanding more close-ups.

Richard would probably say, "That makes sense. Let's have fewer shots of the guy proposing to the girl on the show *about* proposals and let's zoom in on Usher instead. Why didn't I think of that?"

After work, I step outside. The evening air feels cool and dry. Summer has decided to officially pack it in today. I feel a little hurt the city would do this to me at a time like this. I'm not ready for fall. Fall is nothing but a quick pit stop to the long New York winter.

Felipe stands tall as he holds the door for me. "You have a package," he declares and hands me a narrow box wrapped neatly in brown paper.

I'm dumbfounded looking at a very realistic portrait of my face surrounded by bright splashes of paint. It's like I have a colorful halo. And it's gorgeous.

But there's something unsettling about it. It's kinda big, for one. And it looks like me but not *exactly*. She's way too elegant. And glamorous. Like an actress from the 1920s.

This must be how Philip sees me. To be fair, it may have been all the Ralph Lauren outfits. The canvas is mounted in a wooden frame, so I carefully prop it up against the wall.

I look down and see the olive oil blotch on the carpet that TJ made when he spilled an overflowing bowl on his way to massage my toes. The blotch is all that's left of TJ. I have a painting of another woman from Philip. Fernando picked up our book of poems, and I have nothing from Sam.

I've never felt farther from having what I want.

I jump up and rummage through my purse. *Yes. This is a great idea.* I find the Denny's napkin with The List on it.

I light a match, set the thing on fire, and throw it in the sink. It feels surprisingly good to watch it burn. I go back, find my book of lists, and walk back to the kitchen feeling determined. I rip out page after page of lists and add them to the now-growing fire.

Fears to Conquer, Home Renovations to Do, Languages to Master, National Parks to Visit. I feel certain this is what I need. Will be spontaneous from here on out. Spin a globe, close my eyes, and point. No more planning. No more pining. *This feels good!*

I grasp the next page and stop before pulling it out. Bizarre nautical dreams about Landon. I know I just said no more pining, but I pined a little looking at this list. It was brief, and it's passed now, so I rip the page out of the book and throw it into the fire. If I could add a sound track to this moment, it would be something slow and melancholic. Now that the list has evaporated, the song picks up and the beat grows strong. Like the flame in my sink.

Each list smoldering makes me feel lighter. Complex Cocktails to Crush, Tree Species to Identify, Yoga Poses to Master, Things I Don't Want in a Man. I turn this last list over. It's so long it fills the page, front and back. Without hesitation, I throw it into the fire. It floats down into the sink and lands right in the blaze.

I throw the rest of the lists in, including the book cover, for good measure. It's time to live my life without a guide. It's time to be free and wing it. It's time to . . . beeep, beeep, beeep. The smoke alarm has gone off.

I open the front door and both windows. Damn, that alarm is loud. I grab a magazine and start fanning it.

It finally stops as Felipe walks in. "Everything okay?"

"Oh yes. Just a little fire," I say, still fanning the now silent smoke detector. "I've got it all under control."

Tuesday

There are pyramid-size piles of trash bags on the sidewalks all over Manhattan. *Have they always been there?* I'm not saying the sheen has completely worn off the city. It still sparkles, but not as much on garbage day.

Wednesday

I've spent the day watching casting videos for our final season. Thankfully, there is no shortage of people madly in love. And, surprisingly, some of them actually have creative proposal ideas (a ballet proposal = someone's in love with his costume fitter; a stock market trading-floor proposal = the DOW is down, but true love is up; a New York City Marathon proposal = a big finish at the finish line), so it should be a fantastic final season. *If happy endings are your thing.*

Toward the end of the clips, I see a name I recognize. I click on Jorge's old casting video. Man, he was good. So full of hope and excitement. He loved Maria, and I still can't understand why she refused him. What if she was too startled by our cameras or upset with Jorge for having lied to her about what we were filming? What if it's all my fault?

Thursday

I'm in line at the supermarket, and I'm about to cry. Not because the only items in my basket are a pint of mint-chocolate-chip ice cream and an extra-large cube of cream cheese, but because I know I'll never find another friend like Gia. Ever since I met her, she's been like a sister to me. *A difficult and controlling sister who always demands the spotlight.* But also one who adores me.

Friday

I decide to call Gia. She's been on her honeymoon in Bali for a week now, but I don't want to wait until they get home. I hope I'll get her voice mail so I can leave a heartfelt message. But I hear a click on the line like she's picked up.

"Hello?" There's a long pause, and then I hear my voice again in a slightly distorted echo.

"Yeah. I'm here." There's a testiness in her voice. And thanks to the echo, I hear it twice. "Yeah. I'm here."

"I'm so sorry, G."

I envision a list of all the things I need to apologize for (lying, ruining her wedding, hurting her brother) but decide she knows what I've done. Gia always knows. Besides, I don't want to give myself the opportunity to say the wrong thing.

There's a long moment of silence, and for a moment I think we've been disconnected.

I hear her crying. And then there's an echo of her tears. I can tell it's been a long week for her. And she's been worrying she lost her best friend too. I know this because Gia never cries.

CHAPTER 31

I get home early from work feeling all Zen and wise and relaxed. Like burning the lists and taking responsibility for my actions have made me wiser somehow. So I calmly open the large cardboard box at the foot of the bed and tug at the chandelier lamp until it comes out, sending half the foam packing balls all over the place. I am convinced my newfound Zen-ness has given me the ingenuity to finally hang the thing up.

An hour later, I reluctantly admit it has not.

I open the door and find my father standing there holding a stepladder and his rusty toolbox. Within moments, he's inside turning off the breaker, moving the couch, rolling away the carpet, and setting up the ladder in the center of my apartment.

I was enlightened enough to call my father. Calling for backup when you need it is just the kind of thing wise, Zen people do.

"What's this?" He's found the painting of me against the

wall. He picks it up and holds it with both hands. "Wow, you look very nice," he says, but with his newfound thicker Cuban accent it comes out "You look berry nice." He holds the painting farther away. "And *different*."

"Thanks. It was a gift."

"How are things with Mr. Perfect?" he asks, stepping up on the ladder with my chandelier in one hand, his industrial-size electric drill in the other and an assortment of screws he's pulled from his toolbox sticking out of his pocket.

"Over. Turns out he wasn't so perfect after all," I say, looking up at him.

"Then I'm glad it's over. If he's not worthy of my little girl—" He interrupts himself with the *zzzzzzz* of the electric drill.

"You mean if *they're* not worthy..." I say, knowing he can't hear me over the sound of the drill.

"It will happen when you least expect it," he says in between drilling. "*I* certainly wasn't. Elena just walked into the bakery *furiosa* that she had to buy her own birthday cake because her selfish teenage daughter had refused to make one for her, and she thought it was too depressing not to have a cake for her fiftieth. So I said to her, 'Oh, we're all out of birthday cakes today.' She gave me this angry look, and I just cracked up and so did she. And well..." He looks off into the distance. "That was it."

He's told me the story before, but I've never really *heard* it until now. This time I can actually picture them.

"She's great, Dad. Really. I think Elena is great for you. And for us."

He stops what he's doing, and after a moment, he steps off the ladder. He looks at me, takes my hands, and nods gratefully.

His hands feel strong and a little rough. *And chandelier-free.*

"Hey, how did you do that?"

The lamp is hanging securely in place. I know he can build tiki huts and multilayered cakes and anything he puts his mind to, but this lamp has been impossible for me to hang for so long. I had stopped believing I'd ever see it anywhere other than in its enormous box.

"Why didn't you call me sooner?"

"You're right. I should have," I say, staring at the thing in disbelief. "I can't believe you did it."

He walks over to the kitchen, turns the breaker back on, and flips the light switch on the wall.

"Oh wow, Dad."

The chandelier is glowing. The lamp is the perfect balance of a classic shape with a modern twist. It has candle-like lights like a regular chandelier, but when you turn it on, the *entire thing* is a lamp. It's glowing gently now, like a small sun in the center of my apartment.

"That's nice! I like that," my father says, stepping back up on the ladder.

"It's from Sweden," I mumble.

"Que fancy!"

The moment feels like Christmas, warm and special. He adjusts a small high-tech knob at the base of the lamp, and the chandelier smoothly glides down a few inches. "Here?" he says, moving aside to let me see the lamp.

"How did you know it would do that? A little higher, I think."

He turns the knob back in the other direction, and the lamp glides back up effortlessly. Perfect.

"Do you want me to hang up the painting?" he asks as he rolls the carpet back out.

"Oh no. I'm . . . not sure where to put it yet."

"Well, I need to get going," he says as he lifts one side of the couch back into place. We both find ourselves looking at the lamp again for a moment.

"Thanks so much, Dad," I say, feeling more grateful for him than I have in a long time.

"Anytime," he says. "Let me take this down for you." He grabs the giant lamp box still filled with Styrofoam with his free hand.

The thought of having the lamp up where it belongs *and* being rid of its stupid box makes me want to cry.

"Wow, thanks . . . That would be great," I say, my voice cracking.

"Of course." He walks toward the door but then stops and turns around. "It's really nice to be able to actually do something for you."

I go quiet. The tears are getting harder to hold back.

"You know? You just never *need* anything."

Now *he's* tearing up. He puts the box down so I can lay my head on his shoulder.

"I *do* need things." I'm crying now, so he holds me even tighter.

"You just let me know. And I will be there, okay?

Sometimes you gotta give people the chance to show you how much they love you. You're just as stubborn as your mom, you know that?"

My heart stiffens. We never talk about her. My dad and I were never the ones to talk about how we felt about each other. That was always Mom's job. She filled the air with enough love for the three of us.

"She would be so proud of you. She would have loved your show." The thought had never occurred to me. But he's right. "All those romantic proposals." My face lets go into a relaxed smile. "You know, she just wants us to be happy," he says, and I nod.

"*You* especially," he adds.

I feel myself letting go. So much that my legs may give out. But I'm not worried because I know he's got me.

CHAPTER 32

I take a deep breath and press the button next to the bright-green door. Behind me kids are kicking around a soccer ball on the street, and two older men are in a heated game of dominoes at a card table they've set up on the sidewalk.

"Hi! What are you doing here?"

Maria sounds genuinely happy, albeit puzzled to see me. She has her hair pulled back with a multicolored bandana and is wearing a black cotton dress that flows down to her feet. As she lets me in, I can hear Jorge in my mind describing what she looks like when she's watching reruns of *Marry Me, You Fool!*

No makeup. Hair pulled back. A natural beauty.

"I was just in the neighborhood..."

"Really? Come in. Would you like some coffee? Wine?"

I look at my watch. It's 11:06 a.m.

"Wine sounds good, thanks."

We walk through a snug hallway made even snugger with bookshelves on either side and turn into the kitchen. Her East Harlem apartment feels bigger than I remember, but then again, right now it's devoid of our crew and camera and lighting equipment.

"You weren't really in the neighborhood, were you?" she says, taking a bottle of white wine out of the fridge and pouring two small glasses.

"No." I take a seat on one of the benches in the breakfast nook by the window.

Where do I start? *Sorry I ruined your life.*

"Well, I'm doing this thing where I come clean and apologize to people," I say as she hands me the glass of wine.

"Like Alcoholics Anonymous?"

"Yeah." I take a big gulp of wine. "Exactly."

Maria's being nice, but I can tell her guard is up. I don't blame her. My guard would be up too if I were sitting across from someone who had lied to me. The truth is, I never felt bad about lying to the cast on the show before. Why would I?

Soon, they would be proposed to and happy beyond belief. But Maria had missed out on the good part where our production lies are forgiven and even appreciated.

She never said yes, the fountain didn't flow with pink-colored water like rosé, the band never played, and the swans never took flight. For her, it was just lies and nine cameras circling around her as her relationship fell apart.

"I just wanted to say I'm sorry. I feel responsible. Like maybe if the cameras hadn't been there—"

But she doesn't let me finish. "It wasn't your fault. I wasn't ready for marriage. I just wasn't ready."

"Oh."

I see a photo of her and Jorge on the fridge. Does that picture mean he's still *in the picture*?

"Are you and Jorge still talking?"

"We're trying to work things out."

The idea that Maria and Jorge may still have a chance had not crossed my mind, but it makes my whole body loosen up a couple of notches. Maria pours more wine into our glasses, and I feel more at home.

"Why do you think you're not ready?"

"It's stupid. You'll think I'm immature."

"Stupid? What do you know about stupid? You're a nurse! And immature? I'm the queen of immature. If you knew what I've done, you wouldn't have let me in the door."

"What did you do?"

"Well, there was a list. I've always been a big list person..." The words pour out of me. "And I found one I'd made in college, and I just thought it would be nice to feel it, you know? Feel like you finally had everything you wanted. And it worked for a second, I think, but then—"

"What worked?" Maria asks, trying to follow along.

"The list..." I exhale loudly. "It was the things I wanted in a guy. I just knew I'd never find him. Not even close. So I tried to check it off with four different guys, and this is so ridiculous. I told you I was immature."

Maria sits there calmly nodding like a wise sage. The colorful bandana in her hair, her long dress, and the way she's sitting across from me make her look like a gypsy tarot card reader. I want her to have some hidden powers. I want her to tell me what's in the cards. Make some sense of all of this.

She gets up suddenly and walks across the kitchen. "So what happened?" she says, opening the fridge.

"I tried to say yes. You know, open myself up." Maria glances at me as she uncorks a fresh bottle of chilled white wine. "I wanted to be more spontaneous and free from some unrealistic ideal, but that turned into dating four guys at once like a DIY project." It makes me cringe to admit this. Maria nods encouragingly and pours wine into our glasses before setting the bottle down on the table.

"It all ended really badly and was a complete waste of time." I wrap up quickly, as though in fast-forward.

"It wasn't a waste of time," Maria says. "Not if you learned something."

Did I even learn anything?

"If dating required insurance, I'd be...uninsurable," I say without an ounce of energy.

Maria smiles and refills my glass, even though it's still half-full.

"I guess I mainly discovered that I'm a one-at-a-time kinda girl."

"Well, that's something. Which one made you feel the best about yourself?" Maria asks this so warmheartedly, like a mom trying to get to the bottom of her daughter's heart. I shrug and look down at my glass.

TJ made me feel sexy. With Sam I was carefree. Fernando

made me feel intensely romantic. With Philip I was sophisticated.

"I never felt like myself," I say, floored by the discovery. I
mean, except for with Richard. *Not that he was an option.* But
I never had to hold back any part of myself around him.

I look outside Maria's window, mesmerized for a moment
by what I think is a weeping willow. Another random thought
pops up. It's the list of things I *don't* want in a guy and
how Richard checks off a bunch of them. He lives outside
of Manhattan, says "caio," drinks tea, and the last day I saw
him he was wearing a leather bracelet with one clunky jade
bead. For all I know, he's also got a bar code tattoo on
his ankle.

"You said you got to know what it felt like for a moment.
So, what did it feel like?"

"It felt good..." I mutter unconvincingly "...ish. Is it
wrong to expect one person to be all of that?"

Maria takes a moment, holding her wineglass with both
hands.

"I think the right person can be." Maria's quiet for a second.
"And they can be even more." Her delivery is somber, and I
know she's referring to Jorge.

"What happened, Maria? He loves you. And I know you
love him. Please tell me that's enough."

She looks down at her glass and twirls the remaining bit
of wine around for a moment. "You're going to think I'm
pathetic."

"Were you not listening to everything I just said?"

Maria smiles but doesn't look up from her wineglass. "It's

just that"—she finally looks up at me—"Jorge hasn't met my family yet . . . not *everyone*."

"So?" I poke gently because she's finally opening up, and I don't want her to stop talking.

"I haven't wanted him to meet . . . *everyone*."

"Okay. Why not?"

"Wait here."

She walks off into the bedroom, and I prepare myself for something awful. I look around the apartment for clues or photographs on the fridge. Maybe her dad was a serial killer? And now she's going to show me the newspaper clippings she keeps under her bed that contain his ghastly CSI-type murder scenes?

"This," she says and slaps a thick fashion magazine on the table, "is what I'm talking about."

CHAPTER 33

Bzzzzrrr. *Bzzzzrrr.* I wake up to the feel of metal buzzing on my face. *What the? Bzzzzrrr.* It's my cell phone, which is under my laptop, which is under my face. I was up late typing up a treatment for a new show idea and fell asleep on the keyboard. I peel my face off the computer and feel the square-shaped marks it's left on my cheek.

I have a text from Gia. I'm relieved things are back to normal between us. Better actually.

Married life is soooo hard!

She's also sent a photo of Matt and her on their honeymoon. It's a selfie of the two of them in bed. You don't need to be Sherlock to know that beneath those white sheets they are *definitely* naked. The sun is spilling into their adorable hut on the beach in Bali. They both look relaxed and beautiful. I hold my phone out and snap one of myself. Good morning frizzy hair. Check. Keyboard indentations on cheek. Check. I laugh at myself and hit send.

I realize I've slept through my alarm. A record twelve minutes later, I'm out the door and rushing to get to work. The weekly production meeting this morning was the reason I stayed up late writing the treatment in the first place.

I walk into the conference room, and Bianca is deep into her update. She pauses for a moment when I walk in and then continues. I look around the large table, but every single seat is taken. I scan the room again and freeze. Richard is sitting there looking right at me. Crap. I completely forgot I asked him to come in today.

The whole way here I was psyching myself up to deliver this treatment confidently, but having Richard here takes some wind out of my sails. My email to him had been nice and sweet, and okay maybe a *little* long-winded.

Hey,

I just heard we need to do a little bit of reediting to Steven and Elizabeth's episode. I'm sure you are probably busy with your new company (hope all is going great with that by the way!) but I know how editors sometimes get when other editors make changes to their shows, and I wanted to at least give you the option in case you could do it and were free for a day. Plus, the reason for the reedit will be good for a laugh, I promise!

Have a great weekend!!
Ana

Sure. Be there Monday.

R

His brusque reply had made me feel stupid for writing such a friendly email to a colleague. Note to self: Must get into the habit of writing short professional emails.

Now he's here looking pretty good in a fitted cardigan, the sleeves pushed back to his elbows.

He's noticed there aren't any seats, so Richard stands and motions for me to take his before heading out the door. In a few seconds, he's back and rolling in a chair he's nabbed from a nearby desk. Bianca tries to ignore all the fuss but begins to speak louder to make sure no one misses a single word.

"Sooo . . . tomorrow we start taping with a great new couple. It will be so much fun because it's the *groom* who wants to change the way he looks before the wedding. He wants a cross between Tom Cruise and Daniel Day-Lewis, so it's going to be *a-mazing!*"

Bianca's wearing a green button-down blouse that needs to be buttoned *up* a little if you ask me. I can see she has on a matching green bra because it peeks out from time to time. I think people who attend meetings and have to give updates in those meetings should dress more conservatively. And how do redheads know that colors like dark green look great with their hair? Are they born with a manual? *Dear redheaded new baby: Never, ever wear white or yellow, but pink and dark green are your friends. PS: You're too young now, but one day this will also apply to matching bras.*

In a few weeks, Bianca's two new shows, *Mobster Brides*

and *Brides without a Face*, will premiere on the same night on two different networks, which means she'll be able to see her name next to the "created by" credit twice. Flip the channel. Created by Bianca. Flip the channel. Created by Bianca.

"But the big update is that we're working with both networks on a crossover idea for the finale that would merge *both* shows! Mobster brides and grooms who *also* need new faces for their wedding day so they don't have to go into witness protection!"

I catch myself looking at Richard. I want him to roll his eyes. *Roll your eyes, Richard. Come on. Roll them. Bianca sucks, right?* But he's just sitting back in his chair, arms and legs crossed, with his head tilted slightly to the side.

Nina is sitting right next to him, and when she sees me, she tugs at the front of her blouse like she's trying to tell me something. I look down and *oh crap*! My tank top is on backward, and the tag is sticking up out of it. It's one of those that highlights the washing instructions in five different languages, so it looks like a long tongue is licking my throat. I tuck it in and look back up. Okay, no problem, crisis averted. It's just a plain tank top, so no one should be able to tell it's on backward.

"But I *will* say"—Bianca is dramatically intense all of a sudden—"I have already told the networks and Edith, you know." Edith nods in agreement. "It could also be *extremely* dangerous. Mobsters could show up at any moment looking for trouble." She scans around the room to make sure we've all heard her.

"So I told them, if at any time I feel my crew is in danger, we will stop taping. If I hear bullets or see some strange characters, I am not going to let my crew stand in harm's way."

The room is muted, and a few heads are nodding. I can't believe this. Bianca wants a Purple Heart for pretending to care about *her* crew when it's *her* stupid and reckless idea that's putting them in danger in the first place. I look at Richard, and thankfully, he is not nodding.

"Okay, well, that's it for me. I mean, that's a lot. There's so much going on."

"Any . . . other updates?" Edith closes her notebook, which means the meeting is wrapping up.

I feel cold and clammy and regretting the large container of Chinese takeout I devoured last night for dinner. *And the second one I had at 2:15 a.m.*

"Okay then." Edith stands, prompting everyone else to start doing the same.

"Actually . . ." I clear my throat. "I want to."

Richard is closest to the door and was about to open it, but now he's looking right at me. And so is everyone else. They don't know if they should sit back down or if they can just remain standing for what I have to say.

"I have a pitch."

"Go ahead," Edith says, sitting back down, so everyone else shuffles back into their seats.

"Go ahead." Edith's voice is dripping with sarcasm. "You are cordially invited to pitch." Bianca lets out a snort.

I can do this. I open my laptop, pull up the treatment, and walk over to connect my computer into the overhead projection system. Now, up on the wall, everyone can see an image of Jorge on bended knee in Central Park and Maria looking down at him.

"Maria and Jorge. The proposal that *didn't* happen," I say, standing in front of the projection screen and reading the text robotically, word for word. I'm not facing the room and *not* engaging the crowd, which even *I* know is bad.

"But why?" I ask, spinning around quickly. I can do this. I see Richard sitting there and ... Wait a second, is he checking me out? Was he just looking at my ass?

"They were in love." I click to the next image of Maria and Jorge in the kitchen as they prepare dinner. Jorge is saying something and Maria is laughing. "They were clearly meant for each other. And if that's the case, why would someone sabotage her own happiness?" I click on the next photo of the treatment. Maria running away from Jorge in Central Park. "Simple. Maria was scared."

"Yeah, no kidding!" Bianca blurts out, making the production assistant standing behind her giggle.

"Yes, but it's deeper than that," I continue, gaining confidence. "Maria was afraid of *losing* Jorge, but she lost him anyway because she was scared." It feels like I'm going in circles, but I plow forward. "This new show ..." I click through the next few images I found on the internet last night. Women going about their daily lives. Alone. There's a lady buying produce at the market, one drinking tea at home, one riding the bus. "... would help women face their fears."

I look around the table, but no one is nodding the way they did for Bianca. "Their fears ... about men. So they can have meaningful relationships," I say, relieved to have finished my thought. I wait anxiously for the nodding to begin. But there's only a sea of blank faces. Did I skip a page of the treatment?

"How?" Bianca asks, and I see Edith lifting her eyebrows in agreement, like she was just thinking the same thing.

"*Well*. Each episode would be different, depending on what the woman is afraid of." I click to the next slide, but it's Jorge on bended knee again by the fountain. Ugh. I didn't have any time to polish this up. I click again, and a woman appears at the top of a bridge, about to bungee jump over the edge. From the corner of my eye, I see Richard is totally looking at my body. What the...? Why can't he keep his eyes on the presentation?

"If a woman is afraid of taking risks in relationships, we'll help her take that jump." I click again, and the image of a nerdy mom with her legs wrapped around a pole makes a few people laugh. "If she lacks confidence around men, we'll give her pole-dancing lessons." I click again, feeling like I'm on a roll. "Swimming with sharks, if she's easily intimidated." Click. "If she's afraid her new boyfriend will run when he sees her naked"—click, click, more laughter around the table— "she'll have to run through Times Square completely in the buff." I look around and finally see a few nods.

"In each episode we'll meet a woman, find out what's holding her back, watch as she decides it's time to face it head-on...and after we've put her up to that challenge...see if she can get the guy." I nailed it. I feel electricity surging through my body.

"Ehh—" Bianca sounds like a deflating tire.

"Yes, the concept is hard-core and it *is* women facing

their fears, but it's also inspirational, and I think our viewers would really identify with them. Because, ladies..." I look at the tagline I wrote at 3:00 a.m., and though it doesn't sound as clever right now, I still deliver it with confidence. "Maybe the only thing standing between you and Mr. Right is you."

Silence. I try to avoid looking over at Richard, but I can't. There's a smile on his face, but I'm not sure if it's an "I'm so sorry they dropped you on your head when you were a baby" kind of smile or a "Nice job!" smile.

"It's called *Fearless Love*," I say confidently.

"Well..." Finally, Edith is going to say something. "But what if we help her do all that stuff she fears, and she still doesn't get the guy? How can we be sure we'll get a happy ending?"

"I guess we can't. Not always."

Bianca throws her hands up in the air like she's never heard of anything more absurd in her life. This from the woman who's doing a reality-show version of *Face/Off*.

"Well, you can't always tell what's going to happen in relationships. So...the audience wouldn't know what's going to happen either. It would be like in real life!"

"Sounds a little *too* real," Bianca says under her breath.

"Exactly," Edith adds as she begins to put her things together.

"But getting a person to face their fears and *conquer* them...is a happy ending. With or without the guy. Isn't it?"

"Not [mini pause] happy enough," Edith says, stands up, and heads to the door.

I can't believe it. I thought my idea was solid. It was

positive and uplifting. I suddenly feel the urge to let Edith know just how bad Bianca's shows are. I want to yell out, "Hello!? An episode that combines both of her shows? I mean *how stupid* can you get? If a mobster gets a new face and then appears on TV, his enemies will see the new face, so he will still have to go into witness protection. How is that a happy ending?"

But instead, I turn around to let the room empty out behind me. I take my time shutting my laptop and unplugging it from the projection system. This is terrible. I really wanted to *make* this show. I wanted to help that woman on the bus and the one drinking tea by herself while she looks out the window forlornly. And that poor woman with the melons at the market.

Wouldn't getting to see those women release themselves from their own prisons make great television? Maybe I don't know what makes great TV?

I walk into the bathroom to turn my shirt around, but when I look in the mirror, it's like that rack focus effect directors use to heighten drama. The background and the foreground come together quickly as we look into the eyes of the terrified person who has just figured out that there's a shark coming toward them.

I must have been half-asleep when I rushed out of my apartment this morning and didn't bother to look in the mirror. I can't believe this is what I was wearing for my pitch. It looks perfectly fine from above, but from the front it most certainly does *not*. I'm wearing stone-washed jeans and a peplum tank top. I love this top. The peplum aspect gives the illusion I'm wearing something dressier than just a tank top because it skirts out at the bottom like a miniature tutu. The problem is it *must* be worn with high-waisted pants, and these particular jeans are loose on me and drag way down if I don't wear a belt. *And I'm not wearing a belt.*

At this moment, the jeans are down by my hips and the tutu top is flaring straight out, and the entire ensemble is calling attention to about four inches of exposed midriff and some of my yellow thong.

I cannot believe I stood there in front of everyone and pitched my show idea like this. How did I not feel a breeze? Richard wasn't checking me out. He was staring at my belly button. I look at the mirror again and consider sending a company-wide email.

Dear Sirs and Madams, re: This morning's production meeting. Just want to point out that my stomach does not normally look like this. It's just a case of bloated belly caused by an all-night Chinese buffet.

I pull my jeans up as high as I can and open the door to my edit room. Richard is sitting there watching the Steven and Elizabeth episode again. He's up to the montage he begrudgingly edited together of Steven shopping for a new proposal outfit.

When he hears me walk in, he hits the stop button. "Hey."

"Hey." As soon as I sit down, there's a knock at the door.

"Hi . . . You okay?" Nina sounds concerned.

"Yeah, I'm fine."

"That was great. You nailed it."

"Thanks."

"Oh—" She notices Richard and tenses up.

That's the thing about Nina. She's so friendly and fun, but when she has to talk to a guy, she doesn't speak. The last time we went to a bar together, this nice guy approached her and she let him do all the talking and her real, fun self never came out, so the guy got bored and wandered off.

If she were on *Fearless Love*, I'd help her tackle her stage fright somehow. Maybe force her to take a stand-up comedy class. And then deliver her routine to a roomful of single men. She would totally bomb at first, but I know that by the end of the routine she'd be amazing. Cut to a roomful of guys laughing. Cut to Nina feeling more confident onstage. Cut to one particular fella laughing louder than the rest. Cut to Nina noticing him. He smiles. She smiles. That would be a happy ending, damn it!

"I thought you were done with this episode?" Nina says to me.

"So did we, but apparently someone at the network didn't think so," Richard says curtly.

"It wasn't the network. It was Usher," I say, looking at Richard and then at Nina. "He wanted more . . . Usher."

"You've got to be kidding me." Poor Richard. He had wanted to take Usher out of the show completely, and now we have to put more Usher in.

"We'll just get in there," I say, trying to sound peppy and motivational, "and sprinkle a few more shots of him and be done."

"Interesting how you kept that small detail out of your email," Richard says playfully.

On her way out, Nina pops down by my side. "I cannot wait to be back in here with you next week."

"Yeah, me too," I say, looking at the back of Richard's head.

"I've missed you," she whispers. "Sitting in an edit room with Bianca all day sucks the life out of a person. Every time I go to the bathroom, she gives me this look"—Nina distorts her face like an annoyed teenager—"like she's disappointed I have a bladder." I smile and watch Nina shut the door behind her.

"So if I told you what we had to do today, you wouldn't have come?"

Richard turns his head toward me and thinks for a second. "And miss out on ruining the show with you? Never!" He gives me an exaggerated withering look.

Now all I have to do is spend the rest of the day in my seat. My bare midsection will only get barer as the hours go by and my jeans stretch out. I just won't drink any water. Can you die of dehydration in a day?

"Wanna grab lunch?" Richard asks as he stands.

It would be nice. But if he missed my yellow panties earlier, he'll definitely see them now. *Actually, I think I'm okay with Richard seeing my panties.* But my pitch went so bad that it zapped my confidence. I can't risk it. I've humiliated myself enough today.

"No. I'm good. Thanks. I'll just order in." Maybe I can also order a belt?

Once Richard is gone, I open my bag and pull out a small bundle of Zip drives. I sort through them and pop one into my computer. A freeze-frame of Maria appears on my computer screen. She's sitting on a plane, looking out the window. I cannot believe I spent the entire weekend taping what I had hoped would be the pilot for my show idea. I had believed in it so much I paid for a last-minute flight to Houston, a rental car, and a hotel room and actually believed I would be reimbursed once Edith had heard my brilliant idea.

After another bottle of wine with Maria, she felt it was time she faced her fears. And that's when I got the idea for the show. She said I could tape it all, and I didn't want to wait until I got a green light for the show and a budget approved. Plus, everyone involved was going to be home this weekend. I felt I needed to act fast before Maria changed her mind. I was going with the flow. I was trusting my instinct. I was . . . an idiot.

I hadn't mentioned any of this in the meeting because I was waiting for Edith to first say she loved the idea and then I was going to tell her the big news. Surprise! She could have the pilot edited in a few weeks.

I had imagined how the whole thing would play out:

Edith: I LOVE IT! Amazing idea!

Me: Well, guess what? I shot it already.

Edith: What?

Me: Yep, and you can have it in a few weeks.

Edith: Oh my! ANA, YOU ARE A STAR!

I had this whole daydream that Edith would be so thankful I'd found a way to salvage the Maria/Jorge Central Park proposal fiasco.

All she had to do was approve the budget for an editor for a couple of weeks. I was sure that coming up with an incredible idea and making it for very little money was just the kind of thing that got people promoted to head of development.

Instead, she hated my pitch, and she would probably fire me if she found out I had broken company rules to get this done, particularly borrowing a camera and audio equipment without asking.

Note to self: from now on, do the opposite of what my instincts say.

I put on my headphones so no one will hear and press play. My camera coverage is a little shaky, but for the most part it looks good.

"Why am I not surprised?" Richard is standing right behind me, looking over my shoulder at the screen. Crap. I didn't hear him walk back in. "I knew it."

"Why do you say that?"

"Just a hunch. I liked your pitch. I thought it was really good."

"Thanks." I drop my head on the desk.

"You shot that by yourself?"

I nod with my forehead still resting on the desk. "I can't believe I wasted all that money."

"Well, just because one door closes doesn't mean you can't pitch it somewhere else," he says, trying to cheer me up. I hunch my shoulders and sigh.

"Wow, who's that?"

"Huh?" I look up at the screen and see it's still playing. "Oh yeah. That's what Maria was afraid of."

"Well, even I would watch that show!"

I look at him and smile. I can't believe I hadn't noticed until right this second he is *not* wearing a scarf today. Which is bizarre since it's finally starting to get cool out. I can see his neck for the first time and notice his Adam's apple.

There's a knock on the door that startles us both.

Richard reaches across and shuts my laptop for me. The quick-on-his-toes, protective gesture takes me completely by surprise. On the way back, his bare arm brushes against mine, sending a snap of heat through me.

As he catches up with an old friend from the documentary floor, I sit there confused. I can't stop retracing the trajectory of Richard's arm grazing mine, trying to decide if it was intentional. *Or if it's just one of those grazes gone wild.*

"Well, that coulda been worse." Richard gets up to leave at the end of the day.

"Yeah, sorry about that."

"That's okay. What can you do?"

"I know, right? I guess it is what it is." We're talking about our job as if adding a few shots of Usher is the equivalent to coming home from a war only to be sent out on another tour.

"Yep. Sometimes you just gotta get through it." He picks up his bag and walks over to my desk. "Well, I'll be seeing you." He's standing next to me now with his arms extended out in front of him. Does he want a hug? Ugh. My jeans are so stretched out I'm afraid they'll fall straight to the ground if I stand up. I start to move slowly and pull my jeans up as I stand, then tuck my elbows down to hold them in place. Which means I only have my forearms and hands free. *This is how a T-rex hugs.*

"Thanks for everything," he says.

"You too. Thanks. Yep." Our hug is close enough for me to feel his scruffy, barely there beard and smell something earthy. I just can't tell if it's his cologne or if that's just his scent.

My chin's landed on his shoulder and my face has relaxed. It's really goodbye. This time he's gone for good. There simply isn't any Usher left to add. All of a sudden, I hold him for real, no longer caring how low my jeans go or how much of my underwear is visible. I think Richard can sense the difference because there's slightly more pressure. Is he squeezing me? *Can one feel squeezing that isn't there? Okay, I can't be imagining the breathing.* We're both definitely *breathing.* You know, the way you breathe deeply when you're holding someone just before things get more *intimate.*

I need to grow up. For once. People hug goodbye all the time. I have to stop reading into things. I mean, he has a girl-friend. All these thoughts conjured up in the span of a hug are completely unproductive.

This is the perfect time to begin that whole do the *opposite* of what my instincts are telling me thing. Because right now my instincts are telling me I want this hug to last longer and advance into something else. *And so does he.*

My instincts are batting zero right now, so I decide right

then and there that, from now on, I will focus solely on my job. Next week I will work with Nina and be happy and together we'll make the final season of *Marry Me* the best season yet. And I will start to look for a new job. *And always have a spare belt at the office.*

CHAPTER 34

I walk down the long hall to my edit room feeling organized and unstoppable. I sent my resume to three production companies before I even left my apartment. But then I hear something that makes me freeze.

It's still early, and the office is relatively empty. Just a few interns making coffee in the kitchen. I sprint the rest of the way down the hall and into my edit room.

Up on the screen is my show. *The* show. The one I filmed all by myself. The one Edith hasn't approved. *Fearless Love* is somehow edited and scored and playing on the screen. I sit down. Well, more like my butt falls into the chair.

"Hey! This is so awesome." Nina realizes I've come in. "What's the matter?"

"What—*how* is that?"

"Did you not know he was doing this?" Nina looks confused.

"Who?"

"Oh. Even more awesome."

"What are you talking about?"

"The note. I'm sorry. I thought you had left it for me, so I read it. I can't believe you didn't know."

I see an index card on my desk. It has small, neat handwriting. I scan down to the bottom.

Richard

"It's amazing! Here, I'll start it from the beginning." Nina gets up, shuts the door, and hits play.

The large screen fades from black to Central Park. We hear a sweet song kick in as the camera swoops down on a crane from above the trees and past the angel on the fountain and onto Jorge and Maria, who are holding hands as they approach. Jorge gets down on one knee. The music crescendos as he reaches into his pocket, pulls out the ring box, and opens it . . . *screeeeech*. Just as he's about to speak, the music record scratches to a halt.

"That should have been the best moment of my life. But it wasn't. It was the worst." Maria's voice plays over the images as a heartbreaking song begins. "I needed to get away from there, but I also knew that with every step, I was separating myself from the love of my life."

I had given Maria a small camera and a list of questions and left her alone. I wanted her interview to feel intimate, like a personal diary. But I hadn't had time to hear any of this yet.

"But why would I do that? How could I walk away from my own happiness? The reason isn't easy for me to talk about."

How did this happen? How had all of this come together over a weekend? It looks and *feels* like a real show. We see Maria at home in her kitchen, looking through a photo album. The sad song continues as she flips through pictures of her family.

"My name is Maria Garcia, and I grew up in Houston, Texas. My parents emigrated from Mexico just before I was born. When I was nine, my cousin Zamora came to live with us, and my parents eventually adopted her. I was so excited to have a sister, and though she was a year older, we were in the same grade. I thought we'd be best friends, but...life isn't that simple."

She turns the page, and we see a photograph of a nine-year-old, chubby-cheeked Maria standing next to a lanky girl who is a foot taller.

A fast-paced track kicks in as Zamora and Maria get older. We see photographs of them at birthdays, Christmas mornings, proms, high school graduation. Always Maria looking intimidated and small next to Zamora, who only gets taller and more beautiful. I can't believe it. Richard has edited a *montage*!

The girls' photos speed up until they begin to focus on Zamora. The pictures snap, snap, snap as we reach her modeling career on catwalks and magazine covers. Richard hates montages, but it's like he'd read my mind.

The photos end dramatically on one of Zamora on the cover of a magazine in a swimsuit. But this isn't just another girl in a swimsuit. This is a creature from another planet, coming out of the water like a goddess.

When I had first seen that image, back at Maria's apartment, I could almost understand what she was feeling. I was used to walking into a room with Gia. Used to every man noticing her. But there are the *Gia*s of the world and then there are the *Zamora*s. Tan skin, dark-brown hair, bright-green eyes.

On the magazine cover, the water is dripping down her skin but looks like it doesn't want to let go. Behind her, a surfer dude holds her pink bikini top in the air, but she doesn't seem to care. She's covering her bare breasts with her hands and walking toward the photographer with a heavenly look on her face. The grin, the eyes. That's the most beautiful thing about this woman. Her confidence.

"This is Zamora." Maria's narration kicks back in as we see her packing a small suitcase. "Introducing even my *girlfriends* to her was difficult. Everyone wanted to be *her* friend. Hang out in *her* room. And any guy I ever liked fell for her and talked to me only when they wanted me to hand her a love note. Don't get me wrong. I love Zamora and have only ever been supportive of her career and happiness. I just—"

We cut to Maria's interview. She's sitting in the kitchen and starting to cry. "It's funny because I remember when Jorge and I were walking through the park that day, I had just been thinking 'What is he still doing here? Why is he with me?'"

Nina turns around. "This is so good," she says all teary-eyed.

"When Jorge proposed, I couldn't believe it. It was the last thing I expected. I thought if it felt too good to be true, it wasn't meant to be. I felt the only reason he was proposing was because he hadn't met someone better."

Back at her apartment, Maria told me how she had been too scared to introduce Zamora to Jorge. She was afraid he would fall in love with Zamora and break up with her because that's what had happened with every other guy she had ever been with.

I remembered thinking she needed help. Are we *all* this insane? I imagined myself with the Four and thought yes, maybe a lot of us are. And that's when I had the idea for the show.

And now it was playing right in front of me, and it was even better than I had imagined.

I had Maria tell Jorge that I quit my job on *Marry Me* to work on a passion project about Mexican American family life. I felt a little guilty lying to *him* this time, but it was for his own good. Maria had called ahead and told her family the same thing. We had also decided not to tell Jorge about her fears about him meeting Zamora. I told Maria that part of her walking toward her fears was facing this without his support, and she had agreed.

"But I've decided it's time to face this." Maria steps out of her apartment and into a cab waiting outside. Jorge is holding the door for her. He's happy to see her, but their greeting is awkward. "I'm not sure if it's too late to save our relationship. But I have to try. I'm tired of being afraid."

Cut to them on the plane. Maria is looking out the window. "We've been dating for a year, and Jorge has met my parents, but I've kept him from meeting Zamora. We had tickets to go home one weekend, and I lied and said I was sick when I heard she was going to be there."

Maria looks distraught and ashamed. Richard always cuts back to her interview at just the right moments. It starts to dawn on me that he watched all this footage over the weekend. That he must have worked straight through the night. That he had to sort through all my bad shaky cam moments. Because right now it all looks so polished and smooth. But at the same time so raw and real.

Maria and Jorge arrive in Houston and get into a cab. Richard has done an incredible job of making the viewer feel tense. Even *I'm* watching the show as if I hadn't been there. Maria's brow is creased, and Jorge is calmly looking out the window. Right now you're hoping he doesn't even so much as *look* at Zamora for too long. You're hoping Maria's been a fool all this time and she had nothing to worry about.

The taxi pulls up to the house, and Maria looks anxious as they step out. I had asked Maria and Jorge to give me a few minutes alone with her family before they walked in. This way, everyone could get comfortable with me and the camera.

Her parents were preparing a big lunch for Maria and Jorge in their backyard. Her mom showed me the dozens of plants in brightly colored ceramic pots she had hanging from the branches of a sequoia tree. I was glad for the tree because the harsh Texas sun was directly above us, and the shade provided better lighting. Richard selected the prettiest shots of the hanging flowers and the backyard to set the scene of a warm family gathering.

Maria's grandfather and uncle were there too, setting the

table, talking. Zamora was sitting at one end, texting on her phone. Her hair was up in a messy bun and she didn't appear to have any makeup on, but her skin was glowing. She was wearing a white T-shirt and satiny black shorts.

I remember I went back inside to capture how Maria was doing just before the big moment.

"Are you all right?" Jorge asked as he held Maria's hand.

"Yeah, I'm okay," Maria answered convincingly.

"What I felt was this overwhelming sense of relief." We hear Maria's thoughts from her diary cam. "I suddenly understood it didn't matter who was behind that door. I had to be okay now. I had to accept that Jorge loved me now. And that I *was* enough."

The doors open, and Maria and Jorge step outside. Richard has edited the rest of the scene as a montage (I can't believe it, *another* montage!) to an empowering version of Usher's "U Got It Bad" with female vocals I've never heard before. It's slower and more intense than the original, and as soon as the lyrics begin, I feel giddy and emotional. My eyes are glued to the screen, but my mind is going in so many directions, trying to understand why Richard would do all this. Something is dawning on me. There's a chance I was right. When Richard and I hugged goodbye the other day, I *wasn't* imagining things.

Maria and Jorge walk down the steps into the yard, give hugs and kisses to everyone, Jorge is introduced to Zamora, everyone is happy and laughing and catching up and then settling down for lunch. I love how Richard has cut the rest of the scene this way. It just *feels* right. You don't hear any of the conversations because they're not important. The most important part has already happened, just *before* they opened the door.

The music ends, and it's quiet for a moment. "I have a confession to make." Maria looks straight into her diary cam. "When we were at the table, I leaned over and . . ." She pauses, and Richard has added a rising crescendo that makes it clear something is about to happen. "I said yes. I told Jorge that I would marry him. And do you know what he said? 'Well, it's about time.'" Maria laughs as she imitates him, wiping away a tear. "I was so happy he had the ring with him." *What? He had what? How did I miss all this?*

And there beneath the passing of a large platter of grilled corn, Jorge handed Maria the ring from his pocket, she slipped it on, and they went on about their business.

Meanwhile, I was deciding whether I should widen out a little so we could see the stupid hanging plants in the frame, and I missed the little moment when Maria and Jorge got engaged!

No one at the table had noticed either. But still. Bianca's right. Never trust the talent.

Richard then cut to a close-up shot of Jorge about to wipe away some butter off Maria's chin, but then he leans in and kisses it off instead. Fade to black.

My name fades up on the screen along with the words "created by."

"You just shot this, right? Richard must have worked all weekend," Nina says, but I can't respond.

I had thought Maria facing her fears was enough of a

happy ending. But she had gotten an even *happier* ending. And Richard had done something incredible.

It's not a full show, only about seven minutes long, but with the footage edited together like this, I can pitch it to another production company and it will have a way better chance. I can't believe it. *I have a show! I have a show! I have a show! But why? Why? Why has Richard done this?*

CHAPTER 35

On a New York City subway, you can easily figure out where you're headed by studying the people around you. Across from me is a lady with long white hair and a tattoo of a bluebird wrapped around her neck. There's another tattoo of a peacock on her left shoulder, and standing tall on her right forearm is a hot-pink flamingo. So that would make this the L train, headed to Brooklyn.

I pull out Richard's note from my bag, though I've read it so many times I can now recite it by heart.

There's a new production company you should pitch this to. Could be a good fit. Problem is they're in Brooklyn. Do you know where that is? In all seriousness, come by and pitch it to my partner.

Richard

He made me feel so many things in one day. At first it had been a bit disconcerting to see my show put together like that so quickly. Then I felt overjoyed. And when I read his note and realized he was basically telling me that *he* could be interested in producing the show at his new company, I felt ecstatic.

I'm headed out there now because I convinced myself I should thank him in person. I have to let him know how grateful I am. What he did for me was so incredibly *nice*.

I'm not sure I'm ready to pitch the show again at his company, but I did bring colorful printouts of the treatment. *Just in case.*

The truth is, pitching the show is the perfect excuse. The only thing I want to do is see Richard again. I have an overwhelming need to throw out his scarves and wrap *myself* around his neck.

I look at aviary girl and feel a sudden urge to set all those birds free. They seem trapped on her skin.

Who knows? Richard will probably be extremely busy. Maybe I'll make an appointment while I'm there for pitching on a later date. I have, however, made sure I'm not showing any unwanted skin this time.

I'm wearing black jeans (my highest-waisted pair) and a white button-down shirt. *Tucked in.* My hair is up in a ponytail, and the bangs are pinned back. I've given up on them. Or more like I've given up on trying to *force* something that doesn't happen naturally. They'll grow out soon enough.

My ears pop as the train goes under the water. I look out the window at the darkness zooming by, and I try really hard *not* to imagine the worst that could happen. Richard turning me down. Telling me he just wants to be friends or business partners.

The train slows down and then comes to a stop. "There's construction up ahead. We are sorry for the inconvenience," explains the static-filled voice on the intercom. "We should be clear to go in a few moments."

The lack of movement makes me feel weary. I barely slept last night. I kept replaying the show on my laptop. And after I shut it off, I kept playing it in my head.

I feel like Bird Tattoos can see right through me. Like she knows what I'm ashamed to admit. That a small part of me had been relieved when Edith shut down my pitch. Because the show couldn't fail if it didn't even have a chance.

Richard threw a lifeline into the pit I had fallen into, and right now I'm wondering, *Wait, do I want to leave this nice warm pit? It's so cozy down here.*

The train starts to move again, and I pat down the sweat forming on my forehead with the back of my hand.

I check my watch. I've taken the whole day off, but I was hoping to get to Brooklyn early. My plan is to say thanks, pitch the show, and then pitch the idea of us. *In a super casual, hyperorganic way.*

The train stops, and I get up to go. I can see my reflection in the glass door.

Thankfully no hives, but my shoulders are hunched way up to my ears.

———

Richard's new company, Rich in Character Productions, is located on an industrial-looking street filled with old factories that have been converted into swanky office buildings. Dropping by unannounced doesn't seem like such a good idea anymore. He could be busy with actual clients.

I take two deep breaths. Everything is going to be fine. I'll just walk in there and say, "Hey, Richard! Thanks for editing my show, dude! How about you show me around the offices, buddy!" In other words, I'll be totally cool.

I take the elevator to the third floor, and as soon as the doors open, I'm greeted by a guy wearing a flannel shirt buttoned all the way to the top.

"Can I help you?" He's sitting on a stool behind a tall wooden desk. Behind him, the wall is covered with a giant black-and-white photograph of the Brooklyn Bridge and a blue neon sign that says "Rich in Character." It smells like fresh paint in here. And musk.

"Hi. I'm here to see Richard."

"I'm afraid he's out."

"Oh, okay thanks," I say, masking my disappointment. I'm about to spin on my heel and get out of there when he hits me with questions.

"Was he expecting you? Is there anything I can help you with?" He's very put-together and professional for someone wearing flannel.

"Well, I'm actually here to . . . I have a treatment for a show he said I should pitch."

"You can just leave that with me."

"I can?"

I can? That's good! That's the same as pitching it, right? Sort of. I pull the envelope containing a Zip drive and treatment copies out of my bag and hand it to him.

"Just need you to sign this," he says, pulling out a clipboard.

"Okay, thanks." I take it from him. "What is it?"

"It's a confidentiality agreement. We can't accept treatments without it. Just says you're giving us the right to review your idea, and if we are in the process of producing something similar, you can't sue us... You know, the usual."

"Oh right. Of course. The usual." I sign without even reading it because I completely trust Richard. I hand back the clipboard and walk into the elevator. I turn as the elevator doors are about to close and stare at my treatment, still on the receptionist's desk.

Just before they close, I jam my foot in between the doors.

"I'm sorry, I changed my mind. I'll come back later... and pitch it in person. Thanks." He looks at me like I don't ever mean to come back. But I do. I just don't want to leave the treatment all by itself. Without anyone to defend it. I put my show back in my bag feeling more confident than I have in a long time.

"Is there a restroom I can use?"

He points to a door at the end of a long hallway. As I head toward it, I can hear music and talking coming from the edit rooms along my left. To my right, there's an impressive common area with an open kitchen, a dark-brown leather couch, and an entire wall of floor-to-ceiling windows. And there's green everywhere: standing plants, plants on tables, and plants on shelves near the window. The place has a masculine touch but also feels warm and welcoming.

The bathroom door is a modern smoky glass panel. I try to pull it toward me, but it won't budge.

"You have to slide it into the wall," says a voice from behind me.

"Oh, thanks. Oh, *hey . . .*" I turn and freeze when I see the Richard look-alike standing there. He's a little shorter than Richard and has a fuller beard, but this has to be his brother, Max. Nina and I saw his picture in the press release that announced the two brothers' business partnership. She said he was cute, and looking at him now, I'd say he and Nina would make a great couple.

I start to slide the door into the wall and *what the . . .* The glass panel has lost its smokiness. It's completely see-through now. I can see everything inside the bathroom. There's the toilet right across from the door and the sink off to the side. I slide the door back until it's shut, and the glass smokes up again. It's like magic. I can't see *anything* inside. When I start to slide it open again, the glass becomes completely transparent. Now, *that* is fancy.

But once inside, the high-tech door makes me extremely uncomfortable. From the inside of the bathroom, the glass is *completely* see-through even when it's shut. I can see the receptionist all the way down the hall. I can see people walking out of edit rooms, and I can see a guy taking a bite into his sandwich on the leather couch in the main area. How am I supposed to use the bathroom like this? I make sure the door is closed. Like *really* closed. And locked. I triple-check the lock. I find a key hanging on the wall nearby and secure it that way too. *Can't be too careful.*

I'm about to slide off my jeans but decide to tug at the door one more time, to make sure it's locked. It doesn't budge. When I'm finally sitting on the toilet, I spot Richard's brother step out of one of the edit rooms and walk up to the bathroom. He looks right at me. Well, at the door anyway, and then heads back down the hall.

This is ridiculous. This door is some kind of torture device for their clients. I flush and pull my jeans up as quickly as I can.

I look at myself in the boat porthole–styled mirror above the sink as I wash my hands. The big block of soap smells like cedar, and the napkin to dry your hands is nice and thick.

The whole place has been put together with a lot of attention to detail. It's all so edgy but at the same time inviting. Well, except the bathroom door. Other than that, this place *feels* like Richard. He must have put his heart into the design . . . and why is this door not opening?

Why isn't it sliding? I turn the key one way and then the other. I hear clicking sounds, but nothing is happening. I pull and tug and try to get it to slide, but it won't move at all.

I go back to turning the key again. It clicks and I tug. Nothing. I turn the key the other way. More clicking and tugging. Nothing. Through the transparent door I can see a concerned Max approaching.

"You okay in there?"

"Actually, I can't get the door to unlock."

"You just turn the dial and—"

"Yeah no, it's not—" I tug and try the key to the left again.

Max pulls at the door and nothing. "Are you turning the dial to the right?"

"Yeah, but I can't get the key out."

"What key?"

"The one that was—" There's something about his tone I don't like. I look at the key I've been turning. It's so *rusty*. And the glass panel smoky door is so *modern*. *Why would it have such a rusty key?*

I quickly scan the bathroom and see old-fashioned things all around. A vintage set of binoculars sits on a metal table, and a couple of antique fishing rods rest in a tin bucket. I look at the old-time anchor hook on the wall by the door.

That's where the key was hanging when I grabbed it and slipped it into the slot. *Or did I shove it in?*

I desperately yank and pull at the key until it snaps. I am now holding half of the rusty key in my hand.

"What was that?"

I turn the small dial to the right. Nothing. Of course not. How can it work when it's choking on the crumbs of an old rusty key?

"I put a key in the door by mistake, the one that was on the hook."

"That was decoration." Max pulls and pulls at the door harder, making the whole glass panel tremble.

"I can see that now."

"Shit! Hold on," he says and storms off down the hallway.

This can't be happening. I'm so embarrassed. As he walks away, Max takes his cell phone out of his jeans. Who's he calling? Please don't call Richard. I try to turn the dial, but it won't move. *This can't be happening. I'm not stuck in this bathroom, and I did not break Richard's million-dollar state-of-the-art magic door.*

An older woman starts to walk toward me, and Max stops her.

"Sorry, the bathroom is out of commission right now. You'll need to use the one downstairs in the main lobby. Just ask our receptionist for the key."

I rest my forehead on the glass panel. It's clear Max is upset. I can see everything. I can see the receptionist look all over his desk for the lobby bathroom key and not find it. I can see him get up and walk toward Max, who gets even more upset.

Twenty-five minutes have gone by. They've taped a sign on the door. People walk up to it, read it, and then walk away disappointed. So far I've upset six people, one of whom was a pregnant woman.

I take off one of the hairpins holding back my bangs and try to dig the key out, but the rust is packed in tight. I look up and, oh no, Richard is walking straight toward me. My stomach is flipping out. He can't see me. He has no idea I'm in here. Maybe I can change my voice? That's dumb, eventually I'll get out of here. *Right?*

"Hello?" Richard taps on the glass.

"Hi," I say after a moment and watch as his eyes squint up a little. It's so strange seeing him now. As someone who's awfully generous with his time. *Someone who may feel something for me. Something other than loathing.* He's still Richard. Indoor scarf. Annoyingly tight skinny jeans. But something's changed.

"Can you try turning the dial for me, all the way to left?" Aw, he's being much nicer than his brother with his commands. I attempt to turn the dial just so he thinks I'm trying.

"It won't move at all," I say and watch as his eyes squint up even more this time.

"Ana?"

"Hi." For a fleeting moment I think I see him smile.

"What are you doing here?" he says, tugging at the door repeatedly.

"I came by to thank you," I say but wish I could add "you know, for breathing life into something I had dreamed up" without sounding so corny.

"Oh yeah?" He tries to lift the heavy glass panel off the tracks, but it's as if it's been sealed shut with cement.

"So thanks," I whisper.

Max walks up to Richard, panting. "A locksmith is on his way. I told him it was an emergency, so he'll be here in twenty minutes. I've got to get back to this edit..."

"Locksmith? Why did you call a locksmith?" Richard snaps.

"What did you want me to do?" Max yells back. *Uh-oh.*

"You should've just called Derek." Richard doesn't raise his voice, but that doesn't stop Max from raising his.

"Why would I call Derek?"

"Stop yelling. Why didn't you just call me?"

"Because I was *handling it!*"

"Well, you did a great job because now we have to pay an emergency locksmith when we already have Derek coming by to fix the cabinets."

"So?"

"So Derek could have fixed this too for the same money we're already paying him to come out here."

"Well, how am I supposed to know that?"

"Lower your voice, Maxi."

Maxi? So Richard wasn't being rude to his girlfriend all that time we were working together. He was talking to his brother, *who's clearly a spoiled brat.*

"If you keep me in the dark all the time, I can't do *anything around here!*"

Max storms off, and Richard pulls on the door one more time out of frustration.

Oh no, they've got a locksmith and this guy Derek coming in. Plus, I broke their super-expensive door. And I'm obviously stirring up some intense sibling rivalry.

"I'm so sorry." *And I want to flush myself down the toilet.*

"It's all right. Someone will be here soon." He's looking right at the glass, and I think he's trying to see me.

"I feel terrible about this," I say.

"It's okay. Listen, it's not your fault."

He's being so nice, so I have to be honest. "Well, there was this old key on the hook here, and I thought I needed it to lock the door."

"That's just decoration."

"Yep. I heard."

"Why would you think you needed that key?"

"Why would you have a key near a door?"

He laughs and looks intently at the glass. "Good point."

It's strange to be able to see him when he can't see me. *I kinda like it.* I'm looking right at him without worrying about what he's going to say about my outfit or the way I've done my hair.

"I know you can see me," he says suddenly. "You know,

there's something I wanted to tell you, and this is probably as good a time as any." Richard takes a step closer to the door. His face is only a few inches away from mine.

"I wasn't really sure I was going to tell you this, but..." My mind is trying to fill in the rest, but I have no idea what he could be trying to say. "I'm not sure what's going on between you and the lighting guy, but—"

"TJ?" I blurt out without thinking.

"Yeah, him. Well, I'm not sure if you two are *serious*, but..." I'm waving my hands in the air like I need to knock down invisible gnats. No, no, no! Of course, last he heard, I was TJ's girlfriend.

"No, that was, you know...that was never serious."

"Well, that's good, because I overheard Bianca hitting on him at my going-away party, and I wanted to let you know."

"Oh. Interesting." Bianca's incredible. I want to take her Emmy and...

"For the record, I could tell he wasn't really into her. But I thought you'd still want to know."

"Thanks, but it's okay. It's over."

"Oh yeah? That's too bad." He stares into the glass and makes a strange look. Like he's trying to read my mind.

"What are you thinking?" I ask. "What was that look for?"

"You really want to know?"

"Yes."

"I was wondering what you're wearing."

"What!"

"Hey, it's not my fault. I mean, it's always unpredictable with you. You have very *diverse* tastes."

I look down at my outfit. Today it's not overalls or a frilly dress. It's comfortable. It's me. "I think you might be disappointed."

"I doubt that."

"Well, I'm not exposing any part of my stomach, if that's what you're worried about. I wouldn't do that to the professional establishment you've got here—"

Richard laughs a deep, hearty laugh. "No, but breaking my bathroom door is okay."

"That is not funny. I feel horrible."

"I'm kidding. I'm kidding," he says, still trying to see through the door somehow.

"Thanks for editing my show, Richard. I really love it."

"I'm glad. I'm happy with it too. You know, I just meant to put together something quick, like a short teaser, but I got carried away. It's good. I think it really has potential." He puts one hand on the door and leans up against it. He can't see me through the glass, so from time to time he looks around like he's talking to himself. "We'll talk about it some more when you're not in the bathroom."

"That would be great."

"So, you're single now?"

"Uh, yeah."

"So, what are you afraid of?"

"What?"

"Your show. If you were on it. What fear would you need to tackle?"

"Well, let's see, being trapped in small spaces for one," I say.

Richard is quiet for a moment. "Seriously. In your treatment, you wrote, 'Between every single woman and her happiness is a fear that needs to be tackled' or something like that. Is that true?" Behind him, I spot Max walking down the hall with another guy, probably the locksmith.

"Well, yeah, I guess. And mine would need to be a two-hour special."

He smiles, but I can see he's a little disappointed, too. Like he was really hoping I would open up to him.

The locksmith squats down and throws his bag on the ground. From where I'm standing, I can see his thinning hair combed over a large bald spot. He pulls out a long metal pick and gets to work. Max walks off and greets another guy coming down the hall. That must be Derek. They all huddle around the door and the locksmith.

"So..." Richard says, still trying to look directly into the glass.

I was just getting comfortable talking to him. I don't want it to end. What if they let me out now? Richard wants to know what I'm afraid of, and I want to tell him. And it would be nice if that could happen *before* they fix the door.

But what am I afraid of? If I were on my show, what fear would I have to tackle?

"I don't know," I say. The locksmith looks up, confused. "Richard, I don't know."

"No?"

But it's not entirely true. At this moment I'm scared this guy is going to fix the door, causing the smoky glass panel to clear up, which will allow Richard to see me. *But what does that mean?*

"Here, let me." Derek squats down and takes the pick away from the locksmith, who stands up and pats down his comb-over.

Gia said my lists were a security blanket. I think she was right. They were a big wall I built to protect me from what I'm afraid of. But I have no idea what's on the other side of that wall anymore. It feels impenetrable, but until a moment ago, I had no idea it was even there.

I look at Richard and feel a little jab of pain in my heart. What if he likes me?

"I'm afraid of something real."

Richard takes in what I've said for a moment. "Well, that would be a tough episode to edit."

The piece of rusty key falls on the ground near my foot, and the door budges. Suddenly, his eyes find mine, and the expression on his face softens.

He can see me.

The door glides effortlessly into the wall. In a daze of intense relief, I faintly hear Max sigh and Richard thank Derek and the locksmith.

When things clear up, it's just Richard standing there. Looking as though he hasn't seen me in years. Involuntarily, I wave hello with my hand like a windshield wiper.

"Hi," he says with a chuckle and boldly inspects me from head to toe.

My heart speeds up, and there's this unfamiliar feeling. I think it's pure, undiluted happiness.

"You're wrong," he announces, making me wince. "About your outfit," he adds immediately.

"Oh, why?"

"I'm not disappointed." He juts out his chin arrogantly. "This is good."

I pretend to be irked and push him, pressing a hand playfully on his chest. Without hesitation, he grabs it and pulls me out of the bathroom and toward him into the hallway. The feel of his hand perks me up, like I've stepped into a cool lake.

"Unless you'd rather stay in there."

"Oh no, please," I blurt. "I love your place, but that door is—"

"My brother's idea."

I shrug knowingly. He's so close. We both seem calm, but I can feel this force just beneath the surface, like sprinters about to spring into action. I have promised myself not to go into nervous-talking mode or spew facts just to fill the air. I have committed to letting this be whatever it's supposed to be. *I have decided this just now.*

"It's good to see your face," he says, I think referring to my swept-away bangs.

"You too. I mean, you know, I needed to thank you in person."

"I'm glad. I thought I'd just get a long, rambling email from you last night."

"Oh, I can still do that."

"No," he says quickly. "This is better."

My heart is nudging its way up my throat. Someone approaches us, and we part to let them pass. They step into the bathroom, and I hear the clean click of the dial locking the door as it should.

Richard and I come back, pulled like magnets, to the exact

spots we were a moment ago. He parts his lips a few times like he's about to say something but changes his mind. I can hear an invisible clock ticking. *How long can two people stand in a hallway?*

Okay, that's it. I'm doing this. Wait. How do I say "I really want to get to know you better" without sounding too eager? *If only it weren't so bright in here. Stop. Just go for it.*

"I have a proposal to make." The words slip out just as Richard coolly looks at his watch.

"Me too, actually." He sounds distracted. "Can we get lunch? Like, in an hour? I need to do a few things. You know, like, *actual* work." I know he's teasing, so it isn't too hard to appear unruffled.

CHAPTER 36

Brooklyn's not so bad. For the past couple of minutes I've been mesmerized by this fountain. In the center is a statue of a man and a woman wrapped in an eternal embrace as jet streams of water fly over them, shielding the couple from the rest of the world. Across the street is an incredible arch-looking thing like the one in Paris.

This would be such a great spot for a proposal. I mean for *Marry Me*, of course, not for *me*. Unless it's *meant* to happen. I'm just going with the flow now, embracing the unknown and not trying to produce every little detail in my life. I'm honestly relieved Richard said he needed some time because I could use some fresh air.

I should be mortified after the bathroom fiasco. But instead, I feel pretty good. I feel lighter and liberated. Well, technically, I *was* just freed from a bathroom, but still.

I was a little worried about pitching the show to Richard's brother because of what he must think of me. *She can't lock doors—how can she produce a TV show?* But Richard said I didn't have to worry; the show speaks for itself. We'll just let Max watch it on his own and then go in together to pitch it to networks once he's lined up the meetings.

Pitching the show with Richard by my side sounds like a completely different experience. We're *partners*. And, obviously, grabbing lunch together is what partners do. *Nobody* is jumping to any conclusions.

When I walk back into the office, the receptionist greets me. "He's expecting you. Go right ahead," he says, pointing to an open door behind him.

I walk in and take in how unfinished the room feels. There's just a large wooden desk with a laptop on it and a couple of chairs. *Decorating his new office was clearly last on his list.*

"Hey." Richard gets up as soon as I walk in. "Come here. I want to show you something." He walks over to the window, opens it, and steps outside onto the bright-red fire escape.

I look up and see him quickly scaling the ladder. "I'm also afraid of heights," I say, but he doesn't stop.

I climb out the window and see him above me. *Don't look down.* My hands grab hold of a rung. I take a step up and then another. Slowly, I make it up the two flights. Richard is already on the roof, so he extends his hand down to help me, and I take it.

There's nothing up here. Just a black tar roof with a row of large square air conditioners humming. Richard walks over to the elevator shaft surrounded by a chain-link fence and starts to climb it.

"I think that fence is there to dissuade exactly this type of activity."

"Nah." He pulls himself up onto the top of the structure. "Come on."

I can't believe I'm doing this. I climb up the fence. Richard's hand is extended for me, so I grab it. He helps pull me up, but we don't let go for a few seconds longer than necessary. Up here the air is doing that thing where you feel the warm sun and a cool breeze at the same time. This building is five floors tall, plus it's a floor higher on top of this elevator shaft and yet my knees feel steady. Solid. *Conquer fear of heights, check.*

To our left is Manhattan, looking monumental compared to the low Brooklyn rooftops. When I was growing up, the city seemed so far away. Maybe because I was smaller, and things always seem bigger and farther away when you're a kid. From where I'm standing now, the city seems more approachable.

"I grew up with this view. My dad used to take Maxi and me to Brooklyn Heights. He'd always say, 'Best city in the world... even better from a distance.'"

"It's beautiful."

"It's the best view of the city. Hands down."

"Well..."

"What?"

"I don't want to argue with you about your view. I'm sure it was very special and important to you, but my parents used to take me to the Waterfront in New Jersey, and *that* is the best view of the city." Richard has this stupid grin on his face. "What's so funny?"

"Nothing. I just think it's adorable when you think you're right."

"You've clearly never seen it from over there," I say, grinning too.

"I don't have to. *This* is the best view."

I like the idea of a little Richard on this side of the island and a little me on the other. Taking in two parts of a whole and together completing the picture.

"So, how are things with *Bradford*?" He's turned toward me, so I adjust myself and face him. I'm surprised by how comfortable I feel being so close to him.

"Who?"

"No, it was Bradington the First. No, Langley."

"Landon."

"Right. How's *he* doing?"

"Fine. Actually, I don't know. Turns out, he wasn't real."

We're both quiet for a moment, and before I know it, his arms are around my waist. I feel his scruffy, barely there beard on my cheek. *Real stuff.*

"TJ. Langford. Any other guys I should know about?"

"Well..."

CHAPTER 37

What makes a good kiss good? How does a kiss turn the frog into a prince anyway? My new theory is we're all frogs waiting for the person we can kiss well and who can kiss us back well so we can kiss well *together*.

TJ's lips were very nice, but his kiss lacked suction. Like a Jell-O that just wouldn't take the mold. I'd come out the other end all wet and having to find a way to wipe my face with my sleeve without him noticing. Great guy, though, who will no doubt be a great man someday and will meet a girl with enough suction for both of them.

I want to take a moment to say thank you for the butterflies, TJ. And for the access to your very, truly, supernaturally soft skin. Also, thank you for showing me that just because someone is younger than I am (okay, *way* younger), it doesn't mean he can't be capable of having emotional depth. But please refrain from continuing to send me any more inappropriate photos of your body parts.

Fernando's kiss had more serious concerns. It was like he lost his keys and thought *for sure* they were in my mouth. His tongue would search along my gums, behind my teeth, underneath my tongue. They gotta be in here somewhere!

But I was thankful for Fernando's poetry. I wish I had kept a copy of our book of poems, but I'll always keep their passion and excitement in my heart (except for the last poem, which I never read). Fernando taught me love should be passionate and moving like a symphony, but it can be *most* romantic in the silence. When you can just be yourself and don't have to hold anything back. He's currently playing the piano with the New Art Symphony, which is great news. I also heard he's dating a Vietnamese violinist. I have no doubt that when they kiss, he finds what he's looking for in her mouth every time.

Philip's tongue was always an innocent bystander in his kiss. He'd simply press his lips against mine with his eyes closed and then just stand there. Like he was waiting for the bus. Though his kiss was understated, he taught me that we must be fearless in the art we make. He never did what was easy or expected of him. He wasn't perfect for many reasons (age, a wife), but he never tried to be. He always went with his gut. Which he gyrated into beautiful art. One piece of which is now hanging in a special bathroom in Brooklyn.

Now, Sam's kiss was good. But it was good in the way forbidden things are good. Like eating a thick greasy steak *and* fries *and* onion rings and then ordering a chocolate milkshake. Sam's kiss was good because my lips could feel the urgency and excitement of a thing that wouldn't be around long. I heard he and his fiancée recently moved to Los Angeles. I hope he finds an audience on the West Coast, but not a single decent place for tapas.

And then there's Richard. I was standing there on the elevator shaft about to decide how to respond to his question about other men when I realized he was leaning in and so was I. And then he leaned in a little more, and I sank into his scruffy beard, and Brooklyn fell away and Manhattan floated off into the Atlantic.

We were alone. Deep inside a forest. The air was cool and clean, and I could smell the wet soil beneath us. I know what you're thinking... You could smell wet soil? What the heck is wrong with you? But that's exactly what happened.

And I swear that not for one moment did I play the instrumental version of Usher's "U Got It Bad" in my head because there was absolutely *nothing* wrong with the distant sound of a car alarm. Everything was perfect. I was completely relaxed. I had no need to switch out Usher for "How About You" instead. One, because it's September, and not everyone loves New York in September. And two, because I mean, who does that kind of thing anyway? But... yeah, that *did* sound better.

And I absolutely did *not* imagine the camera pulling away slowly above us until we were smaller and smaller with the sun dipping into the Manhattan sky. Because seriously, some folks need to learn to just let things happen and stop producing things and give in to the mystery, and I *did not* add a long, slow cymbal crescendo when he held me tighter because the moment was perfect and it totally didn't need a thing.

Acknowledgments

Writing is a lot harder than producing reality TV. For me, it's more dramatic and way more emotional. *Although there are a lot of tears in TV producing. More than you would imagine.* I know, without a doubt, I've made it to this point (where I'm no longer afraid to open the manuscript) because of the unwavering support of my family and friends.

Liz Nealon, I feel so grateful that you are my literary agent. Your insight and suggestions have made this all possible. Thank you for reading the book over and over and for talking me off so many ledges.

Leah Hultenschmidt, I am so incredibly lucky to have you as my editor. Thanks to you and to Sabrina Flemming, this has been such a nurturing and inspiring experience for me. Thank you both for your passion and thoughtful suggestions and for helping me make the book better.

Thank you, Ralph, Martin, Mel, Maytee, and Gabby for believing in me so much that I had no choice but to believe in myself. Jose Antonio Hernandez, Grettel Jiménez-Singer, Luisa Varona, and Kathleen Rajsp, thank you for reading the first draft—and for the long list of things you've done for me and for this book since then.

The Spanish word for *support* feels more intense to me and closer to what my friends and family have done for me and my writing. Thank you *por siempre apoyarme*, Tommy, Barbie, Rafael Cruz, Martin Jr., Joshua, Serenitie, Andrew, Cary Matilla Villalon, Ali Codina, Aymee Cruzalegui, Lily Neumeyer, Grey Fernandez, Paola Di Marco, Carrie DeCenzo, Nicole Sorrenti, Amy Bonezzi, Jordana Starr, Pamela Faith, Terri Copin, Tula Singer, and Kika Singer.

Thank you so much, Lorraine Babb, for your generous guidance when I was getting started. And thanks to Karen Robinson and Ellie Oberth for your help with an early draft.

And lastly, thank you to my mom, Maria de los Milagros Miranda. You were proud of me even when I'd get an F in conduct for talking too much in class. I can't imagine how proud you'd be of this book. You'd hand out copies to strangers in elevators. Your love fills me up forever.

About the Author

Lissette Decos is a Cuban American executive television producer with more than twenty years' experience in reality TV formats of the love-wedding-relationship-disaster variety. Shows such as TLC's *Say Yes to the Dress*, *90 Day Fiancé*, and Bravo's *Summer House* have helped mold her skills in telling an engaging and oftentimes unconventional love story. In addition to her stint in the "unreal" world of reality TV, Lissette also spent a decade in New York as a staff producer for MTV, which helped her hone her expertise in all things pop culture, while searching for love in the big city. You might say she's got the story and the soundtrack for romantic angst down.

DON'T MISS LISSETTE'S NEXT BOOK COMING IN 2024!